MW00941528

MACPHERSON BRIDES
BOOK TWO

MISCHELLE CREAGER

DEDICATION

To my wonderful husband, Randy, who has gone through this journey with me. I never could have done it without you.

ACKNOWLEDGMENTS

I wish to thank my husband and children for their love
and patience with me through this process.
Also a special thanks to...
My critique partner and mentor, Lacy Williams.
My editor, Lana Wooldridge.
My writers group, OCFW with for all their
encouragement.
And the special ladies at church who read and proofed for
me—Kathy Faulkner, Peggy Hudson, Jean Lowe, and
Terri Wooldridge.

CHAPTER ONE

Central City, Colorado Territory 1862

"Oh, butterflies and pumpkins." Esther O'Brien Sanders jerked her hand back when a splinter caught on the fourth finger of her left hand, the finger that was wrapped in a wedding ring. The ring that was a lie. A lie, like the last name she used, one that hid what had happened to her.

The splinter wasn't deep, just deep enough to irritate. With a nip of her teeth, she pulled it out and spit it away. Looking over her shoulder to make sure no one had seen her act in such an unladylike way, she slipped into the small tack room of the livery owned by her great-uncle, Will Sanders. She pulled the door closed with a practiced flick of her wrist.

Inside the room, she moved past the two bunks nailed to the wall. Uncle Will's lower one was rumpled and messy. The upper one, which belonged to his grandson, Sully, showed no signs of recent use. But that was expected since Sully had been out hunting gold for a week or so. Which was why she was there, helping her great-uncle.

As she pulled her worn work dress over her head, she couldn't help but chuckle when she thought about the words she'd spoken a few moments before. *Butterflies and pumpkins.* Ever since her mother had washed out her mouth with lye soap for telling a whopper when she was only six years old, Esther hadn't been able to cuss. Now she'd made up silly sayings for when something needed to be said. And that splinter was just such a need.

Funny how fourteen years later—five years after her mother had died—that lesson held strong. She swallowed back a sob. At least the name she'd chosen as her fictitious late husband's name, Sanders, had a family connection. It was her mother and Aunt Bonny's maiden name, as well as Great-uncle Will's.

She tugged off her thin petticoat and grabbed Sully's overalls and shirt hanging on the peg. She wished she could have just changed clothes back in her room at the boardinghouse. But if Aunt Bonny's husband, Uncle Ed, heard of her wearing pants anywhere but inside the livery, his anger would pour out on her, and he'd find some extra-horrid chore for her to do as punishment.

She shrugged. Such was the fate of a poor relation. She could take his harshness for her son's sake. And with Aunt Bonny not feeling well, she didn't want to put the poor woman through any more turmoil than necessary.

After Esther hung her regular clothes on the peg, she pulled the knife from the pocket of her dress and slipped it into the overalls. She gave the knife a pat as she did every time she put it in her pocket. Never again would anyone do to her what those two men had done. Since that day five years ago, she'd never been without her knife.

She grabbed an old hat and stuck it on her head, then growled deep in her throat as she caught the button on her shirt cuff in her hair. She hoped she was using up all her bad luck in these few minutes, and the rest of the afternoon would go much better.

Without a mirror in the room to see what she was doing, she tried to work the button loose but instead pulled a thick strand of hair out of the braid that hung down her back. The hair came loose and fell in front of her face. Her eyes almost crossed as she stared at the dull, brown color. Another thing Uncle Ed made her change when she came to live with him and his family.

She had golden-red hair, like her mother, but he forced her to dye it. And she hated the color. She figured the only reason Uncle Ed made her do it was because his daughter, her step-cousin Tina, was jealous of it. Was it Esther's fault so many people made a fuss over the color when she first came to live with them?

She let out a long sigh. At least Uncle Ed offered her and Davey the protection of his house as well as the lie of the ring, considering he'd moved them to a town where the men outnumbered the woman ten to one. And she needed Uncle Ed's protection for her son, since the only jobs for women around here were wives or soiled doves. The first one made her shudder, and the second she'd never do.

With a quick twist of her wrist, she shoved the hair under her hat. If all went well, she should be finished with her work in time to take a bath. Esther slid Uncle Will's too-big gloves over her hands and hurried out of the tack room.

She glanced through the open livery doors and watched her aging great-uncle sitting in the sunshine, eating the noonday meal she'd brought from the boardinghouse. Today's fare— chopped roast between slices of homemade bread with an apple to munch on later. The old man rested on his favorite chair with his swollen foot propped on an overturned bucket. He grinned as he savored the sandwich. Four-year-old Davey sat on the ground nearby, playing with two wooden horses Uncle Will had whittled for him.

Davey looked at her and waved, his little white teeth peeking out of his wide grin as his black hair curled around his head. She smiled and waved back. Davey, that sweet boy, meant the world to her. He was the reason she wore the wedding band.

All was well with Uncle Will as he looked after Davey. Esther turned back to her chore. Using the pitchfork, she lifted the soiled hay from each stall and dropped it into the wheelbarrow that sat in the aisle between the two rows.

Ten stalls and a damp shirt later, Esther grunted when she lifted the handles of the wheelbarrow and pushed it out the back of the livery, then dumped its load by the pile from two days ago. She raised her arm and wiped the moisture off her forehead with the sleeve of the shirt. The smell that greeted her made her glad she'd left buckets of water heating on the stove back at the boardinghouse. Fortunately, wash day wasn't far off so the clothes would get a cleaning before she brought them back for Sully.

"Es, get out here." Uncle Will let out a yell in his gruff old-man voice. "We got us a customer."

From the back of the livery, Esther saw a large man dismount from a pale horse. She rested her fingers against the knife handle as she rubbed the scarred skin of her forearm with her other hand. A scar her attackers carved into her arm as they promised to return for her. She tapped her knife.

"Es, didja hear me?"

Esther moved through the shadows of the livery. The customer was a stranger, but that wasn't new. With so many folks trying to make it rich in the gold fields, most of the men she saw were strangers, both here and at the boardinghouse.

She neared the front of the building and heard some sort of commotion outside. Shouts and racing hooves, and had that been gunfire? A stray bullet whizzed by her head and landed in one of the beams in the side of the livery. She ran for her son. Large hands wrestled her to the ground, right into a pile of muck she'd missed.

The men who'd been shooting raced away.

The air grew quiet.

A heavy body covered her. For just a moment, she stared into eyes the color of spring grass.

A feeling she hadn't felt before raced through her insides. The next instant she realized she was trapped beneath a male body—a large, powerful, male body. Almost without thought, she pulled the knife from her pocket and nudged it into the side of the man over her. "If you don't let go of me, you'll be sleeping in the cemetery tonight."

Her hat slipped from her head, and the warmth of the sun fell on her face. The man's green eyes widened.

She wiggled the knife just a bit, maybe enough to slice though his shirt, but not his skin. "Move."

Before the word had barely left her mouth, the man whirled away and stood.

Esther got to her feet and tugged at the overalls. From the wet feel of it, the muck had soaked all the way to her skin.

The stranger picked his hat off the ground and crushed it over his shaggy blond hair. "Sorry, ma'am. Didn't want to let you get shot."

His voice came out somber, but his eyes twinkled. He seemed to have a hard time keeping his lips from twitching. But it was the way the man's gaze roamed from her head to boots and back that caused Esther to grit her teeth.

She hated to feel so exposed, the butt of jokes and gossip like she'd been in the last town they'd lived. Gossip that ridiculed her for things she'd no control over. Hateful words that had left her unprotected. The leering looks men gave her. Cruel actions that would hurt her son as he grew older, if the truth ever came out.

She rubbed her finger across the gold band on her left hand. Uncle Ed had brought the family to Central City at Uncle Will's suggestion and forced her to live a lie. Maybe it wasn't what she'd planned, but she was thankful the people here didn't know about her past. The men at the boardinghouse treated her with respect.

A deep sigh slipped past her lips. She wanted to rush back to her room and clean up, but she needed to help Uncle Will with his business first.

Esther shoved the knife back into the sheath in the pocket of her overalls, then moved further into the livery, angling her damp backside to the wall. She pointed to the last stall on the left. "You can put your horse there."

The man looked at her. The laughter had left his face. He tipped his hat. "Ma'am, I'm truly sorry if I offended you. It wasn't my intention."

He shifted a bit. His vest moved and revealed a Deputy US Marshal star on his dusty shirt.

She jerked back. Five years ago, it'd been a marshal who came after those outlaws who'd killed her parents and attacked her. A marshal's star had stared back at her while people moved her mother and father out of the yard and into the wagon to take them to the undertaker's place. A marshal's star...she looked into the man's face. It wasn't the same marshal. No, this was a different man. Of course, since she now lived hundreds of miles away from where her parents were killed.

Esther sucked in a deep breath and let it out in little bits while he guided his horse into the stall. Hating the way she'd acted with this stranger, this marshal, she gripped her fingers into small fists and faced him. "Do you want me to unsaddle your horse and give him some feed?"

His lips tipped up the tiniest bit. He shook his head. "No thanks, I can manage. Just point me to the feed."

Forcing her hand to uncurl, she pointed to the box. "There."

"Thanks, ma'am. I appreciate your help."

Esther stood there for just a moment more. It seemed something should be said, but she couldn't think of what.

With nothing else to do, she gave a nod to the marshal and walked to Uncle Will. "I've finished the mucking out. I need to get Davey home."

Uncle Will patted her hand. "Thanks for helping. I'll see you in a couple of days."

Without a backwards glance at the stranger with the star, Esther took her son's hand and walked away from the livery, away from the man who brought back too many memories.

CHAPTER TWO

Colin MacPherson watched the young woman with mousy brown hair take the little boy's hand and walk away. He grinned at the damp spot on her backside that moved with every step. It hadn't taken but a moment after he'd shoved the lad aside to figure out it wasn't a lad at all that he was trying to protect, but a full-grown woman. Then she spoke, and the words came out low and husky. He was sure she hadn't meant to make it sound like that. He hadn't heard a voice as sultry outside a saloon. He touched the hole in his shirt. She definitely wasn't calling him in for any pleasure.

The old man chuckled. "She's a feisty one, all right."

"That she is." Colin turned toward the white-haired man sitting in a wooden chair with his leg propped on an overturned bucket. He'd shoved a pillow beneath his leg like he planned on staying there awhile.

The glittering brown eyes he'd seen on the woman's face when she gave him a final nod still floated in Colin's head. "Who is she?"

"Name's Esther. She's my great-niece and works at the boardinghouse owned by my niece and her husband. Es's been helping me out 'cause my gout's been acting up something fierce lately and my grandson got a fool notion in his head and took off to the gold fields for a spell."

Maybe it was a mite different here than further east, but Colin didn't think so. "Mighty talkative. Figured with all the strangers racing in here to hunt for gold, you wouldn't be quite so free with information about the woman."

The old man set his plate on the ground, then picked up a block of wood and a knife. He started whittling. "Like Es, I seen your star." He gave Colin a quick glance while the knife kept peeling away at the wood. "Got a fair idea of why you're here."

Not many men knew Ray Miller had busted both of his sons out of prison. Word had it they were headed toward the Central City area, but for what purpose Colin wasn't sure. He just knew he had to find the murdering band and see that justice for his wife and son was satisfied.

Colin's hand dropped to his side. Did this man know the Millers? "What would that be?"

"Well, now the country's at war with itself, somebody's got to be sure the gold from here don't end up in those Southern pockets. I read the newspapers. I hear the gossip." He cackled a bit. "I know what's going on around here. Folks seem to think when a man's hair goes white, his hearing takes a trip, never to return."

Colin nodded. The old man might be a good source of information in the weeks to come. "Know of a good place to stay while I'm here?"

The old man shook his head. "Didn't listen, did ya, boy? Es cooks at the boardinghouse just down the road there. The big one." He pointed with his knife to a large gray house a couple hundred feet away, then smacked his lips together. "She makes the best apple pies I ever tasted, 'cepting her ma's, God rest her soul. My niece taught her daughter everything she knew before she passed on."

As the old man sucked in a chest full of air so he could start again, Colin raised his hand in farewell and headed toward the middle of town. *Might be interesting to try the pie. Might be interesting to get another look at that woman —in a dress this time—and see how she acts sitting with me at supper.* But he had a couple of things to do first.

A little while later, Colin entered the sheriff's office and tried to ignore the smell of over-brewed coffee along with the stench drifting from the cells. A man with graying black hair and a matching mustache sat behind the desk. Like Colin, a star was pinned to his broad chest, only that one was a sheriff's star. The man looked up from a stack of wanted posters in his hands. His eyes traveled from Colin's face to his badge and back to his face.

The sheriff stood and held out his hand. "Name's Fred Tucker. Folks around here call me Tuck. What can I do ya for?"

Colin clasped the man's hand and gave a firm shake. "Colin MacPherson. Going to be around for a while. Just thought I'd check in."

"Have a seat." Tuck pointed to a battered wooden chair in front of the even more battered wooden desk.

"Been expecting you. Abe Roper sent word you'd be coming. Don't mind saying I'm happy to have another lawman making sure none of the gold gets to them Rebels."

"Abe speaks highly of you." Colin pulled off his hat as he sat, then ran his fingers through his too-long hair. The chair let out a screechy sound, and he hoped it would hold him. "Says you two go way back."

"We rode together for many a mile 'til the Miller gang got a good shot off leaving me with this." The sheriff stood and slapped his right leg. With a slight limp, he walked to the potbellied stove. "At least I helped get two of 'em in prison, though. The two older boys." He filled a cup with thin brown sludge from the blue coffeepot. "Want some?'

"No thanks." Colin waited until the sheriff got back to his desk. "Did you hear Ray Miller broke his boys out of prison?"

Tuck slammed his mug on the desk but didn't seem to notice the bottom busted out of it. Brown sludge crept to the wanted posters. "What the—" He sucked in a deep breath then let it out slowly as he rubbed his right leg. "Those men should've been strung up years ago."

Colin couldn't have agreed more, only his reason for wanting them hung had nothing to do with the crimes they'd gone to prison for. "Both of them got shot up pretty bad. Stopped at a doc's place to fix them. Miller killed the doc before they left. Must've not wanted to leave any witnesses, but the doc's daughter was hiding. She talked to the posse, told them Blake Miller, Ray's youngest son, was with his pa."

The sheriff mumbled a few heated words under his breath.

Colin got the gist of the sheriff's curses and agreed completely.

"Now they've got another Miller to worry 'bout."

Colin tapped his finger against the hat which rested on his leg. "Not they, us. Rumor has it the whole gang might be headed this way."

"What for? Gold?"

"Not sure. The doc's daughter heard them say something about traveling to Central City. From where she was hiding, she couldn't understand everything, but they seemed real set on finding something here."

"That why Abe sent you?" One of Tuck's eyebrow's rose as if to add to the question. "Abe wrote something 'bout your wife and boy being killed in a poss'ble stagecoach robbery a few years ago. Said you thought it was the Millers but couldn't prove it."

Colin ground his teeth. He'd been through this with Abe more times than he could count.

Tuck shrugged. "Abe said he wasn't sure it was the Millers."

Colin didn't know if the shrug meant the sheriff agreed with what Abe said or didn't care. Either way, it didn't matter. Colin knew what happened out there. "I'm sure."

Tuck's eyebrows jerked upwards.

Colin understood. Even to his own ears, his voice had sounded cold, hard, and deadly. But that's the way he felt.

The sheriff studied him in silence. Colin didn't care. He'd take help getting those outlaws, but he wouldn't abide any interference to him getting justice.

Tuck finally moved and rubbed his hand over the stubble on his chin. "Wish we had the old man's face on a wanted poster so I could show it around town, but I don't get many of them from back East these days. And with all the men coming in to hunt gold, an old man with brown eyes and graying hair wouldn't stand out much. Oh, yeah, did you hear he's got a bad limp in his left leg now?" Tuck chuckled as he rubbed his own leg. "Someone got off a lucky shot. Feels like a little payback for what he gave me."

Tuck glanced at the stack of posters and mumbled something under his breath again only this time the words seemed directed at himself. He grabbed a ragged towel from one of the desk drawers and blotted the mess on his desk. When he finished, he tossed the broken mug in a wooden bucket, then slung the dirty towel in a basket in the corner. "By the way, you related to any of the MacPhersons around here?"

Colin held back a chuckle at the way the sheriff said his name, stressing the middle part and sounding it out as "fear" instead of "fir." Pa always said there wasn't any fear in a MacPherson, but Colin had gotten tired of trying to correct folks.

Tuck dropped in his chair.

Colin fingered the side of his hat. "Might be. I heard my grandparents have a ranch somewhere in the territory, and there's probably a number of the family with them."

"Know a Dougal, Kerr, and Jase MacPherson hereabouts. Might want to check with Drew Hollingsworth over at the Golden Nugget Restaurant. His sister married Thorn MacPherson a year or so ago."

Colin tucked the information away, especially the part about Dougal. "Thanks. I'll check into it." He stood and set his hat back on his head. His long hair rubbed against his neck again. A trip to the barber wouldn't do any harm. He might hear some gossip that could be useful. As his arm dropped to his side, he realized the jail cells weren't the only thing that needed cleaning. He could use a bath as well. "Well, I guess I'll be heading out. Still need to get a room."

"Got a place in mind?" Tuck rubbed his fingers against his shirt, leaving small streaks of old coffee, and stretched out his hand.

"Heard of a boardinghouse where a woman named Esther makes good apple pies." Colin shook the sheriff's hand.

Tuck grinned. "Must have left your horse at Sanders's livery and planning to stay at Mrs. Small's place. You tell her I said you're a good man, and she should take you in. You'll really like it there, clean beds and some of the best food you'll have around here. Her poor niece wears herself out keeping it that way." Tuck's nose twitched. "If you're needing a bath, Mrs. Small's husband owns a barber shop just down the way here. There's a bathhouse next to it."

Colin nodded to the sheriff. "Thanks for the information."

As he walked to the barbershop, his gut tightened. A shiver snaked its way around his spine. He glanced from side to side, trying to take in everything without raising any suspicions.

Something wasn't right, but he wasn't sure what it was. It was a feeling he sometimes had, something his pa told him came from his Scottish ancestry. But he didn't put any credence in fables like that. Still, he looked around, but he didn't see anything. Yet.

Stinking of sweaty clothes along with the smeared muck from the livery, Esther tugged her son's hand as they entered the back of the boardinghouse. At last, her shoulders relaxed. No one had seen them between the livery and the boardinghouse. Now she could have the bath she'd planned before she'd gone to help her great-uncle. With a nudging hand on Davey's shoulder, she directed him to the bedroom they shared off the kitchen. "Go lie down for a little bit while I get cleaned up."

Esther figured Davey would take a nap while she bathed, then she could get him into the tub for a quick bath. She entered the kitchen where she had left several buckets of water to heat and slid on a puddle of water, one of several puddles that led to the stove, where buckets of water no longer sat.

She drew in a slow, deep breath and held it for a moment, then exhaled. With the second deep breath, she fought the urge to scream her cousin's name—no, not her cousin. Tina was not a blood relative of hers. She was Aunt Bonny's stepdaughter and the most selfish person Esther had ever known. Something her uncle allowed and almost seemed to encourage with the way he pampered his daughter, always giving into her demands.

Something thumped. Davey screamed. She ran to her bedroom.

Davey sat on the floor in a puddle of water, rubbing the back of his head. Tears ran down his cheeks. "I falled."

"Frog's legs and—and sauerkraut." Sometimes it was hard to find words that suited the situation without cussing.

She could not believe the mess. The metal tub used for bathing sat in the middle of her room, water puddled around it. Buckets sat empty. Two sopping wet towels lay on the wooden floor. She looked through the murky water still in the tub. The last of the scented soap Aunt Bonny had given her for Christmas lay in a melted glob at the bottom.

Davey cried out again. Esther picked him up and checked out the tiny bump on his head, then rubbed his back until he stopped crying. Finally, his eyes closed, and he fell asleep. She put him on the bed. A glance at the shadows out the window confirmed what she already knew. She didn't have time to heat more water for a bath before she needed to start supper. Preparing a meal for fifteen to twenty people took a lot of time.

She used the buckets to empty the tub. Next, she gathered the towels and dropped them on the back porch, then mopped the puddles on her floor.

With the clean-up done, she went behind the screen cornering off a private area in her room and removed the stinking clothes. Using the water in the pitcher from earlier in the day, she washed herself as well as she could. If only she could wash away her anger with Tina as easily.

Two hours later, Esther wore a large white apron over a worn blue print dress. Davey helped her finish setting the two tables in the dining room, the large one for her, Davey, and the boarders, and the smaller one which Uncle Ed insisted on calling the family table.

Davey set the last fork on the smaller table, then looked at her. "Don't like this table." He pointed to the other table where she ate with Davey and the boarders. "Like eating there."

Esther ruffled her son's hair. "I know what you mean, son." She always thought it was silly to have two tables in the dining room, but she'd overheard Uncle Ed tell Aunt Bonny that he dealt with the riffraff in his barbershop and in his home, but he didn't have to eat with them.

After sending Davey out to play in the backyard for a little bit, Esther sat at the kitchen work table and peeled potatoes for supper. Two large cakes cooled on the counter. The smell of the ham baking in the oven filled the air.

She put the potatoes in the pot to boil, then rubbed her hands on the small of her aching back. With only the cakes to finish, she dumped the butter and sugar into a large mixing bowl for frosting and stirred.

The door from the dining room sprang open. Tina, fresh from her bath, entered wearing one of her newer gowns—a green one this time—with her thin brown hair piled on top of her head and wispy curls floating around the sides of her face.

Esther tapped her finger on the table a couple of times and stared at her cousin. *Going to apologize for leaving the mess in my room, or are you going to keep acting like the princess your father treats you like?*

"Oh, take that silly frown off your face." Tina swatted the air. "Mama Bonny isn't feeling well, so she's resting in the parlor. I told her I'd let you know we have a new boarder. He took the front bedroom."

"How many are in his family? How old are the children?" Esther tried to figure if she'd have enough food for the new family, especially if there were several older boys.

A wide grin spread across Tina's face. "Oh, he's not married...yet."

"Just one man in that big room?" Surprise caused Esther's voice to rise just a tiny bit. She thought about how large it was. Often a family with three or four children shared it. The single men usually bunked two to four in a room. Of course, it was the only one not rented right now.

Tina patted one of her curls back in place. "Yes. And he just loved how fresh and clean I keep it."

No, how fresh and clean I keep it. Esther gritted her teeth to keep from saying anything. It wouldn't do any good anyway. In Tina's world, everything revolved around her.

"By the way, he'll be eating at the family table tonight." She giggled. "And probably every night thereafter."

"Are you sure he won't want to eat at the table with all the other boarders sometimes?" Esther knew the answer before she asked the question, but she did it anyway. Maybe just to irritate her cousin.

Tina stared at Esther for a moment, then waved her hand as if to dismiss the idea. "It doesn't matter if he does. I want him with me, and you know Papa always gives me what I want."

With that said, Tina pranced around the kitchen bopping from the rolls rising to the potatoes boiling in the pot to the unfrosted cakes cooling on the counter.

"Why aren't we having pie for dessert? Earlier today, you said we were having apple pie tonight." She frowned and glared at Esther. "When the new boarder moved in, I told him that he'd just love my pie." She pressed her balled fists on her hips. "What are you going to do about it now?"

Nothing, Esther thought while she bit her tongue to keep from saying anything. She added a little milk to the mixture and stirred some more. Thoughts rolled through her mind. *You're such a selfish, whining baby. With such a devoted father and a loving stepmother, why can't you be content? Start acting like a young woman, not a spoiled child.*

But she knew she couldn't voice any of that for fear of Uncle Ed's anger falling on her. It wouldn't matter anyway. Tina would continue acting the same way.

Esther gripped the spoon tighter. She plopped frosting on the first cake, then closed her eyes for a moment as she thought about all the time it took to clean up the mess Tina had left after bathing.

A thought came to her. It wasn't nice, but she couldn't keep from doing it anyway. Tina hated to cook—hated to clean or do any work—but she loved to take the praise when everything went smoothly or the meal turned out wonderfully.

She opened her eyes and gave Tina a large smile. "I think I'm going to let you bake a pie since you're the one who told the new boarder he'd love *your* pie."

A look of horror filled the girl's face as she took a step back. "No, I'm not going to get covered in flour after I just took a bath." Tina's voice came out as a pleading whine, more appropriate to a three-year-old child than a young woman of seventeen. "You have to make a pie, just one pie for the family table."

"You can use a large apron to cover your dress."

Tina's eyes grew even wider. "But I couldn't do it tonight. I just used my new lily-of-the-valley dusting powder and cologne Papa gave me last week. I don't want to smell like kitchen spices."

Too bad. You've made your choice. Esther spread the frosting on the cake.

Tina's frown turned into a smile as an idea seemed to pop into her mind. "You could bake it while we're eating. That way it'd be all hot and delicious. Oh, I like the idea much better. Just imagine how he'll smile at me when I hand him the pie with steam still rising from it."

"No, supper's the time I eat with Davey."

"You and Davey could eat in here after you have the pie in the oven. You have to do this. After all, you're just a servant in the house. No, not even a servant, since you don't get paid. You're more like a slave, owing everything you have to my father's generosity." Tina's eyes narrowed as she seemed to savor the thought. "And slaves have to do what they're told."

Anger rolled through Esther's blood at the words. *If I'm penniless, it was because your father took everything that had belonged to my family after my parents were killed.* At least, Aunt Bonny insisted they take her in. "There'll still be no pie tonight."

The frosting on the second cake smeared a bit when the knife Esther used slipped, but she refused to back down from her stance against her cousin. *Let Uncle Ed's anger fall on me if need be. I'm just so tired of the way you act, you silly, silly girl.*

"We'll just see what Papa has to say about this." With a determined look on her face, Tina flounced out of the room.

"She's the most selfish, self-centered…Oh, I'm sorry." Esther stopped as her Aunt Bonny slipped into the kitchen. "Sometimes I forget she's your step-daughter and my mouth runs away with me."

"Don't worry, dear." A weak smile crossed Aunt Bonny's face. She rested her balled right hand on her chest. "Even though I love her, sometimes I wish I could forget."

Esther watched as her aunt's fist rubbed in small circles over the front of her dress. *Was it just Aunt Bonny's inner heart that hurt for the selfish person Tina had become or was it more?* Lately she'd noticed how Aunt Bonny seemed to have less and less energy and tired more easily.

Esther left the almost-empty frosting bowl sitting on the work table, so Davey could have an extra treat while she washed dishes after supper. She patted her aunt on the shoulder. "Are you sure you don't need to go to the doctor?"

Aunt Bonny wobbled and grabbed the edge of the table. "No need, no need at all, but thank you for worrying about me." She grabbed Esther's hand. "And thank you for all you do around here. There's no way I could've handled it by myself. I just wish your uncle would pay you something each week. You earn it and more."

Esther couldn't agree more. Her uncle should pay her, but she had nowhere else to go, especially as an unmarried woman and with a son to take care of. Besides, she wasn't sure what rumors Uncle Ed would spread if he lost his unpaid servant.

Oh, she knew there were places that would take in her and Davey, but she'd never lower herself to do what those women did, not if she had any other choice. Here at the boardinghouse, she and Davey had a room of their own and food to eat. And with the egg money each week, she was able to clothe herself and her son. "Don't worry. I'm happy I can help you. It's a little like helping my mother."

Moisture filled Aunt Bonny's eyes. "You're so like my sister." She pulled a hankie from the sleeve of her dress and blotted her eyes. "But promise me this, if the time comes you have to leave for your sake or Davey's, go. Don't look back. Check with your Uncle Will. I'm sending him something tomorrow that will help you. If you have to go, know you have my blessing. I love you and Davey as if you were my own daughter and grandson."

Shivers ran down Esther's back as her aunt walked unsteadily out of the kitchen. What did her aunt know and wasn't telling? And what was she going to give Uncle Will, and would it be safe at the livery stable?

CHAPTER THREE

An hour later, with the same questions spinning through her head, Esther prepared to carry the food into the dining room.

Tina burst in the back door and set a wrapped package on the table. "Papa's home. Hurry and put this in the oven so it'll be hot for dessert." She lifted a pie out of the paper and set it on the table. "And mind you, this is only for the family table. Let the others have cake. Oh my, I need to hurry and let the new boarder know he has to eat at our table."

Without another word, Tina raced out of the kitchen. Esther took the pie and slipped it into the oven. She shook her head because she knew where the pie had come from. Uncle Will had a sweet tooth for this same pie, and she'd seen the same wrapping hidden at the livery when she hadn't had time to make one for him. Tina must have caught her father when he first came home and talked him into going to the Golden Nugget Bakery for a pie.

The clock in the dining room struck the hour. Davey, followed by two of the young boarders, slipped into the kitchen. Early on, Esther had worked out a system so she could have a little help. She gave her helpers an extra serving of dessert. When the young men found out about the reward, they fought over who got to help bring out the food and take back the dirty dishes. To keep everything orderly, Esther had made out a schedule so everyone got a turn and an extra dessert.

The young men grinned and gathered the filled dishes, then took them out to the dining room and placed them on the long dining table.

Esther carried a large tray with four filled plates and a basket of hot rolls. These she'd place on the small square table.

When Esther entered the dining room, she almost dropped the tray. Sitting at her uncle's table was the man from the livery—the marshal—only now it was obvious he'd been to the barber and the bathhouse. As she neared the table, he tapped his dinner knife a couple of times and grinned.

Her scar itched.

Esther bit the inside of her lip. She wasn't sure if she wanted to grin at his playful reminder of her knife at the livery or to frown as she remembered who he was. She kept her head bowed and went around the table, serving her uncle and aunt. *Poor Aunt Bonny. The smudges below her eyes were darker than they'd been earlier.* When Esther placed a plate in front of Tina, her stepcousin dropped her hand below the table and pinched Esther on the leg.

Esther flinched and bit harder on the inside of her lip to keep from crying out. She glanced at Tina. The girl smirked as she narrowed her eyes. Tina needn't worry. This new boarder was all hers. Esther wanted no part of a marshal. Not this one or any other. Not now, not ever.

Esther set the tray by the bench and slipped in next to Davey. They all waited for her uncle to lead them in a moment of silence before the meal, something he insisted on doing to show this was a proper establishment, although he never uttered a word in prayer. Once that was completed, the serving and eating at the long table began while she and Davey said a quiet prayer together.

After she filled her plate and Davey's, she tried to keep her eyes focused on her food because every time she looked up, the marshal was watching her. And every time she answered a question one the boarders asked her about her day, Tina twisted her head around and glared at her. *Oh, the bother of having a deep voice as a woman.*

Esther finished her meal and slipped back into the kitchen. She cut the cakes, kept back the extra pieces for her helpers, and brought the rest out to the long table. The boarders would serve themselves. She stepped back into the kitchen and sliced the pie and set the pieces on small china plates. As she placed the plates on the tray, the kitchen door swung open.

"I'll take those." Tina's voice came out as a low growl. "You just stay out here and clean this mess. Papa thinks you've made enough of a spectacle of yourself tonight with the way you talk. Sounds like a bordello out there every time you open your mouth."

Esther clenched her hands to her sides. She knew her voice irritated Uncle Ed, and she'd tried to speak in a higher-toned pitch, but it always came out sounding false. Besides, this was the voice God gave her. "I haven't done any—"

"And you stay away from our new boarder. He's mine." The sound of Tina's palm slapping Esther's cheek thundered around the kitchen.

Tina grabbed the tray and left the room.

Esther let her fingers glide around the soreness on the side of her face. Her stomach tightened. She fought to keep what little supper she'd eaten from coming back up. Nobody had struck her since those men had come to her parents' farm.

Things were getting worse. If Tina would slap her, what might she do if she got angry at Davey? She needed to find a decent job somewhere else and as quickly as possible. Only there weren't any nice jobs for women in this town. If a young woman worked as a clerk in a store, it was because her father owned it.

Her head began to pound, either from the slap or the worry, she didn't know which. While she placed the rest of the pie in the pie safe, a memory popped into her head. Maybe she could try the Golden Nugget Bakery. The last time she'd been able to go to church, she'd heard the young woman who worked at the bakery was getting married, and she, along with her younger brother and sister, was moving to a nearby ranch.

Esther nodded. Yes, she could go to the bakery tomorrow after she went to the mercantile for her weekly shopping and check out if they'd hire her. Maybe this was her way of escape.

"Marshal MacPherson, since this is your first night with us, please join us in the family parlor. I'd like to hear more of what's going on with the war back East." Mr. Small lifted his hand and indicated the room he wished them to enter.

Colin started to decline. What he really wanted to do was join the boarders while they sat around the table nursing the last of their coffee and talking over the day's happenings, see if he might hear anything about the Millers or anything suspicious around town.

But the young woman didn't give him a chance as she tugged on his hand, leading him to a hard horsehair sofa in the family's private parlor. She plopped herself next to him, and her father took the position on the other side of her. Mrs. Small settled in one of the more comfortable-looking chairs near the sofa.

Colin tapped his finger against the fabric of his pants leg. He hated this kind of thing. It reminded him too much of the way things had been back in Missouri with his former in-laws. But maybe he could gather some information here. After all, a lot of talk passed through a barbershop. Mr. Small might let something slip he wasn't even aware of knowing.

And if he was real lucky, maybe Esther would join them.

Just thinking of the feisty woman seemed to bring her into the room. She carried a heavy tray with cups, saucers, and a pot. He almost smiled. Maybe he'd have a chance to talk with her. But the thought was smashed to bits when she set the tray down, turned, and left the room.

"Ernestina, you may pour for our guest." Mr. Small nodded to his daughter.

For the next hour, the seconds dragged by like two snails running a race and the winner would be the one who came in last. True to his invitation, the barber asked question after question about the events concerning the war, especially the names of the generals and the battle outcomes.

At long last, Mrs. Small stood, wobbling a bit. "I'm sorry to break up this little get-together, but I find I must retire for the evening."

"Yes, of course, dear." Her husband stood. "Ernestina, please help Momma Bonny to her room."

"But Papa, I thought I'd stay here for little bit longer and visit with Marshal MacPherson. I so like hearing about all the excitement back East."

"Ernestina, do as I say. Since I'll be joining Bonny after I lock the front door, it isn't appropriate for you to stay here unchaperoned."

Colin tried to hide the shudder at the longing look the young woman gave him.

"All right, Papa. Here, Mama Bonny, let me help you." She fluttered her fingers in farewell as she gave Colin one last adoring gaze. He breathed a sigh of relief as she linked arms with Mrs. Small and moved out of the room.

After they left, Mr. Small turned to Colin. "I was happy to have you share our family table, as it was your first night with us, and joining us here in the family parlor. I enjoyed the news you shared about the war. But while we appreciated your company tonight, I think you should keep your distance from my daughter. She's at a very impressionable age and could get caught up in the fantasy of the type of life you live. Please make up whatever excuse you wish for sitting with the other boarders, and I will back you up."

Colin almost choked. The barber must have been caught unawares by his spoiled daughter and couldn't refuse her demand to have him share the family table. So now, the man wanted Colin to be the heartless cur to refuse the girl's attentions. What a spineless father. Still, a reprieve from the attentions of the man's husband-hunting daughter had just fallen into his lap. Life here would be a lot more tolerable now. "Yes, sir, I understand completely."

"Good, good. Well, have an enjoyable night. I understand your room has the best bed in the house." Without another word, Mr. Small left the room.

Colin let out a deep sigh. How did he get into situations like this?

When he turned to leave the room, he noticed the tea tray still on the table in front of the sofa. Nobody had bothered to take it back to the kitchen. He blew out a huff of disgust as he stared at Mr. Small. They left it for Esther to take care of. After all the work she'd done, they still expected her to pick up after them.

Moving with speed fueled by anger, he gathered the dirty cups and saucers and set them on the tray next to the teapot. He looked around to make sure he hadn't missed anything, then carried everything to the kitchen. He wanted to shove open the door between the dining room and the kitchen to vent some of his feelings, but he feared the noise would startle Miz Essie, as the other men called her.

Alertness replaced anger when he saw the back door wide open. Had someone broken in? He listened for whimpers or cries of distress, but instead Miz Essie's deep, sultry voice was carried on the night air. There were words, but he couldn't make them out. Just snatches here and there.

"Rest…wait…peace...still...for you."

Then she started humming. It was a tune that tickled the back of his mind. Although he couldn't place the song, it soothed his heart and brought a sense of rightness to his mind.

He set the loaded tray on the worktable, then stepped to the open door.

She sat in a rocking chair on one side of the porch. The full moon shone on her while she stared into the heavens.

His boot brushed against the door facing.

Miz Essie gave a small squeal and pulled the knife from her pocket.

He moved back half a step. "Sorry, I brought the tea things back to the kitchen and saw the open door. I didn't mean to disturb you."

"Oh, Marshal, you scared me. I thought everyone'd gone to bed."

He expected her to slip the knife back into her pocket, but she rested it on her lap with her fingers tightly gripping it. He stepped outside and stood in front of the door. "Mind if I join you?"

She shrugged.

Colin took that for her agreement, but her knife wiggled a little from side to side.

Her eyes flickered from him to the back door. The knife stopped moving.

She's afraid of me. She thought I was blocking her way of escape. He bit the inside of his cheek at his stupidity and moved from the back door and sat on the top step, then scooted as far away from her as he could without falling off the step.

They sat in silence for a while, but at last he had to ask her something, anything just to hear her voice once more. "Do you sit out here by yourself often?"

"It's as far as I can get from the house and all its demands and still be close enough to hear my son if he calls out." She shrugged. "Time to call my own, time to do what I want, even if it's only to sit here and do nothing."

Something twisted in his gut. Many times, he'd heard prisoners say something similar after being in prison for a long time, especially if they were sentenced to hard labor. He hated to think of her as a prisoner in this house, but he could see how it'd happen with the way the barber and his daughter treated her. And as near as he could tell, she did most, if not all, of the work around here. He didn't believe for a minute the barber's daughter had cleaned his room or baked the pie, and Mrs. Small didn't seem well enough to do any work "What draws you out here, on the back porch? Wouldn't you be more comfortable in the front? I noticed the swing on the front porch."

She laughed a little. "That swing was here when we moved in. The first thing Uncle Ed told me and Tina was that under no circumstances were we to sit out there after the sun set. But what he said didn't really apply to me since I'm never finished with my chores until after dark." She shrugged again. "Besides, he locks the front door early. It's my responsibility to lock the back one."

And she'd be the first one thugs would attack if they broke in. "So you just come out here and sit?"

"I like to listen while the world settles for the night. And then there're the stars. Millions and millions of them."

He watched as her lips tilted up into a smile. He was thankful for the full moon so he could see her face.

"Someone told me once my name means 'Star,' and he's called me that ever since. But those stars mean more to me than that. They mean I'm not alone."

Colin had an idea she meant God, but he wasn't going to say anything about it, not with the way he'd pushed that part of his life out of the way for so long.

While he sat there, peace he hadn't known for some time settled over him. He wanted to soak it up. But the longer he sat there, the more restless the pretty woman became. He thought of the way she looked when she left the livery earlier, holding her son's hand, then later while they ate supper together. "You've got a fine son. He seems real bright and polite."

She stood, still clutching the knife. "Thank you. I-I think it's time to go in."

He stood and waited for her to enter the house before him.

Her hands trembled a bit. "Please go on in so I can lock the door. Uncle Ed'll be upset if I don't secure the door before I retire. I have to get up early to fix breakfast."

It was clear she wanted him to go inside and leave her alone.

He would tonight. But tomorrow might be a different story. Curiosity about her ate at him. Maybe it was the lawman in him, but he wanted to know more about her. Halfway across the dining room, he stopped dead in his tracks when he realized what he was thinking. He hadn't been curious about a woman since his wife Jessie died. And he didn't have time now to indulge any personal matter. He swallowed a burst of laughter. What was he in Central City for, if it wasn't a personal matter? One day he would find the Miller gang, and then they would die.

Before the sun had even lightened the sky the next morning, Esther pulled herself out of bed. She hadn't slept well. The dream had come again. And like a thief, it had stolen her peace as well as her rest. Moving quietly in the dim predawn, she dressed and went to the kitchen to mix bread dough. A little while later, she put the sausage patties on to cook. All the while, memories of the marshal sitting on the back porch floated through her head.

She'd been uncomfortable with him when he'd first come out of the house. *First come out of the house.* She laughed to herself. She'd been uncomfortable from the moment he'd thrown himself on top of her.

She flipped pancakes while memories kept taunting her. There had only been one man she'd sat outside with for the last five years, and he didn't count since he was the closest thing to a brother she had. But when the marshal said something about Davey, fear took hold, not knowing where that would lead. What if he'd asked about Davey's father? Who he was? Where he was? If she told him, it might leak out. Secrets, secrets, secrets. For her safety and Davey's, secrets must be kept. So she ran away from him last night.

It was for the best. It had to be.

After washing the breakfast dishes, Esther covered the last loaf of fresh-baked bread on the counter. She let out a sigh, thankful the chore was done for at least two days. That still left shopping today and washing tomorrow.

A knock rattled the glass on the back door. Helga, who lived next door, grinned as she stood on the other side. Esther waved her neighbor to come in.

Helga opened the door just enough to stick her head in. "My brother's taking me to the mercantile. Want to come with us?"

Esther couldn't keep the smile stretching across her face. Not only would the invitation save her from having to walk unescorted to the mercantile, but she could spend time visiting—something she hardly ever had time to do.

And there was so much she wanted to find out now that Helga's older brother had asked Wanda, one of her few friends, to marry him. "Oh, yes. Let me see the shopping list from Aunt Bonny, then I'll get Davey."

A little while later, they entered the mercantile. Esther greeted Wanda's father and handed him Aunt Bonny's grocery list, then joined her friends.

While Wanda stepped from behind the counter to show them the satin she'd picked out for her wedding dress, Esther looked around for Davey. He wasn't nearby like he usually was. She felt her chest tighten as her breath jerked in and out. There were so many strangers in town. Anything could happen to Davey.

She called his name once, then twice. No answer. She swallowed hard. He never wandered off.

She stood very still for a moment and listened. Yes, there off to the right. His little boy's voice whispered something. She rushed around a table filled with miner's pants. In the far corner, an old man she'd never seen before knelt by Davey with his arm around her son.

The man and Davey had their fingers pressed against their lips. Davey dropped his hand and grinned.

She ran to him, the heels of her shoes tapping against the wooden floor.

The old man and Davey looked up at the same time, the grins dropping from their faces.

Esther stopped so suddenly she almost fell. Two sets of dark brown eyes looked at her—Davey's full of merriment while the old man's glared. All at once his face changed. A smile slipped on his face.

"Mama, you found us." Her son giggled in the way only little boys could.

Esther waved her son to her side and brushed back the dark brown curl drooping across his forehead. The scar on her arm itched, but she refused to scratch it. It wouldn't help anyway. It was only a nervous reaction.

But she knew if she started scratching it now, she'd rip the skin right off her arm.

The stranger stood and shoved a lock of gray hair streaked with dark brown from his face. "Sorry, ma'am. Just having some fun with this little fellow. Playing hide-and-seek."

Esther gave the old man a quick nod. She rested her hand on Davey's shoulder and turned him around. "Come on, son. We're going to be leaving in a little bit."

Davey twisted his head and looked over his shoulder, then waved. "Bye, mister."

They headed back to the counter where her friends still looked at the material. All the way, she forced herself not to look back at the man.

The man stood. "Bye, son."

The last word caused Esther's stomach to clench and the scar on her arm to burn. That man wasn't her son's father. In truth, she couldn't say who the father was. She counted the steps until they were with Helga and Wanda.

Over the chattering of her friends, Esther listened to the man's footsteps as he limped across the floor. The bell above the door jingled when the door opened then shut. He was gone.

She let out her breath and looked out the window to make sure the man was truly leaving.

He stared at her from outside for several seconds, then mounted his horse and rode away.

Esther touched Wanda's arm. "Who was the old man just in here?"

"Who? Where?" Wanda looked around. "There haven't been any men in here for the last hour or so, just the Hollingsworth's housekeeper and the red-headed brother of hers." She blushed and ran her fingers across the bolt of satin. "Well, there might have been someone." She shrugged. "Lately, I've had my mind on other things." Wanda looked around the store. "Was he bothering you?"

Esther forced a smile to her lips for her friend's sake and shrugged. "Never mind. I just hadn't seen the man before."

But she rubbed her fingers over the scar that had been carved into her arm by Davey's father. A man she hoped—she prayed—was already in the deepest pit in the afterlife.

CHAPTER FOUR

Colin clutched his hat while memories of Miz Essie's smile at breakfast lingered in his thoughts. As he locked the door to his room, he tried to lock those memories into a closed-off place in his head. His boots thudded on the wooden stairs.

Even though he had his own reasons for coming to Central City, he still had the job he was sent here to handle. The old man from the livery wasn't far off. There had been a few rumors about gold being sent to the Confederacy. He needed to check them out. Best go and have another talk with Tuck.

As he headed toward the front door, he heard someone calling for him. His lips twitched. It was Mrs. Small's voice calling his name and not her daughter's.

He glanced to the hall leading to the family parlor. Mrs. Small hurried toward him but stopped suddenly. Her face turned as pale as one of his ma's fresh-washed sheets flapping on the line. She lifted her hand to her throat and reached for the wall to steady herself.

Colin raced over and took her arm. He led her to one of the chairs surrounding a small table by the front window. "Are you all right, ma'am? Do you want me to call your daughter or something?"

"No. No. Just a little winded, that's all. I wanted to catch you before you left."

He jerked his hat off his head and sat in the chair beside her. "What can I do for you, ma'am?"

Before she could answer, the front door opened, and the sheriff came in. Tuck removed his hat, nodded to Colin, then turned to Mrs. Small. "Morning, ma'am. The kid Sweeney stopped by this morning and gave me a note saying you wanted to see me first thing. Is there a problem?"

"No, not a problem, just something that needs to be handled privately." She looked from the sheriff to Colin and back. "I don't know if you two have met yet."

"Did yesterday, ma'am." The sheriff held out his hand. "MacPherson."

Still unsure what was going on, Colin shook the sheriff's hand. "Morning, Tuck."

They both turned to Mrs. Small.

"Gentlemen, I need to ask a large favor of you both, but we must hurry before either of the girls gets back. Fred, would you get the box on the table in there, please?" She waved toward the family parlor.

The sheriff gave Colin a quick glance, then went to the parlor and returned with a wooden box in his hands. "This what you meant?"

"Yes, thank you. Have a seat while we finish this business." Mrs. Small's hands trembled. She took the box and placed it on the table. With a flick of her fingers, she opened the latch and pulled out a piece of paper, a miniature painting, two daguerreotypes, a bag that made chinking noises, and several velvet-covered boxes.

"Fred, I asked you to come because you're the sheriff. I've gotten to know and love your precious wife when she and I worked together at the church bake sales. Marshal, I trust you wear your badge because you are an honorable and trustworthy man." Mrs. Small eyed each of the men.

Colin nodded as did the sheriff.

"Gentlemen, what I have to say must be kept in strictest confidence for now. You'll know the time to make it known, if it must be." She let out a deep sigh and pressed her balled hand against her chest. "I don't have long left in this life."

The sheriff started to say something, but Mrs. Small held up her hand. "It's what the doctor says, and it's what I feel. My heart's giving out quite rapidly now. But I have to right a wrong and protect someone who's very dear to me."

She slipped a white hankie from the cuff of her sleeve and coughed into it. "Like I said, what I'm going to tell you must stay in confidence, but it'll help explain what I'm doing. When I married, my parents provided me with a large dowry. My husband used it to keep his business going when we lived in Kansas. After…after my sister and her husband were killed, Mr. Small sold their rather large farm and everything else they had. He said since we were taking in Esther, we'd need it to help take care of her."

She shrugged. "I knew it was just an excuse to take the money, but I couldn't fight him about it. He had the law on his side. After all, he's my husband, and I'm just a woman."

Pain carved little lines on her face while her eyes filled with tears she tried to blink away. She let out a shuddering breath, then picked up the paper. "My husband loves his daughter above all else and will do anything and everything for her. So I have to protect Esther and Davey. They're my blood, my family."

She tapped the paper. "This is my will. The only things I've left, that are truly mine, are in these boxes."

She opened them. Resting in one of the velvet cases was a set of diamond jewelry—necklace, bracelet, and earbobs. "My grandparents were from New York and were quite wealthy. They gave the diamonds to their daughter on her eighteenth birthday. She wore them on her wedding day as you can see in this miniature. My sister and I also wore them on our wedding days." She held out the daguerreotypes, one which showed her several years before and a woman who favored her niece.

She opened the other cases and showed the jewelry inside them. "When our parents died, the daughters in the family got the jewelry. The sons got the business and the estates, which was fine with my sister and me. After all, we had husbands who had received our dowries, and they would take care of us."

Colin clasped his hands together under the table. Impatience to get on with his job warred with curiosity over where this story was leading.

Mrs. Small covered her mouth and coughed into the hankie again, then took a deep breath. "In the bag is money. Most of which came from two of my uncles, brothers to Will Sanders who owns the livery. There's also some money from my sister. She wanted me to purchase dresses and such for Esther's coming out since I lived in town."

She let out a small laugh. "My sister was one of the few women in this world who hated shopping."

A tear quivered on her lower eyelashes but never fell. "I never had the chance to dress Esther like my sister planned." She drew in a deep breath and straightened her shoulders. "That's all in the past. What I need to deal with is the present. My will states I am leaving this jewelry, the pictures, and the money to my niece, Esther."

Colin swallowed back a sigh of relief that the woman wasn't crying. He unclasped his hands and watched Mrs. Small take the pen next to an inkwell sitting beside the registry book he'd signed yesterday.

"Would you two please witness my signature on my will, as well as the items I have in the box?" She wrote her name in flowing letters, then looked at the sheriff.

Tuck nodded, then took the pen and dipped it into the inkwell.

As he wrote his name, she looked at Colin. "You may think these are the ravings of an old woman, but let me assure you it's nothing of the kind. In some ways, Mr. Small's been good to me, but he loves his daughter above all else. He's provided a good home for me and allowed me to be a mother to Ernestina. But he also loves money, and he doesn't like having Esther and Davey around."

She pushed the paper toward Colin. "When I'm gone, he'll force her out. This is just to protect her and give her something to start out on her own. I don't want her to have to resort to something unsavory to support herself and her son."

Mrs. Small took the velvet boxes, pictures, and the bag of money and put it all in the wooden box, along with an envelope she pulled from the pocket of her dress.

He spied her niece's name in the same flowing script written across the envelope.

She closed the lid and slid the latch into place. She tucked the will into a pale blue envelope and handed it to the sheriff. "Please hold onto this for me."

She touched the wooden box. "I have one more favor to ask of you men. Will you take this to Uncle Will at the livery? He's agreed to keep it until Esther needs it. And...and if need be he can testify to the ownership of the jewelry. He was there when my grandparents gave the diamonds and the rest of the jewelry to my mother."

Colin gripped his fists again to keep from shaking his head with the craziness of the whole thing happening here in the boardinghouse. Oh, he understood how a father might favor his daughter over a niece or how money might be so important to a man or even a wife wanting to see to the needs of an orphan niece. But the secrecy of seeing all the jewelry and money going into a wooden box to be given to a crippled livery stable owner seemed ridiculous.

So much wasn't being explained. Granted, the private life between a man and his wife was their business, but he'd been brought into it by Mrs. Small. Maybe the sheriff understood and just wasn't saying anything because there wasn't anything illegal about what was going on. Maybe like him, the other man was just trying to calm a woman's fears. But something just didn't sit right about the whole matter. And it involved Esther.

There was some bit of knowledge he didn't have. But he'd find out what it was. The hairs on the back of his neck told him he needed to know.

The two men walked side by side as they headed for the Sanders's livery. Colin balanced the wooden box in his large hands. He tipped his head just a bit toward the boardinghouse. "What do you make of what happened back there?"

Tuck led his horse with one hand as he rubbed his jaw with the other. "In the short time I've been sheriff here, I've seen some mighty strange things, but this is one I understand." He glanced at Colin. "You had much dealing with either of the girls from the boardinghouse?"

Colin bit the inside of his jaw. There was no way in this world he was going to tell the sheriff about what happened at the livery yesterday. "Had supper there last night. Miss Ernestina, uh, asked me to sit at the family table with her parents and then join them in the family parlor afterwards. Her cousin served the meal and sat with the other boarders and her son."

"Yep, sounds about like them. Don't like to gossip like an old lady, but that Small girl isn't the prettiest one around and is a mite pushy. On the other hand, that cousin of hers tries to stay in the background, but all the men notice her first, which I understand has caused a problem or two."

"The cousin a widow or something?"

"Not really sure what all happened before they came here from Kansas. But a husband didn't come with them, and as far as I know nobody's ever spoken about one."

Colin nodded. Something didn't add up. Mrs. Small said Esther was her sister's daughter. She called Esther her own flesh and blood, so why was Esther going by the name "Sanders," which seemed to be Mrs. Small's maiden name? Either some man named Sanders married Esther, then died or deserted her, or... Remembering the knife being held to his belly the day before might give him some of the answer. Kansas and Missouri had been a bad place in the last few years with all the fighting over whether the states would enter the union as free or slave. Then add to that, the outlaws who roamed the states.

"Morning, Sheriff, Marshal. Good to see ya both." Will Sanders sat on the same chair as yesterday, but he looked a bit better and his leg wasn't propped on the overturned bucket today.

"Morning, Will. How's the gout doing today?" Sheriff Tucker shook the old man's hand.

"Getting better."

"Don't understand it all, but we got something for you." Colin held out the wooden box.

The old man frowned, then took the box into his gnarled hands. "Hoped it wouldn't come to this." He let out a deep sigh as he shook his head. "But I'd figured it would, so I got a place to hide it ready." He looked at the Tuck. "She's afraid if she put it in the safe in the bank, her husband'd try to claim it."

He stared at the box as he rubbed his worn hand against the top. His voice lowered to a whisper. "Now Es and Davey'll be taken care of."

The old man raised his head. A grin crawled onto his face. "Did ya take my advice and get a room at the boardinghouse I told ya about?"

The memory of Esther lying in the hay with her brown curls scattered around her head and the freckles dancing on her nose popped into Colin's head. He dipped his head as the heat rose up his face. He didn't think the livery owner had seen what happened until the old man chuckled and mumbled something about knives being good for more than cutting up good-tasting apple pies.

A few minutes later, Colin followed Tuck out of the livery stable. When they got out of earshot of the old man, Colin glanced at the sheriff. "Think what's in the box is safe back there?"

Tuck chuckled. "Depends on what you mean. If you mean, do I trust Will Sanders to hold onto the box for his niece, yep, I do. If you mean, do I think the man can keep it safe and keep his mouth shut about having it? Then again, the answer's yep. That old man sees plenty. He's even helped me out a time or two when I needed some information about the coming and going of certain people around town."

Colin nodded at Tuck's answer. A couple of minutes later, they shook hands before parting ways. The sheriff had a town to take care of, and Colin needed to begin his assignment. He couldn't keep from grinning. Will Sanders had been right about the need to check on where the gold went.

No one needed to know how he'd used all the influence and favors to get sent to this mining town. Protecting the gold from the Confederacy was a good cover for his real motive in coming to Central City. After he completed his personal mission, he didn't care what happened to him. Or his star.

Ray Miller rode to the run-down shack and slid off his worn-out horse. He untied the burlap bag of grub and pulled his rifle from the scabbard, then looked around at the surrounding hills. All seemed quiet. He snorted. Seemed and are—two different things.

The door to the shack creaked open. "Pa, you coming in?"

Ray took a last look around. "Anyone been by while I was gone?' He really didn't have to ask. If there had been anyone, there would've been blood on the ground or his boys would've been dead.

"No, Pa."

"How's Jake? Any change?" Ray entered the shack and pushed past Blake, his youngest. The boy's ma had coddled him for years. Ray snarled at the thought of the woman. She said he'd made outlaws out of their two oldest, but she was keeping her baby away from that kind of life. Well, now the woman was in the ground, and the boy needed to learn what it meant to be a Miller.

His middle son huddled on the dirt floor of the shack. Ray swallowed back a snort of disgust. Prison had changed Harve. Before he was caught, the boy had been the spitting image of him and his older brother, knowing who he was and taking what he wanted. Now he was just a beaten-down pup. OK, so he'd been shot when they escaped, but he needed to get up and get better, or he was going to die.

Ray dumped the bag of grub on the table, then crossed the dirt floor to the wooden bunk by the wall. His oldest boy, Jake, lay there sweating and mumbling. He let out a curse. The boy had never gotten over the wounds he got when they broke out of prison. He'd gotten better several times. But for every time he got better, his fever returned. They were going to have to get a doc to look after him, and soon.

Blake moved to the side of the bed. "Learn anything?"

"Enough. Didn't get too far into town 'fore I saw Fred Tucker. Had to hide out 'til he went back to his office."

"What's he doing out here?"

A deep chuckle burst out of Ray. "With the limp he's got, prob'bly couldn't stay with the marshals." He crossed back to the table and dug into the bag. "Here, heat these while I take care of my horse."

A can of beans flipped through the air. Blake ducked.

Afraid of a lousy can of beans. Ray cursed again. After he got what he came for, he'd have to kill the sheriff. If it weren't for that man, his two sons wouldn't have been sent to prison and be here now, one shot up and the other dying. He started for the door.

"Pa." Blake's voice came out timid as a scared rabbit. "D—did ya find what we come for?"

"Yep." He stopped for a second as a thought struck him. He chuckled. "And I just figured out how to get it."

He went out to care for his horse, plotting all the way.

Esther stood outside the boardinghouse and leaned against the back door, welcoming the humid breeze. The clouds overhead mimicked the way she felt—dark and swirling. The old man at the mercantile still bothered her. Why him? Why of all the hundreds, if not thousands, of men coming to Colorado to find a fortune in the gold fields did this one man bother—no, scare her so much? She'd never seen him before. She didn't even know his name, but then she didn't know the name of the men who'd attacked her either. That whole day was still a blur.

The old man's face floated through her mind time and again, along with the look he gave her just before he rode away. Fear tried to seep in, but she shoved it away. She wasn't going to let the man scare her. She'd worked too hard for the peace she had in her life.

She opened the door and stepped inside. Rain was coming soon, and the pies should be done by now. But before she moved further into the kitchen, she locked the back door, something she usually didn't do during the day. But today felt different.

A few minutes later, she lifted the last pie from the oven just as the first sprinkles struck the windows. The sprinkles turned into a real downpour. The smell of fresh rain floated in the open window by the dry sink. Esther relaxed a little as the smell of coffee and cinnamon joined with the sound of Davey playing in their room with his wooden horses.

Someone knocked at the back door. Esther tried to make out who it was, but the rain running down the glass pane fought against her. All she could make out was a man staring at her with his hat pulled low on his face. Surely the man at the mercantile hadn't come here. She grabbed the first thing her hand touched—her rolling pin.

A nervous giggle slipped past her lips. After all the stories she'd heard of women threatening their husbands with a rolling pin, and now she was arming herself with one. But she'd no husband to protect her, and she didn't know why the man at the back door didn't come in the front door, like everyone else.

He raised his fist and struck the door frame again, then called out something. Star? That voice. She knew it, and he called her "Star." Dropping the rolling pin, she ran to the back door and jerked it open.

"Oh, Dougal, come in." She grabbed her friend's arm and pulled him in out of the rain. "You're getting soaked."

"Wasn't sure you were going to let me in." He took the towel she handed him and dried his face and hands. "What was the matter? Even through the rain on the glass, I could see your eyes wide as an owl's at night."

"I, uh, I thought you were someone else." She turned to get him a cup of coffee, but he touched her arm with the tips of his fingers, not grabbing her like some men might. She turned back to him and swallowed hard at the fierce look in his eyes and the way his hands had balled into fists.

But his anger didn't frighten her. Dougal would never, ever hurt her. "Want some coffee?"

"What man, Star? Has someone been bothering you?"

She let out the breath she'd been holding inside. "No, it was just a man I saw at the mercantile today. He didn't do anything, not really." She shrugged. "I guess I just let my imagination get the best of me, and then I saw someone at the back door and thought it was him. It was nothing really."

Dougal relaxed. His fists uncurled, but the tightness stayed around his eyes. "All right, but tell me what this man looked like. I'll keep an eye out for him."

"Don't bother." She tried to smile.

"Star."

She felt the smile soften a little. Dougal was the only one to call her that, said it was what her name meant, and with the way her eyes shined so much, it just seemed right to use.

One of his eyebrows rose a tiny bit as he tilted his head to the side. "In all the time I've known you, nothing's ever scared you. This has. I just want to check it out. Let me help you, please."

Since I wasn't there for Callie. Esther finished the thought for him. She still remembered the night the sheriff had come and told him the girl he'd planned to marry had been killed.

"All right, as a friend, you can check into it for me."

Dougal grinned. He wrapped his arm around her shoulders and pulled her into a bear hug. "How about like a big brother who has the right to look after you and irritate you at the same time? I've enough experience since I've got five younger sisters."

The kitchen door opened. Tina stepped into the room and rested her hands on her hips. She glared at them as her face flushed an angry red. "Well, here's Mama Bonny's darling, entertaining men not fifteen feet from her bed. Is this how you got your son with no husband?"

Esther tried to pull back, but Dougal only tightened his arm around her shoulders and returned Tina's glare. "Miss Small, it's a pity your stepmother has to tolerate such a vicious stepdaughter. She has my pity and my prayers. Maybe someday you'll have a change of heart." He glanced at Esther. "Now how about that cup of coffee you offered?"

Before Esther had a chance to move, the door swung open again.

CHAPTER FIVE

Colin jerked his hat from his head when he entered the boardinghouse front door and ran his fingers through his matted hair. He'd wandered around Central City most of the day, hoping to catch a word here or there about either Southern loyalty or any of the Miller gang. He heard nothing, although he did make a few contacts, possible sources of information he could check with later.

He sniffed and enjoyed the scent of fresh-brewed coffee, cinnamon, and apples, then followed the smell to the kitchen. Maybe he could get a few words with the lady cook along with a cup of coffee and a slice of warm apple pie. He had his hand on the kitchen door when the voices on the other side exploded.

"Well, here's Mama Bonny's darling entertaining men not fifteen feet from her bed. Is this how you got your son with no husband?"

"Miss Small, it's a pity your stepmother has such a vicious stepdaughter to deal with. She has my pity and my prayers. Maybe someday you'll have a change of heart."

The first voice belonged to a woman he didn't care for and disliked even more for the words she just spoke. The second voice belonged to a man he thought he might find around town somewhere, a man who he'd smashed in the face the last time he'd seen him, a man who said he was wrong to hunt the Millers for killing his wife and son.

Colin shoved open the door. "Get your hands off that woman, or you'll get what's coming to you."

The man glared at him, but he couldn't keep the twinkle out of his eye. "Says who?"

Colin pounded his fist against the star on the left side of his chest. "Says the man who wears this badge, the same man who your ma said to watch after you since you were old enough to stop wearing diapers. No, wait. Ma made me watch your drooling face even when you were in diapers."

"That's only 'cause she loved me best." Dougal released Esther and strode across the kitchen. They clasped forearm to forearm, just the way their pa had greeted family who came visiting, just the way Pa had sent them off when they were ready to leave home.

"Are you saying you know this man, this riffraff?" Miss Small scrunched her nose like something bad floated up it. "Surely, Marshal, he isn't one of your friends?"

Colin glanced at the young woman. "Not only is he my friend, he's my brother."

"Oh, for goodness' sakes." She grabbed her skirt in both hands and stomped out of the kitchen.

Colin punched his brother in the arm. "I take it you and that woman have a history?"

"Let's just say I stayed here for a while when they first opened the place, and I don't like girls who have husband-snatching on their minds." Dougal grinned. "She didn't care for me when I set her straight. I moved out shortly afterwards. Oh, but how I've missed the desserts they serve here, so I sneak back every now and again to get some." He looked at Esther whose mouth was all but hanging open. "Didn't you say something about coffee, Star?"

Colin couldn't help but grin when she looked from Dougal to him and back again. He knew they didn't look a lot alike except their green MacPherson eyes. He punched his brother on the shoulder. "What have you been doing with yourself out here?"

"Not much. Did some mining last year. Found a nice little vein and made some good money before it petered out. Since then, I've worked a few jobs here and there. Thought about going to the MacPherson ranch and working there with Grandda and Thorn. But I've just decided to hang around here and see what happens." Dougal grinned.

Colin felt something shift inside. Was Dougal interested in Esther? Something moved in his gut at the thought. He wondered what the barber's daughter had interrupted when she came into the kitchen. Had they been embracing? Kissing? He fought to keep the image from forming in his thoughts.

"Unca Dewy, Unca Dewy." Esther's son ran into the kitchen and right up to Dougal.

Colin let out a sigh and shoved those thoughts about Dougal and Esther aside. But he couldn't help but raise an eyebrow and stared at his brother. "Unca Dewy?"

"Watch it. Only he gets to call me that." Dougal tossed the boy in the air and caught him, then swung him around.

Colin frowned at the fun his brother was having with the little boy and the way Esther grinned at the two of them. *We'll see about that. Oh, yeah, we'll just have to see about it.*

Esther was filling large bowls with chicken and dumplings for supper when the door to the kitchen burst open. Her uncle entered the room. She set the pot on the table. *Oh, no. What does he want now?*

Uncle Ed closed the door with a snap. His eyes narrowed as he stared at her.

"What is this I hear about you entertaining men in your bedroom? This is a decent establishment, not a brothel." He pounded one fist against his other hand. "I'll not have you ruin the reputation of what I've worked so hard to build."

You don't raise a single finger to keep this place running. I clean. I cook. I do the laundry. Esther bit her tongue to keep from yelling the words. Instead, she waited for a moment, then another to let her anger cool. *Tina's mouth had been at work again.*

At last, she was ready to speak. "I'm not sure what you heard or who said it, but all that happened here today was Marshal MacPherson meeting his brother and having a cup of coffee and a piece of pie here in the kitchen. Oh, and they played with Davey for a while."

He continued to glare at her without saying anything. He'd done it from the time she was brought to his house, bleeding and hurt after her parents were killed. But she'd learned it was just his way of trying to show he was the one in charge, like a banty rooster trying to take charge of the henhouse. There was no reason to continue this silly fight. He had the power to throw her and Davey out, as well as ruin her reputation, if she made him too angry.

She shrugged. "You can ask them if you want. They should be out in the dining room now. The marshal paid for his brother's meal."

The door opened and a couple of the young boarders looked in. "Miz Essie, ready for us to take the food out?"

She looked at her uncle. "Will there be anything else?"

He growled something under his breath and left the room.

"All right, grab the dishes. They're ready." The men took the food while Esther set three plates on the tray and followed them out. But the small family table was empty. She shrugged and took the tray back to the kitchen to keep warm.

Returning to the dining room, she noticed all the men looking at her. No one had started eating.

Davey pulled at her hand. "Momma, can I pray?"

She looked around. The men smiled and nodded.

"All right, son." Davey grinned and clasped his hands together.

She gave a quick silent prayer of her own. *Thank You, God, for the wonderful son You have given me. Please help me to raise him in a way that brings glory to You. I pray this in Your Son's name.*

Esther watched as Davey twisted his head and peeked at the men at the table while he thanked God for each one of them. Some of them grinned. Some of them wiped a tear from their eyes. *How long was it,* she wondered, *since anyone had prayed for them by name? What they could all learn from a child.*

She'd make a point to pray for each of these men by name also, before she went to bed. Everyone needed to know someone was praying for them, asking God to care for them, and during the next few days she'd let them know she was doing just that.

The next moment, a chill ran through her. God hadn't protected her when those men attacked her. Would He protect her if they came again?

Colin bent his head in respect for the woman at the end of the table and the way she was raising her son, but he couldn't—he wouldn't—pray. He wasn't that much of a hypocrite. Hatred and vengeance filled his thoughts. And even though he'd walked with God for many years—had carried his own son on that path for the four years he'd been with him—Colin had followed another path since the day they were murdered.

It hurt even to look at the little boy on his knees, holding his hands together with his head bowed. Five years later, it still tore the heart out of him when he thought of his wife taking their son and leaving him. All because he wouldn't give up his badge. Well, the badge gave him the right to go after killers. And even though the Millers hadn't put a bullet through Jessie and Matty, their attempt to rob the stagecoach ended with it going over the cliff and killing them nonetheless. Colin gripped the bench to keep from leaving mid-prayer.

Dougal poked him with his elbow.

Colin raised his head. He hadn't realized the boy had finished his prayer.

"Let it go." Dougal's eyes said more than his mouth. His brother had been with him when he finally got to the stage.

Suddenly, Dougal smiled. "If you aren't going to get any of those chicken and dumplings, pass 'em on. Others want some of 'em."

Colin loaded his plate and passed the bowl.

About halfway through the meal, Miss Ernestina and her father entered the dining room.

"Sorry we're late." Mr. Small nodded to the men, then he and his daughter sat at the square table. Esther's uncle glanced at her. "We're ready now."

Colin watched Esther interrupt her meal and waited on her uncle and cousin like an employee, not a member of the family. Last night, he hadn't known the connection. After this morning, he did. He also understood why Mrs. Small had done what she did.

Dougal shifted beside him. A dark frown settled on his face.

Colin nudged his little brother in the side while he kept his voice low enough so only Dougal could hear him. "Now, you let it go."

Dougal's frown grew deeper.

Growing up, Colin had seen this side of his brother many times and often had to be the voice of reason to prevent a fight. "I know, but if you do anything, it'll only make it worse." He glanced at the young woman when she sat by her son. "Don't worry. She'll be taken care of."

His brother glared at him, but kept his voice low. "What are you talking about?"

"Nothing I can say now, but the matter's been dealt with."

Dougal nodded and went back to eating.

Colin glanced at the small family table. It was the strangest setup he'd ever seen. In every other boardinghouse he'd been in, everyone—owners and boarders alike—had sat at the same table, but not here. All at once, questions popped into his head when he realized it was just the barber and his daughter at the small table. Where was Mrs. Small? Had she gotten worse? Had her husband discovered what she'd done?

Esther jerked upright in bed. Darkness surrounded her, but something had woken her. Someone pounded on her bedroom door, then the doorknob rattled. She got out of bed. In all the time she'd lived here, no one'd tried to come into her room. But she kept her door locked anyway.

A voice cried out on the other side of the door, a female voice. Esther crossed the room to the door. "Who's there?"

"It's me. Tina."

Esther twisted the key in the lock. Before she could open the door the doorknob twisted again.

Tina burst into her room. "Get dressed. Papa said for you to go for the doctor." She held an oil lamp in one hand as she used her other to grab Esther's arm with enough force to tear her nightgown. "Hurry! Mama Bonny had some kind of attack!"

Esther pulled her arm from her cousin's hand. Was this some kind of nightmarish dream? But once her arm began throbbing from where Tina jerked on it, she knew it wasn't. Davey moved in the bed. If he woke, it'd take precious time to calm him—time she needed to get the doctor.

"Shush, you'll wake Davey." Esther pulled her dress from the peg on the wall. "Give me a minute to get dressed, and I'll do it. Go back and see if you can do anything for your father."

Tina left, taking the oil lamp with her. Thankfully, Esther knew where everything was in her room, so she didn't have to light a lamp and take the chance of waking Davey.

Esther slipped the dress over her nightgown and grabbed her shoes. She'd put them on in the kitchen. In the dark kitchen, she ran into a solid chest and would've fallen if not for the arms that wrapped around her.

Her shoes thudded on the floor. Black fear grabbed hold of her. No, not again. She struggled to reach the knife in her pocket, but his arms kept her from getting it. She fought the man as best she could, beating his chest, kicking his shins.

"Quiet. You'll wake the boy. I'm not going to hurt you."

The voice soothed the fear that the arms had caused. She stopped fighting. "Marshal?"

"I heard voices, someone running in the hall. I passed Miss Small on the stairs, but she didn't say anything. What's the matter? Is it your aunt? Did something happen to her?"

Esther drew in a deep breath. "How did you know?" She shook her head. "It doesn't matter. I need to get the doctor."

The marshal let go of her. "I'll get the doc. I know where he lives. Why don't you make some coffee? I'm sure it'll be needed before the night's out."

The man left through the back door without another word.

Esther wrapped her arms around herself and tried to make her teeth stop chattering. She remembered something her father had said one day. She couldn't even remember what happened, just his words. *Fear leaves a lot slower than it comes.*

When she felt steady enough to move, she built the fire in the stove and started a pot of coffee. By the time the coffee had boiled, the back door opened. Doc and the marshal hurried in. Doc nodded to her and headed to the patient who needed him.

She grabbed a cup and filled it for the marshal. "Thank you for getting the doctor."

"You're welcome." He took the cup. "And thanks for the coffee."

She paced back and forth across the kitchen. "Aunt Bonny hasn't been feeling well lately. I tried to get her to go to the doctor's office, but I don't think she did."

Colin stared at his cup. "She went."

Esther stopped in mid-stride. "How do you know?"

He let out a gust of air. "She told me"—he pulled his watch out of his pocket and pressed a button, and the front of the case popped open—"yesterday morning."

Something was wrong. Esther stared at him, wishing he could give her the answers she needed. Why would Aunt Bonny tell a stranger about going to see the doctor, but not her?

Before she could ask anything else, the door to the kitchen opened. Tina drifted in, her eyes red and her mouth wobbling.

Bands tighter than any corset she'd ever worn tightened around Esther's middle. "Aunt Bonny?"

Tina brushed her balled-up hands across her cheeks and sniffled. "The doctor's with her. Papa told me to come here." She wrapped her arms around her middle. "She can't die. She just can't. I need her. She's the only mama I have." She looked like a little lost child trying to find her parents.

No matter how her cousin had treated her, Esther couldn't let the girl suffer alone. She crossed the room to Tina's side and laid her hand on her cousin's shoulder.

But the moment she touched the girl, the door opened again. Uncle Ed walked in. His shoulders drooped.

Tina ran to her father. "How's Mama Bonny?"

He wrapped his arms around her. "It doesn't look good. The doctor says it's her heart." He pulled his daughter to the table and gently pressed her onto a chair, then dropped to the one beside her. "I didn't know she even had a problem. She never told me she'd gone to the doc." He stared at the table. "Why didn't she tell me?"

Esther poured two cups of coffee and set them in front of her uncle and cousin, then leaned back against the counter and closed her eyes. *Oh God, please be with Aunt Bonny. Guide the doctor as he tends to her. Comfort her. Ease any pain she might have. Please just hold her in Your loving arms. In the name of Jesus, I ask these things. Amen.*

She opened her eyes.

The marshal stood beside her. "I used to help Ma make breakfast. Want some help?"

Shifting from one foot to the other at his nearness, she moved a step away, then glanced out the window. The darkness had started to lighten. The boarders would be down soon. "Thank you."

Uncle Ed stood. "Fix a tray. We'll take it to the doctor. He could probably use some coffee. Add an extra cup. Ernestina will want to sit with her mama."

Esther kept blinking back tears as she fixed the tray. She longed to see her aunt, but knew she wouldn't be allowed, not now anyway. Her uncle and cousin took the tray and left the room. She put sausage patties on to cook, then mixed the dough for biscuits, all the while sneaking peeks at the lawman.

The marshal peeled potatoes and did a fair job of it, too. His mama must have taught him well. While she started the pancake batter, he finished the potatoes, then excused himself and left the room, saying he'd set the table.

Once she was alone, Esther let out a long sigh. She sat at the work table, wrapping her arms around her middle. Now she was alone, she could think of something besides the marshal and his presence in her kitchen.

Fear filled her mind. No matter how much she prayed, no matter how much she trusted God, the fear stayed. She didn't want to lose Aunt Bonny. It was horrible when her parents died, but she had Aunt Bonny to help her through it. If Aunt Bonny died, there would be no one left, just her and Davey.

CHAPTER SIX

Esther sat in the sick room and stitched a rip in Davey's dress shirt. She feared he'd need the shirt soon. Aunt Bonny's pale face rested against the white pillow. It'd been two days since her collapse, and she hadn't woken since then.

Weariness sat upon Esther like a heavy winter coat. The others were eating supper while she sat here. Bless the boarders' hearts. They'd shown such kindness the last couple of days. They insisted that after supper they'd watch Davey, along with washing the dishes, so she'd have time to sit with her aunt until bedtime. She couldn't help but smile. Some mamas had taught their sons well.

She glanced at the cot against the far wall. With Uncle Ed sleeping on the cot during the night and Tina watching over her step-mother during the day, someone was always with Aunt Bonny.

A light tapped echoed on the bedroom door.

"Come in." Esther's voice was just a whisper, but whoever was on the other side heard her. The door opened, and the doctor stepped inside. She stood and made room for him by the bed.

Doc Olson lifted Aunt Bonny's wrist and checked her pulse. "How's she doing?"

Esther stood. "Her breathing's changed in the last little bit."

He tucked Aunt Bonny's hand back under the cover. "It's to be expected. The time's growing near." He glanced at the chair where she'd been sitting. "Why don't I sit with her a bit? I'll wager you haven't had supper yet."

"I wasn't hungry."

The doctor smiled at her. "You have to keep up your strength. There're going to be stressful days ahead."

Esther bit her lip to keep from crying and nodded.

He patted her on the shoulder. "If it wouldn't be too much a bother, could you send along some coffee? It's been a long day—three births, a broken leg, and four miners who got banged up in a small cave-in."

She nodded. "Have you had any supper?"

"Not yet, but my housekeeper usually leaves something for me on the stove."

"I'll bring you a plate with the coffee. The boarders are having ham and beans with cornbread."

He patted his flat belly. "Thank you. Sounds mighty fine."

When Esther passed through the dining room, her uncle motioned for her with a wave of his hand.

"Why aren't you with my wife?"

"Doc Olson's with Aunt Bonny. He hasn't had supper. I'm going to get him a tray."

He tossed his napkin on the table. "Bring it to me when you have it ready. I'll take it up. I want to talk to him."

She nodded and went to fix the meal. A few minutes later, she handed her uncle the loaded tray. She felt the eyes of all the boarders on her, so she went back to the kitchen. There was no way she could swallow any food right then.

In the solitude of the kitchen, she poured water from the stove over the dirty dishes in the small tub. She tried not to notice the little plops of moisture that fell from her cheeks into the wash water. As she rinsed the big pot she'd used for the beans, she heard the door open.

Sweeney, one of her usual helpers, cleared his throat. "Miz Essie, you, uh, you need to sit and have some supper. Me and the boys're fixing to do the cleaning, so we can have dessert."

Esther looked over her shoulder. The cakes still sat on the worktable. "You can have dessert first. I'll eat later."

"Ah, no ma'am. Rule is we clean first, everything but the dessert, then the last one to finish has to wash the dessert stuff." He shuffled his feet for a moment as his face glowed pink. "I usually have to clean up the last of the stuff. But ma'am, your desserts're so good. I just can't shovel them down like some of these yahoos. You cook just like my ma, and I do some remembering as I eat."

She covered her lips with her fingertips and swallowed a couple times. "Thank you, Sweeney. I think I'll fix me a plate."

"That's good, Miz Essie, since Jeb's out there already loading you a plate. Just go on out there and sit with your boy. He doesn't like to eat without you."

The young boarder grinned when she passed into the dining room.

Just as Sweeney said, Jeb had a plate ready for her to eat. Davey rested on his knees with a big grin on his face. Across from him was the marshal, holding a cup of coffee. While she sat, she glanced at the family table. Tina glared at her, then threw her napkin on the table and left the room.

Trouble was brewing with her cousin, but right now Esther was just too tired to do anything about it. Davey wrapped his arms around her neck, pulled tight, and gave her a smacking kiss on her cheek. She drew him close, hugging him back. "Let's eat."

Davey grabbed his spoon. "Yeah, let's eat."

By the time they'd finished eating, the boarders returned with the cakes. They cut and served pieces for everyone, then gobbled everything on their plates. Forks chinked on dishes as each man finished, complimented her on the supper, and left. All except Sweeney. He savored each bite. When his piece was all gone, he stood and gathered the others' plates and forks.

Esther stood. "I'll finish. Why don't you join the others?"

Sweeney looked shocked. "Oh, ma'am, I couldn't. It's against the rules." He glanced at Davey. "And us men gotta follow the rules, don't we?"

Davey puffed out his chest. "Yeah, Mama, us men gotta follow the rules."

Esther couldn't keep back her grin. Sweeney had her, and to think he used her son to do it. "All right, and thank you."

The marshal stood. "Would you and Davey care to take a stroll, a short one? I don't think you've been out of the house in several days."

"Oh, Mama, please?" Davey looked at her with big eyes and hands pressed together.

Esther glanced toward the stairs. Doc might come down any moment. Could she go out for just a few minutes? Poor Davey had stayed inside ever since Aunt Bonny had fallen ill. She took another peek at her son. He held his little hands together with such a look of longing on his face. How could she refuse, even if it meant going out with the marshal?

They left through the front door. Davey scampered the pathway between the boardinghouse and the next three houses. The neighbors waved to them from their porches when they passed.

Esther tried to think of something to say, but her mind was a jumble of thoughts. All at once, she realized this was the first time in five years she'd taken a walk with a man. Not since the time before the attack. Afterwards she hadn't wanted to be alone with any man. Of course by then, her condition made for gossip. What respectable man wanted to be seen with an unmarried mother, much less court her? By the time they'd moved to Central City, she'd become not much more than a household drudge in her uncle's home with hardly any time of her own.

"I hope you got some rest today." Marshal MacPherson seemed to shorten his stride to match hers.

She shrugged. "Not much. I guess I'm too worried about my aunt and…things."

"Is there anything I can do?"

Before she could answer, she heard someone calling for her. They turned around as Sweeney ran toward them.

The young man stopped in front of them and breathed hard for a moment or two until he got his breath. "Miz Essie, Miz Essie, you're needed back home."

The marshal lifted Davey in one arm and rested his other hand against her back. "I got him. Let's go."

Esther nodded her thanks, grabbed her skirt with one hand, and ran.

Sweeney followed behind them.

When they entered the boardinghouse, Tina glared at them. "How dare you go out and cavort with men when Mama Bonny died?"

Esther bit back the cry of pain filling her heart. She knew the time she feared had arrived, but still she wasn't ready for it. "Thankfully, she's with Jesus."

"What do you care?" Tina wiped her face with the back of her hands. "She loved me more than you." She pounded her chest. "I was her daughter."

Tina pointed her finger at Esther and glared. "You were just the girl she took in because you were going to have a baby."

"Tina, don't say anything more. Please, don't." Esther reached out to her cousin, but her cousin slapped her hand away.

Tina turned to the boarders who'd come out of the general parlor. "You all didn't know that about your precious little Miz Essie, did you? She had a baby out of wedlock. Her son there is just a ba—"

Uncle Ed rushed down the stairs and gripped his daughter's shoulder. He jerked her around, pulling her into his arms. "Shhh, little one. Let your papa hold you."

Uncle Ed faced the boarders. "I'm sorry, men. Understandingly, my daughter's upset and is confused in her grief. Please forget her outburst."

Uncle Ed ushered his daughter to the stairs without a word to Esther.

No one said anything, but Esther could feel all the boarders' eyes on her. Pain pressed in hard on her head, on her heart, on her soul. Grief fought with humiliation. Esther stood still as a statue for several seconds, then she pivoted on her foot, grabbed Davey from the lawman's arms, and rushed out of the room.

Burning fire filled Colin's gut at the gall of the man and the selfishness of his daughter. Esther had to be hurting from the loss of her aunt, then the young vixen spewed out her poison. And the worthless uncle seemed more concerned about his daughter than the devastation she'd caused. He watched Esther stand before the boarders, her face pale, cold, and unmoving. Suddenly, she grabbed her son away from him and ran out of the room.

He started to follow her, but stopped when Sweeney spoke.

"I don't care what that little biddy says about Miz Essie. She's one of the finest women I know. And I'll say right now, I claim her as my little sister, and if any of you men so much as insult her or try to take advantage of her, you'll answer to me."

Two other men stepped beside Sweeney. "Us, too."

The other men raised their voices in agreement.

Sweeney looked at each man. "And I say we never repeat what we heard any more than we'd say something like that about our own mas or sisters back home."

The men agreed again.

Colin left and headed for the kitchen. The fire in his belly had changed to ashes over what Esther had gone through in the last few minutes. Thoughts of the knife she carried and her skittish actions when she was around him raced through his mind. He was pretty sure he knew what had happened to her years before.

God help me. I'm scared. Esther sat in a rocking chair on the back porch with Davey in her lap. Thankfully, he was too young to understand what Tina said. But now that Aunt Bonny was gone, the time had come to move on.

But where would she go? Why hadn't she gone to the bakery to see if they had an opening, like she'd planned?

With little more than three dollars in egg money, she didn't have near enough to set up a home anywhere for Davey, not for long anyway.

Aunt Bonny's funeral would probably be tomorrow or the next day. Would she have time to find a job and a place to live before Uncle Ed forced her out?

She leaned her head against the back of the rocking chair and tried to make a plan.

After breakfast was finished tomorrow and the men left...a flood of heat filled her whole body. The men. What must they think of her now? How was she going to face them? Surely they wouldn't say anything in front of Davey. All the more reason she needed to leave soon.

The back door opened. The marshal stepped out.

Colin stood in the kitchen at the back door, his clenched fist resting on the wood facing. His gut tightened as he watched the woman who had been so cruelly spoken about by someone in her family. Families should stick together, cling together, stay together.

His breath burst out in a huff. If Jessie had stayed, they'd still be a family. Matty'd be almost nine and might've had several more brothers and sisters to play with. But Jessie took it all away. Jessie and the outlaw bunch who killed them. Ray Miller and his sons. Maybe one of them was dead now from injuries from the escape. It'd even the odds a bit, but he'd find the others and give them the justice they deserved.

He eased his fist to his side and willed his muscles to relax. He couldn't do anything for Jessie and Matty right now, but there was a woman out there who needed a little comfort. And though he couldn't give her the comfort she needed, he figured he could ease her mind a bit.

Colin opened the door and stepped out onto the porch. "I didn't get a chance to tell you how sorry I am for your loss. Although I haven't been here long, I could tell you meant a lot to Mrs. Small and she to you."

"I loved her almost as much as I loved my own mother." She sniffed a bit like she was trying to hold back tears.

He hoped she would for now. He knew she'd need to cry out her grief. But like his own pa, he didn't handle women's tears none too well. "And I also wanted you to know none of the boarders are taking to heart what...what Miss Small said about you. The fact is, your boarders love you like a sister and all pledged to never repeat what she said. I'm not sure any of them believed her anyway."

"But it's true. I've never been married. Some men came to the farm when we lived in Kansas...Mama..."

The moon wasn't full any longer, but it still shed a lot of light. And the light showed him the pain filling her eyes.

"You don't have to say anything more." He'd seen firsthand the results of the raiders in Kansas and Missouri who stole and burned, raped and killed. "I figured you'd had...trouble, what with the way you act around strange men. Along with the knife you carry in your pocket. But you needn't worry the boarders'll say anything. Your secret's safe."

Esther rubbed her son's back. "Secrets never stay hidden forever. They have a way of coming out when you least expect them to. Just look at tonight." She looked so alone sitting there holding her son.

Colin tightened his hands to keep from grabbing her and offering her some comfort, rubbing her back like she was doing to Davey.

She sniffled. "I appreciate you telling me what the boarders said." She stared at the stars. "There are some things I'm going to miss about living here. Those men are one of them."

"You don't have to leave right now. Give it a few days. Your cousin'll get her grief under control, and everything'll get back to normal—well, as normal as can be without your aunt."

She shook her head and looked at him. "No. I've been thinking about this for several days, but I couldn't leave with Aunt Bonny, well, while Aunt Bonny needed me." She took in a deep breath. "Besides, I don't think Uncle Ed'll give me a choice."

Colin agreed, but he wouldn't say so. "Whatever you do, just know me and the men in there want the best for you, and if you need help, let me know."

She nodded and stared back at the stars, all the time stroking her son's hair while he nestled against her chest.

He bit his bottom lip. He wanted to say something else, but there was nothing more to say right now. He'd go to her great-uncle at the livery tomorrow and let him know about his niece's death. Esther would need him, along with what her aunt had left her. With the matter settled in his mind, he went inside, hopefully to sleep. Hopefully to sleep without dreams of this woman sitting outside all alone except for the child she loved. Hopefully without dreams of his own son lying in the cold ground back in Missouri.

CHAPTER SEVEN

Early the next morning, Esther pulled herself out of bed. She hadn't slept much, but breakfast needed to be cooked for the boarders. Using the tepid water still in the pitcher in her room, she washed, then dressed for the day.

By the time she heard the first of the boarders coming down the stairs, she had the coffee ready along with hotcakes, ham slices, and biscuits with redeyed gravy. She even had the men's lunch pails filled and ready for when they left.

Sweeney stuck his head in the kitchen. "Ready for me to take in the food, Miz Essie?"

Esther smiled at him. "Yes. And, Sweeney, thank you for what you and the other men said last night. Marshal MacPherson told me. I—I appreciate your support."

The young man blushed from his neck to his forehead, especially his ears. "Like I said to the others, I claim you for my sister. If anyone does anything against you, he'll answer to me."

She wiped a tear from her cheek. "Well, big brother, why don't you take out the biscuits and gravy so the others can get started?" While he gathered those things, she grabbed the coffee pot and the first platter of hotcakes. She'd return for the rest of the hotcakes and the ham slices.

In the dining room, the men greeted her with nods and smiles, then their condolences. Her chest eased a bit at their welcome. While she returned with the rest of the food, her uncle entered the dining room and sat at his usual place at the small square table.

When she returned with his plate, he stopped her before she returned to the kitchen.

"When I'm finished, I'll take breakfast to Ernestina. She isn't feeling well today. Please prepare a tray of toast and tea for her. Also, add some of the berry jam Ernestina made. I think she'd like it." He turned back to his meal.

Esther bit her lip. *Oh, yes, the berry jam.* Weeks before, on her last day off, she and Helga had gone berry picking and made the jam together to use for gifts at Christmas. Ernestina discovered the jars in a sealed box at the back of the pantry and gave some to her father saying how she had made it. Esther hadn't corrected what her cousin said. It wouldn't have made any difference. She'd learned through the years Uncle Ed would've believed his precious daughter no matter what she said and Esther would've been punished for lying.

She went back to the kitchen. Once breakfast was done, she needed to go and let Uncle Will know about Aunt Bonny. She lifted the tray as her uncle entered the kitchen.

"Is it ready?" He took the tray, then gave her a look that made her uncomfortable, a look he'd never given her before. "Your aunt's funeral will be this afternoon at two. Be ready. I've sent word about the funeral to Bonny's uncle."

After a sharp nod to her, he headed for the door, but turned back and gave her one more of those looks before he left.

Esther pressed her hands together to stop their trembling. She'd gotten that same look from some of the men when they'd first stayed at the boardinghouse, but they stopped when she didn't respond to any of their advances. A deep shudder shook her body. She remembered how five years ago two men gave her that same look, then did more than look.

She drew in a deep breath. It'd taken lots of tears and her aunt's love, but she learned to accept the harsh realities of life. And whatever happened next, she'd be able to handle it, too. She had to, for Davey's sake.

"Are you sure they did it?" With the way the muscles in Colin's gut twisted round and round, he was thankful he hadn't had any breakfast yet. It looked like the Miller gang had struck again and not too far away.

"According to what the miner who rode into town described just before he died." The sheriff held his horse's reins as they headed toward the livery. "'Course, there was that mark."

Colin carried his saddlebags and rifle. The Millers had struck again, and just like it was back in Missouri. Hold-ups, robberies, and rapes. But no one ever lived through the attacks so there weren't any witnesses to testify. Just the Millers leaving their mark on the dead.

As they neared the livery, a young man opened the large doors to the big barn.

"Morning, Sheriff."

"Sully. Good to see you back. This is Marshal MacPherson." He waited while Colin shook the redheaded man's hand. "He's got a horse here."

"Yep, Gramps showed me which ones were boarding and which ones he owned."

"Sully, can you put some grain in these? I don't know how long we'll be gone. Just add the charge to my bill." Colin tossed the young man the bags, then saddled his horse. With the news the sheriff had, they needed to get moving. When he was done, he led his horse to the entrance.

The young man handed Colin the saddlebags.

The sheriff looked around. "Where's your grandpa?"

"He got word 'bout a man twixt here and Denver who had some horses for sale. Since he's feeling better and I'd gotten back, he lit out yesterday real early. Figured he'd be back tomorrow or the next day or the next."

"Didn't he get word about Mrs. Small's passing?" Colin hated to think about Esther grieving alone, even worse being at the mercy of the barber. He felt a small tug to go back to the boardinghouse to see if she was all right, but a greater pull to go after the Millers.

"Oh, Mr. Small had Sweeney come by and tell me yesterday morning, but Gramps had already left." He shrugged. "I got busy and couldn't make the funeral."

Sourness rose up in Colin's throat, but he swallowed it. He'd see what he could do to help Esther and Davey out when he got back. But for now, they needed to track down the Millers.

Colin mounted his horse and wasn't surprised when Dougal rode up beside him. They nodded to each other. Maybe together they could put all the Millers away for good. Hopefully, before they killed anyone else.

Colin, Tuck, and Dougal rode hard to the miners' camp. They didn't have much information, but enough. It was the bloody detail which caused Colin and the sheriff to think Ray Miller and his sons had done the killings.

They neared the miners' camp.

The stench of death hung heavy in the air, surrounding Colin—filling his nose, his mind. He willed himself not to gag.

A brown-haired stranger wearing a buckskin shirt rode toward them.

"Marshal MacPherson, meet Adam Lone Eagle, one of the best trackers in this part of the country. Matter of fact, he's the one who tracked your cousin Thorn's wife last year."

Colin wasn't sure who Thorn was, so he glanced at Dougal.

His brother nodded. "Thorn lives on the family ranch with Grandda and Granny south of here."

Colin didn't have time to hear about the Colorado family now. He looked back at the tracker. "Good to meet you."

The stranger nodded, then glanced at Tuck. "It's safe. No one's around."

They rode closer to the shack and stopped at the sight that greeted them. The miners lay where they'd died, one just outside the crude cabin, one by the small corral, and the third just outside the lean-to, next to the corral where their donkeys stood in the sun.

Colin, along with the other men, dismounted and checked to see if any of the miners were still living. There really wasn't any real need to do it, not from the color of their faces and the pools of blood around each one of them, but they did it anyway. "They're all marked the same way."

"Yeah, every one of them." The sheriff slammed his fist against his leg. "Just like in Missouri." He walked to the lean-to and grabbed a couple shovels and a pickax. "Adam, could you look around and check out where they're headed? We'll bury these poor boys."

Colin didn't want to take the time, but he understood the need, so he grabbed the pickax and pounded the ground where the sheriff indicated.

By the time they had the dead men buried, Adam had returned and dismounted.

"There're just two of them. One has a horse with a double notch in its shoe. Saw where they spent the night. Don't seem to be hiding their tracks." The man rubbed the back of this neck. "Something doesn't seem right, but I can't figure out just what it is."

After the funeral, Esther set out the cakes, cookies, and pies the neighbors and people from church had brought.

Several sweet ladies had brought dishes for supper. Neighbors and businessmen came by with their condolences.

While Uncle Ed and Ernestina welcomed them, Esther served coffee and tea. She was surprised when a few people offered sympathy to her. She figured most people didn't even know that Bonny was her aunt because she wasn't able to attend church very often. She figured they thought she was just a maid who didn't believe in God.

But that would change. She knew she and Davey would have to move out. As soon as they got settled somewhere else, they'd start going to church services every Sunday, no matter what.

These thoughts helped her through the afternoon, then supper.

After all the visitors had left and the supper cleanup was finished, Esther sat on the back porch in the rocking chair holding Davey as he fell asleep. Her body ached with tiredness.

She leaned her head against the back of the chair and looked up at the nighttime sky. Aunt Bonny loved the stars, too. She said their twinkling reminded her of God's love—glimmers of His care in a dark world. Even though Esther had taken to looking at the bright North Star as her special one, watching them all gave her peace.

At last, that peace settled over her. She could fall asleep and let tomorrow's worries wait until the next day.

The back door opened. Uncle Ed stepped out.

And that precious peace fled like a rabbit being chased by a fox.

The pale moonlight shone on his face. He glanced from her to Davey, then stared at the sky. "I thought it best if we talked out here."

He stood over her. She didn't like the feel of it and started to stand. He pressed his hand on her shoulder and forced her to stay seated. "As of last night, your place in this household has changed. While your aunt was alive, I was forced to take you in as part of her family. Now that she's gone, you're nothing more than a servant."

Davey shifted in her arms. She was gripping him too tightly and forced her hands to relax a bit. She knew Uncle Ed wouldn't let her stay, but she hadn't expected him to throw her out tonight.

"You have two choices, go out and find a new place to live, probably a saloon since no one'll want to take in an unmarried woman with a child to show how far she has fallen. Make no mistake. If you leave here, you'll leave without the lie that's protected you. People *will* learn you've never married. On the other hand, you can stay here, continue living like you have. But there'll be one change. I'll come visit you when I feel the need. You needn't worry about my daughter finding out. I'll come late at night when she's asleep."

His hand tightened on her shoulder. "You'll keep silent about the arrangement. If you don't, I'll throw you and your brat out, again making sure word gets around that you aren't a poor widow, but a loose woman who I had to get rid of to protect my innocent daughter."

His fingers loosened and moved in a rubbing motion on her shoulder as he looked at her. "You have until tomorrow night to make your decision. Late tomorrow night, and make sure your boy has something to keep him asleep."

Esther shifted sideways and pulled out from his grip, then stood with her son in her arms. "I don't need until then. I'll leave first thing in the morning."

His lips formed into a cruel smile. "So be it. But know if you leave, you can't come crawling back. I don't want the leavings of miners and cowboys."

He went back into the house.

Esther drew in a deep breath. Once before, she'd lost everything. She had to do it again, not just for herself, but for Davey. He depended on her. She couldn't let him down.

Early the next morning, Esther used the last of the sausage for the boarders' breakfast and the last of the ham for their lunches. When Sweeney came in to get the coffee, he stopped and stared at her.

"What's the matter, Miz Essie?"

She raised her eyes and tried to blink, but she was too tired to even do that. During the night, she had packed everything she and Davey owned, before snatching a couple hours' sleep. "I'm moving out."

"Where'll you and Davey go?"

"Great-Uncle Will's livery, for now." She forced herself to smile, then looked at him. "Do you think you or one of the other boarders could take my trunk to the livery before you go to work?"

"Do you have anything else besides the trunk?"

"Just my chickens, but I've nowhere to put them so I guess I'll just have to leave them here." Esther blinked back tears. She hated to leave the chickens. Aunt Bonny had given them to her the first Christmas they were here in Central City. The money she got from the eggs was all she'd had of her own since she'd come to live with Uncle Ed.

Sweeney grinned. "You won't have to leave 'em. We'll take 'em with us for now and figure out something later."

"Mama, trunk in bedroom?" Davey stumbled into the kitchen, rubbing the sleep from his eyes.

Sweeney nodded to her and took the coffee into the dining room. He returned a few moments later for the rest of the food. "Looks like there'll be one less for breakfast. The sheriff just came and got the marshal. And don't bother with the small table. No one's there."

Esther nodded and took Davey into the dining room. They needed to eat a good breakfast. And she needed to let the boarders know how much she would miss them all.

Then she'd be ready to leave. After all she did have a little money, enough to get by for a few days.

After that, she wasn't sure what would happen. She would just have to trust in God to help her.

Esther held Davey's hand while they walked to the livery. If the future wasn't so scary, she'd laugh at the sight they made—she and Davey leading their band of merry men as Sweeney and another boarder carried her trunk with all her earthly belongings between them, and four other boarders each toting two wood-and-wire chicken crates filled with squawking hens and one crowing rooster.

Sully, her second or maybe third cousin on her mother's side, stood gawking at them.

When they got to the front of the livery, the men set down their burdens, and Esther thanked them for their help. They waved good-bye and hurried off to their jobs.

Esther turned back to Sully. "Where's Uncle Will? I need to talk to him."

"Sorry, Es. He's not here. Won't be back for a day or three." Sully shrugged. "Sorry. He left before we heard 'bout Bonny."

"Oh, no." The strength she'd drawn on since last night slowly leaked out and flowed into the ground beneath her feet. She started to drift downward.

Sully grabbed her arm and pulled her to the chair his grandpa sat in while waiting for customers. Davey followed her and patted her hand. She tried to smile at him, but it took too much effort. Sully raced around and got her a dipper of water.

She sipped the water and tried to plan what to do next. She couldn't stay here. Sully and Uncle Will slept in the tack room, and there was no other place to sleep.

Something tried to push through the exhaustion in her mind. Something she'd been thinking about just recently.

Suddenly she remembered—the bakery. Maybe they'd still have that opening to replace the worker who was leaving.

"Sully, do you think I could borrow a buggy for a little bit? I won't be long."

"Sure. Gramps said to let you have a buggy anytime you wanted." He hurried off to hitch a horse to the small buggy at the back of the livery.

A little while later, Esther held Davey's hand as they walked into the Golden Nugget Bakery and Café. Only a few men sat around drinking coffee.

Davey's eyes grew wider and wider as he looked at the cookies and doughnuts on display.

An older woman, who was restocking the display case, looked over the counter. "Would you like a table or did you want something from the bakery?"

Davey tugged on Esther's skirt. She patted his hand. Much as she'd love to get him a cookie, she needed to watch what little money she had until she could find a job and a place for them to live. "I was wondering if the owner or manager is available."

"Just a moment." She turned around and went to the kitchen.

A minute or two later, two men followed her back as they talked to each other. They shook hands, and the older one went back to the kitchen area.

The younger man came toward Esther and stopped. "I'm Drew Hollingsworth. My wife and I own the Golden Nugget. Is there a problem?"

Esther smiled but felt it wobble a bit. "Oh, nothing like that. It's just…"

He held up his hand. "Let's have a seat while we talk." He held out a chair for her. "Ruth, would you get us some coffee and milk, please? And some doughnuts."

Mr. Hollingsworth lifted Davey onto a chair next to her, then sat across the table from her. "Aren't you Esther Sanders?"

Esther nodded. How could he know that? He had never been to the boardinghouse.

He smiled. "I thought I'd seen you at church a time or two with your aunt."

Aunt Bonny's still watching over us. Esther nodded. "I haven't been able to go to church as much as I wanted. There was too much to do at home with the boarders and all."

The woman who'd been behind the counter brought a tray with a cup of coffee, two glasses of milk—one big and one little—and a plate of doughnuts, along with a large cookie. She handed the cookie to Davey whose face lit up like a child at Christmas.

Esther chanced a quick glance at Davey. "What do you say?"

He grinned. "Tank you."

The woman smiled back and ruffled his hair. "You're welcome, kind sir."

Esther played with her glass of milk. She feared taking a drink of it since her stomach was in such knots. What if she didn't get a job here? Where would she go? She wasn't sure she could even make it back to the livery in order to return the buggy.

Mr. Hollingsworth placed his cup on the table. "You have my condolences on your aunt's passing. She was a truly wonderful example of a Christian woman."

"Thank you. I miss her so much." Esther blinked hard to keep back the tears filling her eyes.

He nodded. "Now, what do you need to see me about?"

Esther swallowed hard. The time had come. "I'm in need of a job. With my aunt's passing, I, uh, I find myself without a position. I'd heard one of the young women who works here is getting married and will be leaving. I was hoping I could fill her position. I don't care what it is. I'm willing to work at any job here."

He frowned.

Her hopes crashed.

"No, Linda isn't getting married. The young man decided he didn't want to marry her." His fingers tightened around the handle of his cup while a deep frown pulled his lips downward.

"Uh, well, thank you for seeing me." She stood, trying to decide where to go from here.

"Please, sit. I'm sorry I seemed upset. My anger wasn't directed towards you." He forced a smile to his face. "It's just the way some people think. In this case, I'm talking about the young man who didn't have the sense of a donkey."

Esther returned to her seat and gave Davey, who was still munching on his cookie, a smile.

"As far as a job here, we don't have an opening here. You see, I've just hired a manager and his wife to run the Golden Nugget. They have three daughters who'll be helping them." He loosened his fingers and fiddled with the handle of his coffee cup for a moment, then seemed to come to a decision.

"But I think I've something else in mind, something you'll like much better. Next week, I'll begin reading law with a lawyer who's recently moved to Central City, which is why I hired a manager here." The grin grew on his face while he watched Davey eat his cookie. "Also my wife and I recently were blessed with twins, a boy and a girl."

"Congratulations." Esther nodded, not sure where exactly this was leading.

"Thank you." He took a sip of his coffee. "We have a cook who comes in during the day and the young woman who'd planned to marry is now going to be our housekeeper, but we find ourselves in need of a nanny. And with you having a young son who seems happy and healthy, I think you may be a perfect person for the position."

"But, sir, I've never been a nanny. I wouldn't know what to do."

Mr. Hollingsworth smiled. "You've raised your son, right?"

She nodded and let go of the table so she could grip her hands tightly together.

"I've heard your aunt praise your work, your lifestyle, and your love for God often. And I held your aunt in the highest esteem. I saw how she worked with the less fortunate around town. She's reference enough."

Hope broke out of its shell. Could this be the answer to her situation? But what if Uncle Ed carried through with his threat? She'd find herself in just as bad a mess as she was in now. The only way to stop the damage from Uncle Ed was to tell the man before her about her past.

Esther prayed God would be with her and truth would win out. She cleared her throat, glanced at Davey, then at Mr. Hollingsworth. She forced her hands apart, ready to break free from the lie her uncle forced her to live, and pulled the hated wedding ring from her hand. The words came out soft and low. "I've never been married. My name is Esther O'Brien."

CHAPTER EIGHT

Esther held onto Davey's hand while they rode with Mr. Hollingsworth to his home. She remembered Aunt Bonny talking about the man and his wife, how they'd helped her with some of the widows of the miners. She thought at the time how much she wished she could have worked with them, but Uncle Ed told her she didn't have the time, then added additional chores to prove it.

The gentle love of her aunt outweighed the harshness of her uncle. For without that love, Esther knew she would never have come to peace about the murder of her parents, the attack, and the result of it.

She smoothed her hand over Davey's dark hair. No, she'd never call her son a result. He'd been the blessing which came from the loss. But without Aunt Bonny's love and teaching, she'd never have seen that. Blessings, her aunt had often said, were whatever brought one closer to God, no matter how terrible. So Aunt Bonny and Davey were both great blessings in her life.

They turned off the road to a path which led to the back of a large two-story house.

Esther looked around. It was a well-kept home with a barn in the rear. Maybe there would be a place for her chickens, if she was allowed to keep them.

Mr. Hollingsworth stepped out the buggy and came around to help her down. Davey tugged on her hand. "Mama, we gonna stay here?"

"I hope so, son."

A few moments later they walked up the steps to the back porch. A swing sifted in the breeze. They entered the kitchen. A woman, a little younger than Esther, looked at them while kneading the dough on the table.

"Drew, I didn't expect you back so quickly."

"Didn't know I'd be back so soon, but I'd like you to meet someone." He lifted his hand toward Esther and Davey. "This is the twins' new nanny, Esther O'Brien. And this young man is her son, Davey." He smiled and glanced at the woman at the table. "This is Linda, a good friend to our family. My wife's helping her to learn to be a housekeeper, but she's doing double duty since our cook, Pippa De Lucca, couldn't be here today."

Esther recognized the name as the young woman who wasn't getting married. It seemed Drew Hollingsworth and his wife helped everyone. A bit of tension, she didn't even realize had built up in her chest, eased.

"Helen has the children in the parlor. If you want, I can bring in some coffee." Linda gave the dough a pat and wiped her hands on a towel.

The smile dropped from his face. "She didn't bring them by herself?"

"Of course not." Linda chuckled. "As if she'd go against your orders."

"Good." He glanced back at Esther. "My wife had a hard time when the children were born, and she hasn't regained all of her health yet." He turned back to Linda. "I'd appreciate the coffee. I'll go introduce Esther to Helen." He held out his hand and waved them forward. "Let's go see my wife."

A spark of energy wove its way through Esther. This would be a wonderful home to work in.

They walked down a hall and turned to the right into a parlor. A lovely woman, a little thin and with dark shadows under her eyes, sat on the sofa. Her eyes lit up when she saw her husband. She put her finger to her lips.

"The babies have just fallen asleep." She kept her voice low and pointed to two cradles near the fireplace.

Mr. Hollingsworth directed her and Davey to a chair while he sat next to his wife. "I've someone I want you to meet. I thought she'd make a good nanny for the children."

His wife's eyes widened. "So quickly? We only talked about this last night."

"And look at how fast the Lord has provided for our needs." He settled back against the sofa. Barely touching her skin, he ran his finger down the side of her cheek.

Heat flooded Esther at the intimate gesture, but heat turned to chilling cold as she saw a long thin line running from the temple of Mrs. Hollingsworth's face to her chin. She wondered what caused such a scar.

Mr. Hollingsworth cleared his throat and his wife's face turned pink. They both looked at her. "Helen, I'd like you to meet Esther O'Brien and her son, Davey. Esther, this is my wife, Helen. Esther is Bonny Small's niece."

Esther nodded. "Please to meet you, ma'am."

Mrs. Hollingsworth nodded. "I've heard Bonny speak of you so many times I feel I already know you. I'm sorry for your loss. We'll all miss her." A sweet smile settled on the woman's face. "And I hope we'll become good friends. I think I need that as much as I need a nanny."

Esther looked at Mr. Hollingsworth to see what his reaction was. He just nodded. "All right."

"Good, now let me show you the babies."

When Helen stood, so did Esther. Davey slid off her lap and held onto her hand as if he didn't know where they were going next. She gave his hand a small squeeze. His whole world had been turned upsidedown since he woke this morning, and it wasn't even noon yet.

They stood by the matching wooden cradles. Helen touched the baby with tufts of light brown hair. "This is our son, Andrew Elijah Hollingsworth the Fourth, but it's too big a name for such a little fellow, so we just call him Andy." She touched the black curls of the other baby. "This is Sarah. She's named after her aunt, Drew's sister, Sarah Rose MacPherson."

Esther's head jerked up. "MacPherson? A deputy US marshal just came to town named Colin MacPherson. Are they related?"

"Probably." Helen laughed softly. "Sarah says Thorn, her husband, told her that he has eighty-one cousins spread from here all the way back to New York, plus his brothers as well as two sisters back on the ranch."

"I know Dougal MacPherson, the marshal's brother. He stayed at the boardinghouse for a while when we first moved here, and he became a good friend." Esther felt like slapping her hand across her mouth. She hoped Helen wouldn't think anything was going on between her and Dougal. But then she always felt she was on trial when her name was linked with any man.

"He's a good friend here, too. Even more so since he helped save my life as well as Sarah's last year." Helen leaned closer to Esther and dropped her voice. "And between you and me, I think he is a bit sweet on Linda."

Before Esther could say anything, Helen dropped beside Davey and pointed to the babies. "When they get a little bigger, you can play with them."

Davey jerked closer to Esther and pulled on her skirt. "Mama, don't wanna play with dolls."

"Oh, sweetie, those aren't dolls. They're babies, just like you were after you were born. But they'll grow just like you."

He grinned. "Me a big boy."

"Yes, and when they're bigger you can play together and be friends."

Davey stared at the twins for a moment, then nodded like a old sage. "Me be friends."

Linda entered the parlor and set the coffee tray on the table in front of Mr. Hollingsworth. Helen joined her husband on the sofa.

Exhaustion rolled over Esther, and she grabbed a nearby chair.

Mr. Hollingsworth stood. "Esther, why don't you go to your room and rest? With all you've been through in the last few days, I think you need a little time to get settled."

"But the babies." Even to her own ears, Esther's voice sounded weak.

"Don't worry. They'll be here tomorrow." He glanced at his wife who nodded, then turned toward Linda. "Could you show Esther and Davey to the bedroom on the other side of the nursery, please?"

Linda wrapped her arm around Esther's waist and urged her to the door. Davey tagged along beside them.

Esther looked over her shoulder. "Thank you. For the position, for the home, for everything. Thank you."

Linda directed them across the hall and up the stairs. "I'm glad you're here. Helen had a difficult time even before the birth of the twins."

"I noticed she was rather pale." As well as the scar on Mrs. Hollingsworth's face. Esther's own scar didn't seem so bad. At least she could cover it with her sleeve. Still, Helen didn't seem disturbed by the mark on her face.

At the top of the stairs, Linda pointed to the first door on the left. "Drew and Helen's room. This next door is to the nursery." She stopped and opened the second door and stood back so Esther could peek inside.

It was a beautiful room, filled with sunlight. A couple of rocking chairs rested across from a comfortable sofa, but the loveliest things in the room were the cribs. They were lace-trimmed and sat side by side. What lucky children they were to be born to such a loving couple!

Esther looked at her son. But then, she was a blessed woman to have Davey.

Linda moved back and closed the nursery door. They headed farther down the hall to the third door on the left and opened it. "This'll be your room."

Excitement filled Esther. This room was so much better than the one she'd had at the boardinghouse. Centered on the far wall in the sunny room sat a large poster bed covered with a beautiful quilt. A pretty oil lamp rested on a small table next to a comfortable chair. The hardwood floors had been well cared for. There was even a door connecting the nursery so she'd be able to hear the babies during the night.

"I never imagined living anywhere so nice when I left the boardinghouse this morning." Esther couldn't keep from looking at everything in the room, from the scatter rugs on the floor to the pictures on the wall to the small pot of ivy on a stand next to the window.

Linda nodded. "I felt like that when Sarah and Drew took in me and my brother and sister."

A huge yawn pulled Esther's mouth wide open. She quickly covered it with her hand. "Excuse me."

"Why don't you and Davey take a nap?" Linda pulled the covers back. "When lunch is ready, I'll come and see if you're awake. If you aren't, it's fine. And if you're still asleep, I can take Davey to the kitchen for something to eat, if it's all right with you. Later this afternoon, my brother and sister, along with Helen's brother will be home from school. Drew sends them to a widow who teaches in her home since there's not a school in town yet. So there'll be someone for Davey to play with."

Esther was so tired she couldn't keep the people straight. She just nodded.

Linda seemed to understand and slipped out of the room.

With fumbling fingers, she pulled off her dress. Davey crawled onto the bed. She followed him. Her son's little body snuggled against hers, and she closed her eyes. As she drifted into the hazy place between drowsiness and sleep, a voice crept into her mind calling for her son. The old man in the store, the one with the dark hair and eyes, called out Davey's name. She wrapped her arms tighter around the little boy as exhaustion pulled her into darkness.

Colin could just make out Adam Lone Eagle sitting outside the light of their campfire as he took the first watch. Good thing too, since Tuck's snores could cover any approaching attackers.

They'd ridden until even the tracker couldn't follow the Millers' trail in the darkness. And even though Colin needed the rest before his turn to watch, he couldn't sleep. Memories of holding his son's broken body joined with the ever-present hatred of his killers and refused to let him have even that brief period of reprieve. He shifted again on the hard ground, cushioned by only his bedroll.

"Let it go, brother." Dougal kept his voice low. "Do your duty in getting the Millers for what they did to those miners. There never was any proof they—"

"Stop." The word came out low but harsh. Colin's gut tightened. He and Dougal had had this argument before, and he couldn't go through it again, not with the Millers so close. This time he'd get justice for Jessie and Matty. He had to.

"Jessie wouldn't want you to destroy your life like this."

"Jessie wouldn't care what I do. She left me, remember? If she hadn't, they'd still be alive." Colin sat up and pulled on his boots. "Get some sleep. I'm spelling Adam early."

A few minutes later, Colin sat in the darkness, a rifle in his hand. Only this time it wasn't the memories of the past which haunted his mind. No, those torturing memories were chased away by ones of a different woman and child. He tried to push them away, but thoughts of the woman with the sultry voice and a little boy with dancing brown eyes stubbornly wouldn't leave. He refused to question why. But for a short, precious time, he had peace.

CHAPTER NINE

Esther groaned and reached for Davey. The other side of the bed was empty. She jerked upright. Her heart pounded in her chest. Breath ripped out of her lungs. She looked around the room. The tightness eased out of her muscles. Her trunk sat by the door. Linda must have come and gotten Davey. She glanced out the window and realized she'd slept for several hours, although it didn't feel like it.

She shook her head at her crazy mixed-up dream where the man from the store had tried to take Davey while Uncle Ed had chased after her. She felt she'd fought them both the whole time she'd been asleep.

Needing to get to Davey, Esther hurried out of bed, pulled the covers back in place, and dressed. She smoothed her hair, then took a last look around the room before she headed toward the stairs. The doors to the nursery and the Hollingsworths' room were closed. She hoped Helen was resting.

No one was in the parlor, but sounds of laughter and children's voices joined the tasty smells of roast and fresh-baked bread drifting from the kitchen. She entered the room. Five sets of eyes turned towards her.

Davey jumped from a chair and raced from the far side of the table. He grabbed Esther's hand. His eyes sparkled. A grin split his face. "Mama, Mama, got friends. Carl, Jack, my friends. Nancy too, she's a girl."

Linda covered her mouth and tried to stifle a giggle. She moved from the stove to the table and rested her hand on the girl who looked a lot like Linda and seemed to be about eleven. "Let me introduce the others who live here. This is my sister, Nancy." She moved onto the older, redheaded boy, who was a little older than Nancy, and rested her hand on his shoulder. "This is my brother, Jack." She nodded to the last person at the table. "That's Carl. He's Helen's brother. His room's across the hall from the nursery. Children, this is Esther. She's the nanny for the twins."

Jack and Nancy both greeted her with "Nice to meet you," but Carl, who looked to be about seven, just stared at her for a moment. His eyebrows drew together just a bit while his nose wrinkled. "What's a nanny?"

Linda smiled and ruffled his hair. "A nanny is someone who helps look after babies. That way your sister can get more rest."

"But I help Helen." Carl looked from Esther to Linda.

"But you have to go to school, and Esther can get up in the night when the babies are crying so Helen can sleep. You'll still be their uncle and do all the things you do now. It's just your sister'll have some help when you're not here."

"All right." Carl nodded and grinned at Davey. "'Sides, it'll be fun to have someone upstairs to play with. Wanna see the soldiers Drew got me for Christmas?"

"Yeah." Davey's head shot up and down like a bobber on a fishing line with a fish nibbling on the other end. He started to follow Carl out of the room, but stopped and looked from Carl heading out of the kitchen to his mother. "Can I go?"

"*May* you go. And yes, you may. Just be quiet so you don't wake the babies."

"Me be quiet." He raced after his new friend.

A hollow feeling rolled around Esther's middle. She'd been so busy at the boardinghouse she hadn't realized just how much Davey needed a friend near his own age. He hadn't complained, but then he hadn't known any differently. She'd always kept him by her side since there hadn't been anyone else to look after him.

Linda set a cup of coffee and a slice of warm gingerbread on the table. "Have a seat. This should hold you until supper."

Esther's stomach grumbled. Her mouth watered at the smell. She realized she hadn't eaten anything since breakfast. And even then she hadn't eaten much, worried about where she and Davey were going to be staying the night and how they'd be able to pay for food. She dropped her head. *Thank you, God, for providing a position and a place to live for Davey and me.*

When she raised her head and took a sip of coffee, Nancy stood.

"Is it all right if I go and sit with the babies?" Her eyes lit up. "I'll be quiet. But if they wake, I'll take care of them until Helen comes in." She waited for her sister to nod, then hurried out.

Linda sat across the table. "That girl loves babies. Think she'll make a good mama someday." She gathered the dishes from the children's snack. "I'm glad you're here. Like Davey, I'm glad to have a new friend." She wiped a spill, then waited a moment. With her head still lowered, she refolded the cloth. "Dougal has mentioned you a few times."

Esther recalled some of the things Helen and her husband had said before her nap. "Mr. Hollingsworth said they knew him. I didn't realize you knew him, too."

"He's been a good friend for a long time." She scrubbed at a spot on the table which only she saw. "He didn't think I should marry the cowboy I was engaged to, and it looks like he was right."

Esther wasn't sure what to say. She'd never been engaged or even courted. Sometimes she thought she'd like to keep it that way, especially seeing the hurt the cowboy had caused Linda. But then there were other times when she wasn't sure.

Suddenly the marshal's face floated into her thoughts. She swallowed the last bite of gingerbread, then stood. "I better go check on the babies."

She hurried out of the kitchen, but the marshal's face came with her.

Warm light knocked on Esther's eyelids, drawing her from sweet dreams. *If the sun's shining, I'm late getting up. The boarders'll be hungry. Uncle Ed'll be angry.* Her eyes popped open. She jerked upright and realized she wasn't in the bedroom off the kitchen in the boardinghouse, then fell back on the pillows. Excitement rolled through her. She was getting ready to start a new position with a wonderful family.

Davey shuffled around under the covers. It wouldn't be long before he woke, but she had a few minutes to think about how her life had changed in the last twenty-four hours.

During supper the night before, Mr. Hollingsworth repeated so many nice things that Aunt Bonny told him about her. The words he said were bittersweet, making her miss her aunt all the more. Yet hearing what her aunt had said soothed her hurting soul.

After supper, she put the babies to bed so Mr. and Mrs. Hollingsworth could have a little time to themselves. Once the twins were down, she had the rest of the evening to spend with Davey. She couldn't remembered when she'd been able to read so many stories to him.

Davey made a little snorting sound in his sleep.

Esther bowed her head. *Dear Father, I come to You this morning with my heart full of thankfulness. Thank You for this position. Thank You for letting me work for employers who love You. Thank You for letting us live in a home where love flows all around Davey and me. Help me to do the best I can for You as I work for the Hollingsworths. In Jesus' name. Amen.*

Esther knew it was time to begin her duties. She rolled out of bed, then glanced at Davey. Even though Helen had told her that she could use the small bedroom next to her, Davey hadn't wanted to sleep there. And she understood. Her son had never spent the night anywhere except her room. One day he'd need to. But with all the changes happening in his life right now, she didn't want him to wake in the night and not know where she was.

Esther quickly washed and dressed, then stepped into the nursery.

Helen sat in one of the two rocking chairs in the room, feeding her son with a bottle. "Andy tends to rise first. I can usually get him changed and fed before Sarah wakes up."

A fussy wail announced the other baby was awake.

"I'll get her, ma'am." Esther picked up the little girl, changed her diaper, and dressed her in the clothes lying on the end of the crib.

"That's something I want to talk to you about."

For a moment, Esther couldn't breathe as she braced herself for whatever was to come.

"Don't look like that." Mrs. Hollingsworth chuckled. "I told you yesterday I needed a friend as much as I needed a nanny. Friends call each other by their first names. So, I want you to call me Helen, not ma'am or Mrs. Hollingsworth." Her employer smiled and tilted her head slightly to the side as if asking a favor. "Please? After all, we will be raising our children together. And my husband said to call him 'Drew'."

"But ma'am—" Esther stopped when Mrs. Hollingsworth raised her eyebrows. "All right, Helen."

Another chuckle burst from Helen. She held out her son. "See, it wasn't so hard. Now, if you take and burp him, I'll feed Sarah."

Esther sat in the other rocker and lifted the baby to her shoulder.

Davey stood in his nightshirt by the open door, rubbing his sleepy eyes. "You gone."

Esther held the baby securely against her chest and waved her son forward. She slipped her hand over his head, then gave Davey a kiss. He smiled at her, and she went back to patting the baby's back.

Davey pointed at the baby. "Me little like that?"

"Yes, sweetie, except you had darker hair, like you do now."

"Me play with him?"

"When he gets a little bigger."

The baby burped loudly.

Davey's eyes got bigger and bigger, then he shoved his fists on his hips and glared at Esther. "Bad baby."

Even though Helen tried to smother them, her giggles crossed the room.

Esther smiled at her son. "Davey, he's just a baby. He's got to learn to burp so his tummy won't hurt. When he's older like you, you can help me teach him not to do it when others are around."

Davey seemed to think about it for a moment, then nodded. "Me help. Play ball, too."

Drew came upstairs to tell them breakfast was ready. He took both of his children, and together with his wife, left the nursery. Their hushed murmurs drifted behind them.

Esther took Davey's hand and followed them. Maybe someday she could experience that closeness with a man. All at once, Marshal MacPherson's green eyes flashed into her mind. She shook her head and kept walking.

In the middle of the afternoon, Esther visited with Helen in the nursery while the babies slept in their cribs. After all the years of work under the harsh hand of her uncle, she felt almost guilty just sitting here and talking. The door to the hall edged open. Drew slipped in, a frown marring his face.

"What's the matter, dear?" Helen kept her voice low while she continued hemming a tiny shirt for one of her babies.

Drew kept his voice low, too. "While Pippa cooked breakfast this morning, she mentioned she was late getting here because something happened at the Smalls' boardinghouse last night." He glanced at Esther. "I don't know if you knew she lives about three houses from there. The town deputy said the room you slept in was torn apart, the mattress slashed, the dresser drawers pulled out and smashed, the curtains ripped to pieces."

Esther's stomach churned. She wrapped her arms around her middle. "Who would have done such a terrible thing?"

Drew glanced at his wife, then back at Esther. "Your cousin said you slipped back in after you left and damaged whatever you could."

"I did no such thing! You know I didn't! I went from the boardinghouse to the livery, then to the Golden Nugget. You brought me here, and I never left." Esther's stomach rolled into knots but she refused to give into fear. She was free of Uncle Ed. She would not let him have any power over her again.

The scar began to itch, like it was laughing at her. She rubbed her right fist against her left sleeve.

"I told him that, so he's going back to talk to your uncle and cousin. Hopefully nothing more will come from it as far as you're concerned." Drew kissed his wife. "I just wanted to let you know what is going on." He turned to Esther. "I believe you."

Helen smiled at Esther. "And I'd believe you, but since I was with you from the time you came to the house, there's no believing, just facts."

The tightness in her stomach eased a bit. "Thank you."

Drew nodded, then waved as he left the room. "See you both after I close the Golden Nugget."

Helen set the shirt into her workbasket. "Pippa and Linda have gone to the mercantile to do some shopping. Why don't we do like the children and take a nap? After all the turmoil you've been through in the last few days with your aunt and moving and all, I think you could use a little extra sleep. I know I need to rest after dealing with the children today even with all the help you've been."

She stopped at the door to her room, looked over her shoulder, and smiled at Esther. "Don't worry. Just trust God. Everything'll work out."

Esther slipped into her room, but found no peace. She paced with her hands clasped together. Her fingers fidgeted across her middle. Thoughts pounded in her head—thoughts of anger, thoughts of hatred. But they weren't her anger and hatred. No, those ugly things were what filled Uncle Ed and Tina.

She let out an unladylike snort. The destruction of her room at the boardinghouse could only have been done by one of them, especially after she left like she had yesterday. Tina hated doing any work. There was no way she was going to take care of the boardinghouse and do all the cooking. Uncle Ed didn't get his way with her, and now he was going to have to pay for someone to clean and cook.

Stopping for a moment, she rubbed her fingers in circles over her temples. She wished they would stop blaming her for what they did. She hadn't done anything to hurt them. Why did they have to continue hurting her with their lies?

She lay on the bed next to her son. Right now she needed the comfort of his little body. He snuggled next to

THE SCAR AND THE STAR   97

her, and she let out a sigh. As long as Davey was with her, and she could provide for him in an honorable way, everything else would be fine.

A half hour later, sleep still eluded her. Even though the mattress was the softest she'd ever lain on, she still couldn't relax. Too many memories pounded in her thoughts, too many losses tugged at her heart. Too many *what-if* and *if-only* jabbed at her mind.

She finally gave up the idea of sleeping and sat in the comfy chair by the window. She pulled a tatting shuttle from her pocket. It was an ivory one Aunt Bonny had given her for her last birthday. She worked with the pattern she'd been tatting before her whole world had turned round and round. The handwork relaxed her, and she let her mind wander back to happier times, times before she was fifteen, before the men came, before so much was taken.

One tear leaked out of the corner of her eye. If she didn't take notice, maybe another wouldn't follow. She had to stay strong. Davey depended on her, needed her.

All at once, the quiet of the house was shattered by the pounding on the front door. She had to stop the noise, or the babies and Helen would wake.

CHAPTER TEN

Esther leaped off the chair. Not bothering to take the time to put on her shoes, she grabbed them and ran out of her room. The pounding stopped. Still, she rushed to the hall, dropping her shoes behind her, and swung open the front door just to make sure the pounding didn't begin again.

A young man with a star pinned to his chest stood on the front porch with a deep frown on his face. Behind him was Uncle Ed, his lips parted, showing his clenched teeth. He glared at her with near hatred in his eyes.

Tina held onto her father's arm, pointing a finger at Esther. "That's her. She's the one who did it."

"Miss O'Brien, I'm Deputy Trent Ellis, ma'am. You've been accused of stealing some very valuable jewelry."

Esther clasped her hands together in front of her to keep from rubbing them down the sides of her skirt. The people had no control over her. She would not cower before them. Her whole body tightened as she realized Uncle Ed had done what he threatened. The deputy had called her Miss O'Brien, not Mrs. Sanders.

She refused to move and let these people into the house. "I didn't take anything. I don't know what you're talking about."

"I told you she'd lie about it, didn't I, Deputy?" Tina looked at her father. "I want what's mine, and those diamonds were mine. I've always planned to wear them when I get married. I've dreamed of it since I was a little girl and saw Papa and Mama Bonny's wedding picture. Make her give them back."

The deputy pulled on his shirt collar. "May we come in and talk about this?"

Esther looked over her shoulder. Helen was coming down the stairs. The muscles in Esther's neck relaxed just a bit.

"Deputy, may I help you?" Helen scooted in front of Esther, but she reached behind her and touched Esther's icy hands.

The deputy jerked his hat off, then pointed to Esther. "Sorry to bother you, Mrs. Hollingsworth, but I've a complaint against this woman here."

Helen tilted her head slightly. "This woman is my nanny and shall be addressed as Miss O'Brien."

The young man's face flushed red. "Yes, ma'am. Sorry. As I was saying, Mr. Small and his daughter have accused Miss O'Brien of robbery."

"That's the most foolish thing I've ever heard, but come in so we can get this matter straightened out." Helen waved the deputy, Uncle Ed, and Tina into the parlor. "Have a seat, but we must be quick about this before my babies wake from their afternoon nap."

While the others moved into the parlor, Esther pulled on her shoes, then hurried after them.

Tina jerked on her father's sleeve. "Papa, make her give the jewelry back. I don't care about anything else. But those are mine. Mama Bonny wanted me to have them. She told me so lots and lots of times."

"I've never stolen anything in my life." Pounding in Esther's head joined the twisting in her stomach. Tina had always been a manipulative, spoiled child who'd grown into an even more manipulative, spoiled young woman. She'd lied about things in the past so she wouldn't get into trouble, and Esther took the punishment for most of them.

"Don't worry. We'll clear up this misunderstanding." Helen patted Esther's hand, then looked the lawman in the eye. "What proof do you have that Miss O'Brien stole anything?"

The young man swallowed. "Um, well, Mr. Small said she did."

"And Miss O'Brien says she didn't." Helen stared at the deputy.

Silence filled the air for several seconds, only to be replaced by Tina's whine. "Papa, do something."

Esther glanced from the deputy to Helen, then back to the man who could take her to jail. "I don't know about any diamonds other than the ones my mama had from her mama, but Uncle Ed said he'd sold them when he sold my parents' farm."

Tina jumped up. "It's a lie. I saw you playing with them when you were cleaning Papa and Mama Bonny's bedroom. You put them on and acted like you were a bride. Then I saw you sneak into her room the night Mama Bonny died. You slipped something from her jewelry box and put it into your apron pocket."

"Ma'am, I got two people who are accusing her." The deputy stood. "I gotta take her in."

Esther trembled when she realized that she was going to jail for the lie these two people were telling. "I—I didn't do it." Her head felt like a spinning top. She looked from Tina to Helen. "Believe me. I didn't."

"I believe you." Helen patted Esther's hand. "Deputy, can't you leave Miss O'Brien here in custody of my husband and me? From what I've heard, your jail is no place for a young woman."

Redness crept across the young man's cheeks, but he looked directly at Esther. "I'm sorry. Mr. Small's made a charge against you, and he has a witness. He's also said your great-uncle owns a livery, and you can get a horse anytime you want, so he's afraid you'll skedaddle out of town."

He swallowed hard. "Since the sheriff's gone, I'm gonna have to take you to jail until the judge can hear your case. Sorry, I got no other choice."

Fear, like a cold, narrowed-eyed snake, wrapped itself around Esther when the deputy took a step toward her. "Couldn't you—"

"No, I have to take you."

Davey ran into the parlor, crying. "Don't go, Mama! Don't go!"

Esther knelt and wrapped her arms around her trembling son. She kissed his forehead, then glanced at Helen. "Will you keep Davey? I have no one else."

Davey clung tighter. "Mama!"

Her tears joined his. "You have to stay. Please, mind Mama and stay with Miss Helen. Can you do that for Mama?"

Helen wiped tears from her eyes. "Of course, we'll keep him. And Drew will be here shortly to see about getting you out of this misunderstanding."

Still wearing her bonnet with her reticule dangling from her wrist, Linda rushed into the room and knelt by Esther and took Davey in her arms. "We'll take care of him."

Esther bit her bottom lip to keep from crying out for Davey. Her heart ripped in two.

"Oh, keep the brat quiet." Uncle Ed stood and helped Tina from the sofa.

Helen stood and glared at Uncle Ed and Tina. "Leave my house. You've done your filthy work, but you won't get away with it. Esther's innocent. We'll prove it."

Father and daughter left in a huff.

The deputy took Esther's arm and led her away. Once outside the house, fear coiled tighter and tighter around Esther with each step she took. If Tina could lie so easily about her, what else would she and Uncle Ed accuse her of?

Esther stood in the middle of the cell. The floor was stained with so many colors. The walls reeked of stale whiskey, dirty bodies, and something so horrid she kept her hankie over her nose and mouth. The bed, covered with a tattered blanket, was even worse. It was still rumpled from when the last prisoner had lain there.

Her back ached. Her feet hurt. She refused to touch the bed, and there was no other place to sit.

Vibrations rattled through the cells as the front door to the sheriff's office banged open and smashed against the wall.

"Just what do you think you are doing arresting Esther O'Brien and hauling her off to jail?" Drew's voice rang out. "What proof do you have that she committed any crime?"

At her employer's voice, Esther let out a large sigh, then took in a deep breath. She smashed the hankie back over her nose and mouth at the smell that surrounded her.

"Well, I've got a written complaint and the sworn testimony of an eyewitness." The deputy's voice sounded a bit shaky.

"An eyewitness to the theft?"

"Well, no, but with what I had, Mr. Small insisted I arrest the woman so she couldn't leave town with the stolen jewelry."

Drew's shoes pounded on the wooden floor in the outer office. "In that case, I want her released to me. I'll take full responsibility for her and her actions until this matter is settled."

Joy filled Esther at the thought of leaving this pit.

"I can't. Mr. Small's already had someone ride to the judge in Mountain City, and the judge ordered no bail be set. She gotta stay in jail 'til the matter's settled."

Sorrow and anger gobbled the joy Esther felt just moments before.

The thud of a fist pounding wood echoed back into the cells. "This is complete nonsense. Let me see Miss O'Brien. I want to see how she's doing for myself."

The screech of a chair scratched across the wooden floor in the office, followed by boots pounding on the floor and drawing nearer.

Drew almost gagged when he entered the cell area. A frown tugged deep into his face as he looked at her in the cell.

Esther lowered the hankie and tried to smile at him, but she couldn't make her mouth work. She forced herself to stand still.

He glanced from her to the bed, then around the small cell. "Deputy, is it possible to give Miss O'Brien a chair to sit on?" His voice came out tight and hard. He pointed to the filthy bed. "There's no way she can be expected to rest on that."

"Well, normally we don't. Can't let a prisoner break it apart and use it as a weapon, but I guess with her, I can." The man left and in a few moments returned with a straight-backed, wooden chair." He waved at Drew. "Step back there so I can unlock the door. Then you can push the chair inside, but don't try anything funny. I'll have my gun on you."

Esther almost laughed. What did the deputy think? Drew was going to bust her out of jail and race out of town with guns blazing?

Drew rolled his eyes, but did what he was ordered.

Once the chair was inside, Esther dropped onto it. Her feet screamed as her weight came off of them. "Thank you."

Drew stared at the deputy. "Would it be acceptable for my wife to send something for Miss O'Brien to eat and a quilt to keep her warm since the one in the cell is entirely unacceptable?"

The young man shrugged. "Fine by me. Saves the town the cost of a meal. But just know I'll have to check out anything she sends before it's given to the prisoner."

"Don't worry. She'll send enough for you, too."

"Now I didn't mean that. I just wanted you to know, it's, aah..."

The young man sputtered to a stop when Drew turned away from him and shifted toward the cell. "Helen and I'll be back here shortly. Know you are in our prayers every moment."

Drew nodded to her and walked past the deputy, who followed him out.

As the men left, the muscles in Esther's back relaxed. Her head dropped to her hands which rested on her knees. She bit her lips to keep from crying. Why was this happening to her? What had she done to Tina to cause her to make up such a lie? None of it was true. She'd never even seen the jewelry, much less played with it like her cousin said. What did Uncle Ed and Tina hope to get out of all this?

She drew a shuddering breath. Drew's words drifted through her mind, saying they were praying for her. It was what she needed to be doing also. She sat upright, then bowed her head and clasped her fingers together. *Oh God, I'm so scared. Help me, please help me. You know I didn't steal anything, not from Uncle Ed or Tina or anybody. Please protect me. Please look after Davey. We need You so much. In Jesus' name I pray to You. Amen.*

Esther raised her head, but still kept her eyes closed. She didn't want to see the warped wood of the ceiling. Note by note, a tune started in her heart and went to her head. Peace seeped into her. She hummed for a moment or two, then sang softly. "My faith looks up to Thee, Thou Lamb of Calvary, Saviour Divine! Now hear me while I pray, take all my guilt away. Oh, let me from this day be wholly Thine."

She scrubbed her cheeks with the balls of her hands and kept on singing. "May Thy rich grace impart, strength to my fainting heart, my zeal inspire. As Thou hast died for me, oh, may my love to Thee, pure, warm and changeless be, a living fire."

Quiet sat in the room around her. She knew the next words and right now they were so true. "While life's dark maze I tread, and griefs around me spread."—she swallowed the tears running down her throat before she could sing any more—"Be Thou my guide. Bid darkness turn to day, Wipe sorrow's tears away. Nor ever let me stray, from Thee aside."

She couldn't finish the song, so she sat there letting thoughts of Davey run through her mind. Her fingers twitched to touch his face. Her arms longed to hold his little body next to her and feel him hug her back.

She wasn't sure how much time passed while she let the sweet memories of Davey float through her thoughts. The sheriff's office banged open again, causing her eyes to jerk open. Footsteps padded across the office.

"Helen, wait a minute so the deputy can check out what you have." Drew's voice rang out. The padding stopped.

"See, it's just a quilt for Esther. No gun, no knife to help her escape. Just a quilt. My husband told me how horrid that cell is. I need to see how Esther's doing." Helen's voice grew louder the longer she talked.

"All right, Mrs. Hollingsworth, you can go back there and see the prisoner. I'll be back there as soon as I check out this basket."

Helen's very unladylike snort sounded just before she entered the cell area carrying a quilt over her arms. She hurried to the cell door.

When Esther stood, her legs trembled so much that she had to wait a few moments before she could move the few feet across the cell. She clasped the hands Helen pushed through the iron bars.

A few minutes later, the deputy carried a basket into the cell area. "Mrs. Hollingsworth, could you kindly move back a few steps so I can unlock the cell and give this to the prisoner?"

Helen's eyes flared and she waved her finger. "Don't use that word for her. She's a young woman, falsely accused. You are just too—too—too young to see that. Just wait and you'll see. Then what will the sheriff say about what you've done?"

The deputy's face flushed a bright red. "Be it as it is, ma'am. I gotta job to do. So if you want her to get this basket, you're still gonna have to move back."

Helen let out a loud huff and stepped backward a few feet.

He unlocked the cell, handed the basket and quilt to Esther, then stepped out of the cell.

Esther cringed when the door clanked closed again, and the lock slipped in place. She let out the breath she didn't even realize she was holding.

The deputy turned on his boot heel and went back into the office.

At last she raised her head. One hand tightened on the handle of the basket while her other gripped the quilt. "Thank you for this. Thank you for looking after Davey. But you need to get home to your babies." She couldn't hold back the sob at the end of her words.

Helen gripped the bars so tightly her knuckles grew white. "Oh, Esther, I can't leave you here like this."

Esther shrugged. "You have to. You need to be with your babies." She drew in a large jerky breath. "Ple— please leave and go home. Please."

"Our prayers are with you. We'll get you out." Helen turned away. A few moments later the office door closed with what seemed like a lot of force.

Esther shuddered. She felt more alone than she had in all her life.

Darkness covered their movements, just the way Ray Miller liked it. It'd taken most of the day to find out where the boy was, but now he knew. He jerked on Blake's sleeve to get the kid to come up the back porch steps.

If they worked it right, they'd be in and out in just a few minutes. Then he'd have what he'd traveled so far to get. He cursed when he tried the doorknob and found it locked. City people never trusted their neighbors. It didn't matter. He knew how to get it unlocked. A few minutes later, he laughed to himself when the door swung open.

He slugged his youngest son's arm to make sure he got his attention. "Let's get the boy."

Before either of them had taken more than two steps inside, a flash burst in the darkness, a shot rang out, and Blake screamed like a stuck pig.

Ray heard a swish and felt a sharp pain smash into his chest. "Get out, Blake! Get out!"

The two of them ran out of the house. It took a little while to get to their horses, but the night covered their getaway.

They stopped at the edge of town where there were some lights breaking through the darkness—the businesses of the night were still selling.

Ray Miller pulled a knife from his chest. It was a puny one, not a killing kind. Still, it'd gone in a ways, not enough to take him to his grave, but enough to cause some bad hurt. He shoved a wadded-up handkerchief inside his shirt to keep the blood from dripping. Once he got his wound taken care of, he turned to Blake. "You hurt bad?"

"Don't think so, Pa, but it's bleeding something fierce."

"Well, wrap it up good. Don't want to be leaving a trail for the law to follow."

Ray cursed the darkness, his useless son, and the people in the house. He didn't get what he came after. The boy was his—his flesh and blood. And he'd get him. Nothing'd stop him from getting what was his. Nothing and no one.

Early on the second morning, after the dying miner had ridden his mule into town, Colin sat at the long table at the stage station halfway between Central City and Denver. Frustration boiled inside him, hotter than the steaming coffee in the cup sitting in front of him. They'd tracked the murderers of those poor miners all day yesterday, following a clear but wandering trail and now this.

They'd stopped at the station for a bite to eat and any information they could find. The manager of the station remembered the two men, one old and one young, but he didn't know when they left or which way they traveled.

"Feels like we've been played like some kinda puppets." Tuck rubbed his leg while he sat on the bench alongside the table. "The trail leading us here was clear as the sky after a spring rain, now nothing. Makes my skin crawl to think those men are out there waiting with us in their sights when we leave here."

Adam rested his buckskin-clad arms on the table. "If they'd wanted us dead, they had many chances to attack. We passed many good ambush places."

Dougal raised his head. "Why would they mark those men like that?"

Tuck grunted. "I can't answer for certain, but there's been a rumor about it. Seems Ray Miller had a place back in Missouri, the Lazy M. He lost it for back taxes. Then all the men on the stagecoaches the Millers were thought to have held up were killed and left with a carved brand on them. If you remember the mark, it looks like a tilted M."

"That's just plain evil." Dougal turned a tad pale.

"Now you know why we've gotta catch these men. Can't let them do here what they did in Missouri." Tuck let out a deep sigh.

"Did he mark the women in the same way?" Dougal's hold on his cup tightened, and he glanced at his brother.

Colin could feel Dougal's eyes on him, but it didn't matter what the sheriff said. Colin knew who caused the stagecoach carrying his wife and son to tumble over the cliff. He didn't need a mark to prove it.

"Nope, but like the men, they killed them, so there weren't ever any witnesses. Except once." Tuck slammed his empty cup on the wooden table. "Happened when I was laid up after tangling with some other outlaws. Anyways, rumor has it there was one girl the boys left alive, and they marked her. Seems the older son had taken a shine to her and planned to come back for her when a posse wasn't on their tails. Never did get her to testify though 'cause her family left the area right sudden. Some thought Ray Miller got to the pa and threatened the whole family or else got them out of town and killed them, although they never found any bodies."

Colin jumped up. "We've been tricked." He smashed his balled-up fist against his thigh. "What if this whole chase has been to get us out of town?" He threw some money on the table and headed for the stable. The place in his gut that told him trouble was brewing had twisted tight. He'd known something hadn't felt right, the way the Millers left such a clear trail, but now they needed to get back.

The other men followed. In minutes they were on the road back to Central City.

CHAPTER ELEVEN

The sun barely reached overhead when Colin and the others raced into town. For the last few miles, a gut-tightening dread had woven its way through his insides. Were they right in thinking the Millers wanted them out of town? But why? They'd never struck a town before, just stagecoaches and outlying farms, and now the miners. Something wasn't right. He just didn't know what it was.

They rode down the main street. Everything seemed fine—no crowds, no gunshots, no cries for help, just people going about their regular activities. Colin let out an uneasy breath when they stopped in front of the sheriff's office.

The town deputy stumbled out of the building, his eyes red-rimmed, his chin and cheeks bristle-covered, and his hair sticking out like he'd run his hands through it more than once. A cup dripping coffee dangled from his fingers. "Sheriff, I'm mighty glad you're back."

Tuck dismounted. "What happened?"

"Plenty." The young man turned on his heel and went back inside. Colin followed him while Dougal and Adam took the horses to the livery.

The sheriff dropped on the chair behind his desk with a sigh. He rubbed his leg. "All right, spit it out."

"Had a break-in at one of the boardinghouses. Leastways, we thought it was a break-in, but later the owner accused someone who used to work there of doing it out of spite and greed." He handed Tuck and Colin metal cups, then filled them with coffee which looked like it'd been brewing since the night before.

Colin set his cup on the window ledge next to where he stood. No way was he going to drink the sludge.

The young deputy set the pot back on the potbellied stove and turned back to the sheriff. "Then sometime last night, someone broke into the Hollingsworths' house. The woman from the bakery had moved back there with her brother and sister. Brother threw a knife, and the woman shot a gun at 'em. Must have gotten one or both of the thieves 'cause when they got away, they left a trail of blood to their horses."

The door burst open. Tuck jumped to his feet. Colin's hand dropped to his side where his gun rested. He let out a snort of disgust when Mr. Small barged in. Colin leaned back against the wall.

The little man strutted into the room. "Good, I'm glad to see you're back, Sheriff. Now maybe we'll get something done around here."

Tuck lifted his hand and rubbed the back of his neck, then glanced at his deputy. "Was it the Smalls' boardinghouse that was broken into?"

The deputy nodded.

The sheriff turned back to the barber. "Look, Mr. Small. I'll look into your break-in and see if we can catch the thief, but I've got a couple of things to handle first."

"Oh, we've caught the thief. She's sitting in your jail right now." Small grew more red-faced the longer he bellowed. "What I want now—no, demand—is you go and look through her things at the Hollingsworths' house at once and get back the diamonds and other jewelry she stole."

Colin's head jerked around the room and looked first at Tuck, then to the back of the jail where the cells were. He raced across the room and into the cell area. What he saw there made him jerk to a stop. His hands curled into fists. He gripped the cell bars to keep from grabbing Small by the neck.

Esther O'Brien sat on a wooden chair in the middle of the cell, surrounded by stink and metal bars. Her chin rested on her chest. Even though a quilt wrapped around her shoulders, she trembled—either from hurt or fear.

"Tuck, get in here with the key."

She raised her pale face. Dark shadows rested beneath her red-rimmed eyes. Her lips wobbled, but no words came out. The heels of her shoes hooked around the bottom rung of the chair as if to keep from touching any part of the cell.

"Now, just a minute. You can't let her out until she tells me where she hid my things." Small followed Tuck into the cell area.

Colin shifted toward the bully barber and kept his voice low. "One more word—just one—and you'll need a doctor." He stared at the other man's blustering stance. "Or the undertaker."

The door screeched as Tuck swung it open.

The woman didn't move. She just sat there, shaking.

Colin ignored the other men and entered the cell. He lifted Esther in his arms, carried her out of the cell and into the office, then placed her on the sheriff's chair.

Tuck shooed Small back into the office, then sat on the corner of his desk. "Now, Mr. Small." He raised his hand when the boardinghouse owner opened his mouth. "I'd advise you to keep quiet until I say my piece. Now just get things straight—this jewelry? Where did it come from?"

Colin took a bit of pleasure when Small took a quick glance at him before he answered Tuck.

"They were my wife's. I, uh, I gave them to her." He said the words, but his face had lost a bit of its color. "I want them back." He tipped his head toward Esther. "She stole them the night my wife died."

Tuck stood and folded his arms across his chest. "Before we get into where the jewelry is, let's get back to where you got them?"

"What does it matter? They were my wife's. She's gone, so they belong to me."

The sheriff shrugged one shoulder and tipped his head to the side. "All right. You admit the jewelry was hers then?"

"Yes, it was Bonny's." Small's face reddened as he scowled. "Look, I don't care what you do with her." He pointed his finger at Esther. "I just want my property back. My daughter always planned to wear it for her wedding."

"Well, Mr. Small, I'm sorry your daughter's gonna be disappointed. Your wife left a will leaving the jewelry to her niece here." Tuck moved to the desk and pulled open the bottom drawer. He took out a metal box with a lock. From his pants pocket, he took out a key and unlocked the box. Next, he took out an envelope.

Colin recognized it as the same pale blue one Mrs. Small had put her will into and given to Tuck.

The sheriff drew out the will and showed it to Small. "This is your wife's will. See for yourself."

Colin couldn't keep from grinning while he kept one hand on Esther's quilt-covered shoulder.

Small's face turned even redder.

"As you can see, Small, the sheriff and I both witnessed it for her." Colin didn't even try to keep the satisfaction out of his voice. From everything he'd seen, the man deserved this.

"She'd never—she'd never—" Small's eyes narrowed. His nostrils flared. "She'd never do that. She loved Ernestina too much. She knew how much my daughter wanted the jewelry."

Colin tightened his hold on the woman's shoulder just a bit, not enough to hurt, just enough to let her know he was standing by her. "But Mrs. Small loved her niece, too. Seems she wanted her protected, in case you threw her out. And it looks like your wife knew you very well."

"I, uh, I never threw her out. It was her choice to leave."

Even through the quilt, Colin felt the young woman's reaction. He held her in the chair so she wouldn't jump into the fray. "No, you just made it impossible for her to stay. What'd you do, offer to make her your mistress in exchange for room and board?"

Small's face paled, then grew red again. He glanced at the woman in the chair then back at Colin.

"I don't have to stand here and take her crazy accusations." The small man glared at his niece.

"Never said she said anything. It was all my supposing." Colin stared Small right in the eye, wishing the man would take a swing at him for the words said, but it'd never happen. The barber was a bully and a coward.

Small turned on his heel and stomped out of the office.

Tuck tapped the will and chuckled. "Always did admire that wife of his for her gentle, helping ways. Now I understand why she did what she did when she called us over."

All at once, the woman in the chair stood. Colin stepped back. A touch of guilt jumped in his gut. He'd gotten too caught up in Small's frustration and forgot about her for a moment. Now, his face felt a bit hot.

Esther stood and tried to brush the wrinkles out of the dress she'd been wearing since yesterday morning. She swallowed when the stink of the cell, woven into the fabric, taunted her. "Sheriff, am I free to go? I need to see about my son."

"Certainly, Miss O'Brien. I'm sorry Sanders wasn't here to clear your name."

She caught hold of the desk as she tried to keep her balance. "What has Uncle Will to do with this?"

"He has the wooden box from your aunt, the one that contains the jewelry. The marshal here and me took it to him just before, uh, before she passed."

A wave of exhaustion swept over her. She raised one hand to the side of her face. "I need to get home and see Davey."

Before she could take a step, a man opened the door and stepped back. Pippa hurried into the office carrying a basket and glanced at Tuck. "I wanted to make sure how Esther's doing so I brought dinner for her. But like last night, I brought enough for you and your deputy."

She sniffed and glared at the young man, then turned her frown to the marshal. When she saw Esther standing by the desk, she scurried over. "Oh, child, why do they have you out here? What are they doing to you?"

"She's been cleared. She's free to go." The sheriff huffed out, then glowered at his deputy.

Exhaustion dripped off Esther as her legs trembled.

"She never should have been brought here." Pippa gave the deputy a disgusted look. "You need to teach this young man who the real criminals are." She turned to Tuck. "Now you're back in town, you need to come to the house. Someone tried to break in last night."

Esther felt her legs weakening. She just wanted to leave and see Davey, feel his little arms around her neck.

Pippa wrapped her arm around Esther. "Let's get you home."—she gave the lawmen one of her best glares— "Where people care about you."

Colin stared at the man who'd followed Pippa in and was now holding the door open for her and Pippa.

Tuck tipped his head toward the man. "Kerr MacPherson. Probably a cousin or something."

The man stepped forward. "Kerr, son of Bernard, grandson of Angus MacPherson."

Colin held out his hand. "Colin, son of Alasdair, grandson of Angus MacPherson. The two men clasped forearms. "Dougal mentioned you. Good to see family."

Pippa mumbled something about men and their crazy traditions, then pushed them aside and helped Esther to the door.

Esther didn't care about any man now. She just wanted to get to Davey. A few minutes later, she thanked God for freeing her while she sat between Pippa and Kerr MacPherson on a padded buggy seat. It seemed like forever until they stopped at the back of the Hollingsworths' house, near the barn.

The back door opened. Davey ran out. "Mama, Mama." The little boy held up his arms. "Hold me."

She scrambled over Pippa and jumped to the ground just in time to catch her son in her arms. She held him as tight as she could. "Oh, Davey, oh, my baby."

An arm slid around her shoulder. Pippa nudged her forward. "Let's get you and Davey inside."

Esther nodded, but held onto Davey while she walked to the house. At the bottom of the steps to the porch, Drew lifted Davey from her arms while Helen helped her to the porch.

Once they were inside, Drew sat Davey onto a chair, then helped her to another one next to her son. Helen poured coffee while Pippa filled a plate.

"I'm so glad you're home." Helen smiled. A baby's, then two babies' cries filled the air. "The twins're in the parlor. I'll be back in a few minutes."

Esther's hand shook when she lifted the fragrant coffee and took a sip. She was home with her son. God had seen her through her trial. She felt a new strength flow through her. He would be with her wherever she went.

Davey pulled up on his knees and rested his head against her shoulder. He wrapped his little arms around her. "Don't go 'way 'gin."

She bent and kissed the top of his head.

The kitchen rang with the sound of filled pots and kettles being set on the stove while Esther ate. When she finished her coffee, Pippa turned to Drew. "Why don't you join Helen while Esther gets cleaned up? When she's done, I'll bring coffee to the parlor."

A while later, Esther left the kitchen, her dirty clothes and the stench from the jail left behind. She walked hand in hand with Davey to the parlor, then stopped so quickly Davey almost fell. That was until he saw one of his favorite persons, then his lips jerked up into a wide grin, and he jumped up and down.

"Unca Dewey. Unca Dewey." Davey tugged on Esther's hand. "Mama's home! Mama's home!"

Dougal smiled at Davey, then turned back and joined in the discussion Drew, the man named Kerr, and the marshal were having by the fireplace. Helen and Linda sat on the sofa. Davey pulled Esther farther into the room.

Helen waved to the chair next to the sofa. "Please be seated. We have something we need to discuss."

Pippa entered the room, carrying a large tray with a coffee service. She set it on the table near Helen and handed out the cups Helen filled.

The minutes passed like snails on a Sunday morning stroll. Butterflies fluttered around in Esther's stomach. When she was handed her coffee, she set the cup on the small table next to her chair, all the time sneaking peeks at the men standing at the fireplace.

She wrapped her hands together, as they trembled slightly—unsure if the reaction was the result of getting out of jail or worry over why the men were huddled at the fireplace.

Helen turned to her. "I know you must be exhausted and need to rest, but we need to discuss something."

Drew cleared his throat. Everyone turned toward him. "Esther, I'm sorry for what you went through the last couple of days, and I'm happy you're back here with us. My wife and children really need you."

Esther nodded. That was good to hear, but there still seemed to be an undercurrent of something not right.

Drew set his cup and saucer on the fireplace mantle and turned to her. "What you probably haven't heard is that we had a break-in here last night."

Esther wrapped her arms around Davey and pulled him onto her lap, then looked around at the people gathered, making sure she hadn't missed any sign of injury.

Drew glanced toward the back of the house for a moment, then back to Esther. "They snuck in the kitchen door after everyone was in bed. But thanks to the fast thinking of Linda and her brother, Jack, the men didn't get far into the house. Which reminds me."—he slipped his hand into his trouser pocket, pulled out a pocket knife, and handed it to Linda—"Will you give this to Jack to replace the one he lost, please?"

"Thank you." Linda dropped it into the pocket of her apron.

"You're welcome." Drew nodded. "Now, what bothers all of us is what one of the thieves said: 'Let's get the boy.'"

Esther's arms tightened around Davey as the face of the man in the store flashed in her mind. Had he followed her here? Did he want Davey for some reason?

Drew let out a deep sigh. "I fear a man named Stanley Snodgrass might be behind this. He's in prison for kidnapping Linda, my sister, and her daughter last year, but there're people who'd do his bidding, if he'd paid them enough. He knows my sister is wealthy and would pay any ransom for her nephew. I've asked Dougal and Kerr for help."

He nodded to the two men. "They helped out last year when we had problems with Snodgrass before he went to prison. And they've agreed to guard the house and those living here again."

Esther knew this was all important, but exhaustion was weaving its web around her. All she wanted to do was go to her room and sleep.

Drew's voice droned on. "Like before, they'll take turns guarding the house day and night, but this time they'll have the bedroom across the hall from Helen and me. Now, while we're talking about MacPhersons moving into the house, I've invited Marshal MacPherson to share our home. After all, he's family, too. And the only request my sister made when she signed this house over to Helen and me was that all MacPhersons, by name or blood, be welcomed here.

Drew nodded to the man who'd been in Esther's thoughts more than she wanted.

Esther's hand fluttered across Davey's back. She glanced at the man with the star on his shirt. When he stared back at her, she dropped her eyes. Her hand gripped Davey's shirt. Why did he bother her so much?

Drew started again, "Colin will have the room at the back of the house. My wife and I have talked about it and feel better having two men upstairs at night, especially after what happened last evening."

Esther covered her mouth as a huge yawn struggled to slip out. She felt heat flood her cheeks until she saw Helen raise her hand to hide her yawn.

Drew smiled. "I've said all I needed to say to you ladies for now. Why don't you take a nap or just rest for a while? This has been a disturbing twenty-four hours for all of you."

Esther tried to rise. But with Davey now asleep in her lap, she couldn't do it. Two of the MacPhersons came to her aid. Dougal took Davey from her arms while the marshal helped her stand. At the feel of his large hand wrapped around her arm, her mind went numb even while warmth returned to her cheeks, then the warmth grew hotter when she stumbled. He wrapped his arm around her waist and helped her to the stairs.

Once she had her hand on the railing, he dropped his arm from her waist but cupped her elbow. He took the stairs one step at a time with her.

"You don't need to go all the way upstairs with me."

"Just being a good lawman, ma'am." He let out a small chuckle. "Besides, there's something I need to get in my room."

She wondered if he knew his room was across the hall from hers, but got her answer when he walked straight to her bedroom door, no hesitancy at all. Drew must have told the MacPherson men where everyone slept, since Dougal, who still carried Davey, followed right behind them and never asked directions either.

Dougal handed Davey to her, then stepped back while his brother opened the door.

She entered her room, then looked into the hall as she raised her hand to close her door.

The marshal stood at his bedroom door. His eyes were on her.

Her hand shut the door, and she wished she could shut him out of her thoughts just as easily. But she couldn't because no matter how much she'd tried to push him away, he'd been there for her again and again. And she wasn't sure what to do about him.

CHAPTER TWELVE

Once Esther and Davey were safely tucked into their room, Colin signaled Dougal to follow him. When they were both inside his room, he unbuckled his gun belt and set it on the dresser. "All right, tell me about the girl."

Dougal's face reddened while he looked around the green-and-gold decorated room, then took the only chair. "Star, I mean, Esther? You met her at the boardinghouse. You know she's a good cook." He leaned back and rested the ankle of his left leg over the knee of his right one. With his right hand, he patted his flat stomach. "Sure did hate to leave there, really missed her cooking."

Passing by his brother, Colin flicked his wrist and dropped Dougal's booted foot to the floor. "You know I don't mean Esther. The other one. Linda. You couldn't keep your eyes off her. What's her story?"

Colin's gut clenched when he saw the pain for just a moment in his brother's eyes.

Dougal shoved off of the chair, walked to the window and pulled back the curtain. He stared outside for a moment, then turned back to his brother. "I met her when our cousin Thorn brought her and her family to Central City after some outlaws killed her pa and..."—he bowed his head and sucked in a deep breath. He let it out and raised his head but kept his eyes closed— "and attacked her." At last, he opened his eyes. "By then, Thorn was married to Drew's sister. He asked Kerr and me to watch

after the family." He shrugged. "So I got to know Linda
while I was here."

"Why didn't you do something about it then?"

"She was too young and still hurting. By the time I
figured I could begin courting her, some other yahoo had
gotten there first, the son of some new rancher who
started a place a few months back. Anyway, they were
supposed to be married next month, but she felt she
needed to be honest about her past, with the outlaw and
all." He rubbed the back of his neck. "Well, when she
did, he left her with some harsh words about soiled
goods. He's engaged to another girl in town."

Colin felt like he was back in the barn at his folks'
place giving his little brother advice on girls again.
"What's stopping you from taking up with her now?"

Dougal shrugged again. "It'll be a while. She's gotten
over the hurt to her body, but it'll take a while to get past
the hurt to her heart." A grin spread across his face, the
one he always wore when he had a plan to get his way.
"In the meantime, I plan to make myself a good friend to
her. And maybe a bit more."

With Dougal's words about Linda, the shadowy sense
of jealousy about Esther floated away, but Colin couldn't
resist a small jab. After all, what were brothers for? "All
right, Unca Dewey."

A disgusted snort burst out past Dougal's lips. "Like I
said, only Davey gets to call me that." He stood and
headed for the door. "Don't know about you, but I gotta
get to work. See you at supper."

The door closed, and Colin dropped onto the chair and
leaned his head back until it rested on the wall behind
him. Thoughts of the last few days rolled through his
mind along with the questions.

The sight of the dead miners still shook him. They
weren't killed for their gold. Each of the miners had a
small pouch of the dust in their pockets. Their supplies
had been destroyed, not stolen. Why had the Millers

killed those miners and left such an easy trail to follow only to disappear at the stage station?

The only major thing to happen in Central City while they were gone was the break-in here at the Hollingsworth house, but Drew was sure it had to do with someone from his family's past. He didn't even know about the Miller gang until Colin asked him about them.

Somehow the break-in seemed important. Two men had tried to sneak in the kitchen. Two men had been at the miners' cabin and at the stage station. Colin shook his head. Was he grasping at dust motes drifting in the air? He thought about the people living in this house. Linda along with her brother and sister, Esther and her son, the Hollingsworths with their son and daughter.

Linda reported the man last night had said something about getting the boy, but which boy? It seemed foolish to break in and try and kidnap a baby on the second floor with a woman and two youngsters just off the kitchen and a nanny upstairs. But Esther wasn't upstairs. She was in jail. And according to Drew, Linda and her brother and sister had just moved back from above the bakery the day before. So maybe the men who broke in didn't know about these people.

Harve Miller's face flashed into his thoughts. He had seen the man before, several times in fact. He had brown hair with a reddish cast in the sun. Linda's brother had red hair. Could it be the boy was family to the Millers in some way? Of course, lots of people had that same color of hair.

Colin tapped his fingers on the arm of the chair. He was running in circles around the circles, trying to find reasons for the Millers to come to Central City, reasons for them to attack the people in this house.

But who were they after? And just as important, why?

Esther rose before the sun the next morning, then hurried and dressed for the day. Since it was her only good one, she put on the same dress she had worn after her bath the previous day. A new dress was the first thing she'd buy when the Hollingsworths paid her the first time. After all, she couldn't look like a scullery maid if she was a nanny.

She made sure Davey was still asleep, then rushed to the kitchen. She wanted to have everything ready before the babies woke.

When she entered the room, one MacPherson sat at the table with a mug in his hand while Linda handed the children their school lunch pails. Another MacPherson stood at the back door. Neither one of the men wore a star on his shirt.

The back door opened. Pippa came in.

"Good morning, Linda, Mr. MacPherson, Pippa." Esther waved. "Bye Nancy, Jack, Carl."

The children headed for the door with Dougal following behind them.

Seeing Kerr MacPherson sitting there, yawning and a bit droopy-eyed from guarding them all night, reminded Esther of the possible danger they all could be in, especially her two little charges. "Goodness, this is a busy place back here."

She nodded to Pippa. "I just wanted to get the bottles for the babies before they wake. Hopefully, they won't disturb Helen, and she'll be able to get a little more sleep."

"So far you're in luck, but I found this little fella wandering the hall upstairs." The marshal stepped into the kitchen holding Davey. Her son's mouth wobbled, but he clung to the man with both arms.

Something moved inside her at the sight of the man and the trusting way her son clung to him. Other than Dougal, Davey wasn't used to men holding him, having learned early on from the way Uncle Ed always shooed him away whenever Davey got too close. But Davey trusted the lawman, and that meant a lot.

"Mama, Mama." He reached out for her. "I scared. You gone."

Esther lifted her son from the marshal's arms and rested him on her hip. She pulled a hankie from her apron pocket and wiped his face. "Oh, sweetie, I thought I'd be back before you woke."

Davey wrapped his arms around her neck and gave her a big hug. He nodded his head against her shoulder. How easily children forgave. Tina's face flashed into her mind. If only it was as easy for adults. She knew she'd forgive her cousin eventually, just like she had the men who'd hurt her even worse five years before, but not yet. The hurt from Tina and her father was too fresh. But with the memories of Aunt Bonny's sweet counsel and with God's help, one day she'd be able to put it behind her.

"Star man carried me." Davey pointed to the marshal.

Esther bit back the chuckle which threatened to burst out at the look on the man's face. "Thank you."

"He can call me Colin." He glanced at her. "After all, he calls my brother 'Unca Dewey'."

She couldn't keep the chuckle locked in this time. "Is this a contest or something?"

She couldn't believe it. The man blushed.

"Not really. Just thought since we'd be staying in the same house for a while, it might make things easier. I'd like if you'd call me Colin also. It could become a little confusing if you refer to all of us as Mr. MacPherson."

Before she could answer, the MacPherson at the table stood. "Well, then, you have to call me Kerr."

She looked back and forth between the two men and shrugged. Normally, she didn't use a man's first name until she knew him a lot longer, but they were all living in the same house, and three MacPhersons might get a little confusing. "All right, then you can call me Esther."

Colin grinned. "Or Es, like your Uncle Will calls you?"

She tapped her shoe on the kitchen floor. "Only family gets to call me that."

The marshal nodded. "All right, Essie."

Esther's chest ached at the name her parents, as well as the men at the boardinghouse, always called her. Putting the momentary sadness behind her, she forced a smile to her lips. "Sounds good to me, Collie."

She grabbed the glass baby bottles Linda held out, turned on her heel, and walked out of the room while the big man sputtered behind her.

After Esther dressed the babies, she brought them downstairs to the parlor. She liked how the Hollingsworths wanted to use the parlor daily instead of keeping it just for company like many folks did. Helen had said there was another room they could use for a family parlor, but Drew used it for his office, since he needed a quiet place to read his law books.

While the twins napped, their cradles positioned near the front windows overlooking the road, Linda brought in the tea tray.

"Helen thought she'd spend the morning in bed. She had a bit of a rough night." Linda poured tea for the two of them. She held out a small ginger cookie for Davey.

The little boy dropped his wooden horses, grinned, and took the cookie. "Tank you."

"You're welcome." She handed Esther a cup and saucer with another ginger cookie on the side. "I'm so thankful you're here to help with the twins. I tried, but the house takes a great deal of my time, even with the two daily girls Helen has come in." She shrugged. "Anyway, it's good that you're here."

Someone knocked on the front door.

Esther started to stand.

Linda motioned for her to stay seated and went to the door. "Yes, may I help you?"

"Came here to see my niece, if you please."

Esther knew that voice. Uncle Will had come back to town. She set down her tea and hurried to the door. "Uncle Will."

He tried to smile at her, but it was a bit wobbly. He had a wooden box under one arm. The fingers of his other hand rubbed the top of the box as he blinked back tears.

"I'm sorry, Es, I wasn't at the liv'ry when you came to see me. I coulda saved you all that misery."

Esther reached out to her uncle. She wove her hand through his free arm and kissed him on his wrinkled cheek. "Oh, you've nothing to take the blame for. Everything worked out as it should. I'm away from Uncle Ed and Tina. My name's been cleared, and I've a wonderful place to work, for the kindest people you've ever met. I think I can see God's hand at work here."

He pulled a faded bandana from his pocket and brushed his nose. "Ah, you're your mama and grandma all over again. Always giving God the praise for the good and the devil the blame for the bad."

She shrugged and smiled. "I've learned it's just the way life is."

Linda stood back and waved them in. "Why don't you two go into the parlor so you can visit a while? Would you like some tea or perhaps some coffee, Mr. O'Brien?"

"Thank ya. Tea's fine."

Linda disappeared down the hall to the back of the house, while Esther took her uncle to the parlor.

When Davey saw his great-uncle, he jumped up, but started tiptoeing when Esther touched her fingers to her lips, hoping the babies would stay asleep until her uncle left. She needed this time with him.

Once seated, he took off his straw hat. His wispy white hair floated around his head for a moment. He handed her the wooden box he'd brought. "This is from

Bonny. God rest her soul." He blinked several times. "She asked me to keep it for ya."

"Thank you." Esther took the box while Davey climbed onto the sofa beside her. Like her uncle, she rubbed her hand over the top of the box. Her aunt had loved her enough to leave her something. And if what had been said in the sheriff's office was true, she wasn't penniless now. If she were desperate enough, she could always sell the diamonds, but with the position here, she hoped to be able to pass them to Davey's bride someday.

Linda brought in a pot of fresh tea, along with a cup and saucer for Uncle Will. She smiled and removed the other set. "Davey, why don't you come in the kitchen with me? Miss Pippa is making some bread and she has some dough you can play with."

His eyes widened. He looked at his mother. "Can I?'

"*May* you."

"May I?'

"Yes, you may." She nodded.

The boy rushed to Linda and walked out with her. In truth, she walked, while he hopped and skipped.

The fire crackled in the fireplace. She rubbed the wooden box again.

"Go on, open it." Uncle Will lifted his cup to his lips.

Esther raised the lid. An envelope with her name written in her aunt's hand stared back at her. She brushed her finger across her name, then slipped the envelope into her pocket. Later when she was alone, she'd read it, for she knew it'd bring tears to her eyes.

Next, she touched the velvet-covered box. "I remember this on Mama's dressing table. She'd gotten them out to show me. She planned to wear them at my sixteenth birthday party." She opened the velvet box. The light from the window danced on the stones in the jewelry. She blinked back the moisture in her eyes. It almost seemed like rainbows after a spring shower.

She bit the inside of her bottom lip as it quivered. Oh, how she missed her parents. It'd taken a long, long time before she stopped waking up at night, screaming from the nightmares of them being slaughtered in front of her. They still came occasionally, but she no longer woke up screaming.

She shook her head. That was not the place she wanted to go while she looked at the gift her aunt had left for her. With a snap of her wrist, she closed the jewelry case and set it aside on the sofa. She lifted the other jewelry and gave the pieces a quick look, then set them aside also. A heavy bag lay flat on the bottom of the wooden box.

With great care, she lifted the bag. It jingled. Uncle Will chuckled as she tilted the bag and poured out its contents. Her heart pounded as coin after coin fell into her hand, then through her fingers and onto her lap. When the bag was empty, she looked at her uncle as he cackled. His tea sloshed over the edge of the cup and would have landed on his worn pants if not for the saucer.

Esther dropped the bag and touched the pieces, mostly double eagles—twenty-dollar gold pieces, along with a few other coins. "Where? How?"

Uncle Will pointed to her apron. "Might want to check the letter Bonny wrote you."

She jerked the envelope out of her pocket and ripped it open. She skimmed most of the words—they were for later. Right now she just wanted to find out about the money. What did it mean? Why was Aunt Bonny leaving it to her? And most importantly, would Uncle Ed try and get it back, maybe send her to jail for robbery?

At last, she saw the words that answered her questions. *The money in the bag is all yours. Your Uncle Ed knows nothing about it. You know what your mother was like, not liking to leave your father and the farm to come to town and shop for party clothes. So she provided me with the funds to purchase what you needed. Only we never got to do it. Those men saw to that.*

Most of the money in the bag is from two of your great-uncles on your mother's and my side of the family. Neither Uncle James nor Uncle Titus ever married. They were "too busy increasing their businesses for dealing with such things" as they were known to say. Anyway, they both sent me money for your dowry, money that I was to hold for you. Money your mother didn't even know about. They said they wanted it to be a surprise so no man would want to marry you just for your dowry. They said since they had no children to provide for, they wished you to have it since you were the only one of your generation in the family.

Esther bowed her head and closed her eyes. "Thank you, God. Thank you, for looking after me and Davey."

"Amen." Uncle Will grinned at her. "Got your answers?"

She nodded as she counted the coins. "Did you know my Uncle James and Uncle Titus?"

He harrumphed. "Those two old codgers. Work. Work. Work. That's all they ever thought about. No fun a'tall."

"Maybe they were, but they left me most of this." She finished the count. Her chest tightened to the point she wasn't sure she could breathe. All at once the air burst from her lungs. "There's fifty double eagles here, a thousand dollars. How did Aunt Bonny keep all this from Uncle Ed?"

"With love, Es, with love. She knew you'd need it someday. So out of love, she hid it away from her husband so you'd have it. And it's all yours, right and legal." His knees cracked as he stood. "I gotta get back to the liv'ry. Sully's in an all-fire fit to get back to hunting for gold." He gave her a bear hug. "Don't forget where I live, ya hear me?"

She kissed his cheek. "I won't."

He reached in his pocket and pulled out several animals along with three or four people he'd whittled. "Give these to Davey. The boy seems to enjoy them."

Esther wrapped her fingers around the gift. "He'll treasure them. Thank you."

She closed the front door after he left and walked back into the parlor. There was a lot of thinking and praying to be done. She had choices, but which would be the best for her and Davey?

Ray Miller stood beside the bunk where his firstborn burned in fever. The boy was getting weaker, and nothing seemed to help. He'd been gut-shot in the escape, but he hadn't died outright. So there'd been hope. Even the doc who'd seen to him told him Jake might survive, but he needed a lot of rest if that was to happen. Right. The doc just wanted them to stay put until the law could catch them. And they almost did. The medicine man must have sent someone for the sheriff when he wasn't looking. Good thing he had the brains to set Blake as a lookout or they would've been caught.

The doc deserved the bullet in the heart for trying to turn him and his boys in.

Now they needed to get what they came for. And they wouldn't let anyone stand in their way this time.

CHAPTER THIRTEEN

Once supper ended, everyone gathered in the parlor. Esther walked over to Drew. "Is it possible to speak to you privately?"

"Of course, let's go to my study." He glanced at his wife. "I'll be back in a few minutes."

Helen smiled and nodded.

Drew waved her to the door at the back of the parlor. In the room, Esther followed him to a pair of chairs. She rubbed the scar on her wrist. It'd been itching ever since Uncle Will had brought her the wooden box.

After they sat, Drew folded his hands together and waited for her to begin.

Esther took a deep breath and wiped her hands along her skirt. "My uncle came by today and brought me the box my aunt had the marshal and the sheriff take to him. Like they said, there was a set of diamond jewelry inside. There was also a bag of money, about fifty dollars in small coins, and, uh, and a thousand dollars in gold double eagles."

His eyes widened, but he nodded for her to continue.

She explained about the letter from her aunt and what it said.

When she finished, her hands fluttered in front of her. "What am I to do?"

"What do you want to do?" He smiled at her. "It's your decision. Do you want to go back East, back to where you lived before your uncle and aunt moved you all here? Do you want a home of your own? The choices are yours."

The future loomed out in front of her like a huge, scary monster. She didn't know what she wanted to do. She wasn't sure she'd ever want to marry. The thought of a man's hands on her still bothered her, but not as much since those moments in the livery with the marshal. She did know she didn't want to go back to the town where everyone knew what happened to her. She also didn't want to live in a house with just her and Davey here in Central City. They might not be safe living by themselves. What she wanted was what she had now, but would Drew still let her stay?

"Could Davey and I stay here just like we'd planned? I'd still work for you as a nanny and take care of your children."

"Are you sure it's what you want? You can now afford so much more."

"Oh, yes. Davey and I are happy here." She ducked her head for a moment, then raised her face. "And protected."

Drew nodded. "I understand. And yes, it'd be fine for you to remain here as a nanny. But I also wonder if you've thought of how you want to handle the money and the jewelry?"

"I've thought of hardly anything else since I saw it. I can't keep it in my room, and I'm not sure I trust banks. I know they can be robbed."

He rested his chin on his hand and tapped the side of his cheek. "I agree you can't keep it in your room. Davey might find it and think it's a toy." He grinned. "Don't get me wrong, I look forward to the day my children are big enough to play with the toys they've already been given. But the money and diamonds need to be protected. What about this? I have a small safe here in this room. I don't have anything in it now. It was left by the man who built this place. There is also a safe at the law office where I am reading law. You can put all of your valuables here or split them between the two safes."

Relief raced through her veins, chasing away some of the worries that had troubled her during the day. She wouldn't have to hide all those things in her room. "I'll put them in the safe here for now. Later, I might split them." She stood. "I'll go get them now. Thank you."

She felt as if the weight of the world had been lifted off her shoulders. She'd keep the money her mother had given Aunt Bonny and buy things she and Davey had been needing for some time. The gold double eagles, she'd put in Drew's safe along with the diamonds and other jewelry.

Her arm itched. She tried not to rub it, but it itched all the more. Was God giving her a reminder not to put her trust in earthly wealth? Or was he warning her about something else?

While Colin sat on a chair by the parlor window, he couldn't get past the feeling he was missing something, something to do with Ray Miller and his sons. Had they been the ones to break into the house instead of someone trying to kidnap one of the babies? Neither Linda nor Jack said they got a really good look at the men.

He sat there with his hands folded across his middle, and let his mind wander down different paths, jumping from one to another when each led to a dead end. He glanced from one person to the next around the room. Something flickered in his mind. Suddenly, he locked onto each person for a moment, then moved to the next. At last, he stopped at Jack, the housekeeper's brother. He remembered talking to Dougal after Esther got out of jail. He'd wondered at the time, if Jack, with his red hair, might not be related to the Millers.

He studied Jack even more. The boy didn't look at all like his sisters. He was heavier with dark brown eyes. His sisters both had brown hair and green eyes.

Something hopped around in the back of Colin's head, something he heard a dying man say after he'd been attacked by Ray Miller outside a brothel in Missouri. Something about Miller liking redheaded women. His gut tightened. Jessie's face crept into his mind. She had red hair. Had that been why the Millers attacked her stagecoach?

Bile rose from his stomach. Even though he swallowed it back, the taste remained. The outlaws had tried to hold up the stage, but it went over the ledge into a crevasse below. His wife's neck was broken. She hadn't been forced to live through any torment at their hands before they killed her.

Suddenly, memories of Matty jumped into his thoughts. The way his son begged him not to leave to go after outlaws, the way his son clung to him when he came back home, the way Matty said he wanted to be just like his Pa when he grew up.

Colin tried to shove the memories back, but they wouldn't quite go all the way back into the dark hole he kept them in. Bracing his hands against the arms of the chair, he shoved himself out of it. "Think I'll go see if either of my cousins needs anything."

He hurried out of the room, but the memories of his son ran right beside him.

Early the next morning, Colin left his room. He hoped to talk to Linda before anyone else got up. Maybe she'd have some of the answers he was looking for.

He pushed open the door to the kitchen and watched Linda wave good-bye to her brother and sister, along with Helen's brother. Kerr left with them. When Colin glanced at the table, he stopped dead in his tracks. His jaw clenched. Dougal sat at the table with a cup in his hand.

"Morning, brother. Thought I'd join you for a bit of coffee."

Colin swallowed back a few choice words that popped into his mind. Dougal knew he planned to talk to Linda this morning. They'd discussed it in the barn last night, and Dougal didn't seem to have any objections then.

He didn't need his baby brother joining in his investigation. For just a moment he thought about telling Dougal to leave, then Linda stepped over and sat by him at the table.

So be it. Colin let out a deep sigh and took a chair. "Has my brother told you what I want to talk to you about?"

She nodded, shook her head, then shrugged. "He just told me you needed to ask me some questions, and I might want to have Jack and Nancy leave for school a bit early." She snuck a quick peek at Dougal. "He had Kerr take them to the bakery for a doughnut. They thought it a great treat and were eager to go." She blinked several times. "They aren't in any trouble, are they?"

Her hands twisted together on top of the table. Dougal laid one hand on top of hers and stilled the movement. She thanked him with a smile.

Colin couldn't believe the change in his little brother since he'd left home five years before. Little kids loved him. Young women looked to him for comfort. What happened to the wild kid who always got into trouble? And when had Colin, a deputy US marshal sworn to uphold the law, become the man who women and children feared? The one who made them cry?

"If Dougal had just let me talk to you first, you wouldn't have had time to worry." His brother frowned, but Colin ignored him. "It's just something I wanted to get straight. Now, don't get upset. After what you reported when the men who broke in here said about getting the boy, I just wanted to make sure of something."

Linda looked puzzled, but at least she wasn't crying.

Colin's muscles relaxed a bit. He took a sip of coffee. "I know this sounds farfetched, but could I ask what color hair your mother had?"

A blank look filled her eyes as she tilted her head slightly. "Red. What's that to do—?"

Colin raised one hand and tightened his grip on his cup with the other. "Just another question or two, then I'll explain why I'm asking these things. Dougal says you haven't lived around here but a couple of years. Where did you come from?"

She turned her fingers around and gripped Dougal's hand. "We moved around a lot, Texas, Kansas, Missouri."

Colin hesitated. He'd thought all night how to ask this question of the young woman, more of a girl really. She couldn't be more than nineteen. He tapped the table a couple of times. "Is Jack your brother?"

She stood and stumbled back a few steps. "Of course, Jack's my brother. I was there when he was born. Preacher Bob was there and Grandma made a big cake and—and—no that's not right." Confusion, then fear crossed her face. "Wait a minute." She ran to her room off the kitchen. Thumping and thudding sounds came from her bedroom.

Colin looked at his brother. Dougal shot him a glare rivaling the sun on the hottest day of summer. His brother got to his feet, crossed the floor, and followed Linda.

Before he got to her bedroom door, she came out, holding a black book in her hands. "This was Ma's. She used to keep all the family information in it until—until she lost the third baby after Nancy was born. Then she just closed it and packed it away. I used to ask to look at all those names, grandparents, great-grandparents, but she'd always cry, and I stopped asking."

She shoved it at Colin and let Dougal help her back to the table. "Look at it. See if you find what you want to know."

Colin felt like a trespasser to her family memories, but he needed to find out if his suspicions were correct. Flipping through the Bible he found the page where someone had written Linda's birthdate, then in a different hand Jack's and Nancy's births were recorded along with the births and deaths of three more children. But there was nothing recorded about marriages or even her mother's death. It was like Linda said, after the death of the last baby, nothing else was written. So he still didn't have the answers to his questions.

All at once, Linda let out a gasp and touched her half-opened mouth. Her eyes grew huge in her pale face. She dropped her hands onto the table. "I, uh, I just remembered something Pa said. I was only four when Jack was born, but I remember Pa sitting me on his knee as he sat by the bed where Ma held baby Jack. He said...he said I now had a new brother and a new ma. How could I not remember that before? She wasn't my real ma."

Dougal wrapped his arms around her while her shoulders shook and the tears flowed. He narrowed his eyes and glared at his brother. Dougal motioned Colin to leave.

Guilt ate at Colin's gut as he left the room. Had he really proved anything other than he could hurt a young woman when he ripped her world apart? He let out a snort of disgust at himself. He just couldn't seem to keep from hurting women. He should've remembered that about himself. His wife told him often enough before she died.

He stopped mid-step in the hall. What about Esther? Memories of her being in the jail cell jabbed into his mind. The sight of her there still left a sour taste in his mouth and a crushing tightness to his chest.

His boot finally dropped to the wooden floor. He cared for her. And that scared him. Could he chance losing someone else he cared about? Even more important, was there room enough inside him for the caring to live with the vengeance he had to mete out to the Millers?

Esther held Davey's hand while he carried his bag of wooden horses. She followed Helen out of the nursery. The twins were finally asleep for their morning naps.

"You have such a well-behaved son." Helen smiled at Davey. "I just hope my two will be like that when they get older."

"Davey's learned to be quiet. Uncle Ed would scold him horribly if he wasn't." Esther watched her son move down the stairs, gripping the side rail before taking each step. "He's much happier here."

"I'm glad, for him and for you."

At the bottom of the stairs, they headed to the parlor, but stopped at the entrance.

Linda stood by the wooden cradles, her shoulders shaking. Her hand covered her mouth. Moisture quivered on her eyelashes.

Esther touched her son's head and bent so her lips were close to his ear. "Please, go to the kitchen and ask Miss Pippa to make some tea. And tell her I said you could have two cookies." She kissed his cheek and didn't have to nudge him on his way. Grinning, he took off like a bear was nipping at his heels.

After he left, she walked with Helen into the room.

Linda heard them and quickly wiped her cheeks. Helen wrapped her arm around the younger woman's waist.

"What's the problem?" Helen drew Linda to the sofa, and they both sat.

Not wanting to interfere, Esther turned to leave.

"Don't go, Esther." Linda sniffled. "You live here, and I don't want any more secrets."

Esther hesitated. She had plenty of secrets in her life, but she didn't think she was ready to share all of them, even with these women with whom she was becoming friends.

Helen patted Linda's hand. "Bad memories?"

"Not about that." She shook her head. "I hardly ever think about what happened anymore." She sucked in a deep breath. "Well, I guess it has been on my mind some, since Hank refused to marry me because of it."

Esther wondered what they were talking about. She remembered Drew saying something about it when she'd met him at the bakery the first day.

Linda glanced at Esther. "Just so you know, before I came here—actually it was part of why I came here." She stopped for a moment and swallowed. "Anyway, Drew's brother-in-law helped us after two men rode in, killed my pa, and attacked me."

Esther's stomach tightened. She knew what Linda had gone through without her saying another word. Snatches of memories, sounds of heavy breathing, pain, oh, the pain. She wrapped her arms around her middle to keep them from shaking. *Don't say any more. Please, don't say any more.*

Helen lifted her hand. "One of them gave me this." She touched the scar on the side of her face. "They joined a man named Snodgrass and kidnapped me and Drew's sister." She let out a sigh. "But it's all behind us now. Snodgrass is still in prison, and the other two are dead."

Esther rubbed her arm.

"I know you can't understand what it'd be like." Linda clasped her hands in her lap.

Yes, I can. I really can. I just don't know if I can talk about it like you.

Pippa brought in the tea tray. "What did the lawman say that upset you so much this morning? You weren't responsible for what those men did to you. And if he said otherwise, I think his welcome to this house should be questioned." She glared at Helen. "I don't care whose relative he is. And if you think differently, Helen, then I don't need to work here. You should have seen the mess the lawman left." She raised an eyebrow and looked at Linda. "Although Dougal looked real good comforting you."

Linda blushed. "Oh, no, Pippa. You have it all wrong. The marshal helped me remember something about my mother." She raised her palms upward and shrugged. "But that's the thing. I don't think she was my ma. Oh, it's all so confusing."

"Well, as long as he was acting like a gentleman." Pippa huffed a bit and walked out.

Linda and Helen giggled like two school girls.

Esther began rethinking secrets. Maybe these two women would understand what she had gone through. With Aunt Bonny gone, she had no one to talk to, no one who wouldn't judge her because they didn't understand, no one to help support her when the nightmares woke her at night. She needed to step out in faith that these women were the friends she needed.

"I want—no—I need to correct something you said earlier." She looked Linda in the eye. "I understand what you went through. Outlaws came to our farm in Kansas, killed my parents, and attacked me." She turned her eyes to Helen. "And before they left, they did this to me." She jerked back her sleeve and showed the scar the men had carved into her arm. "The only good thing that came out of it was Davey." She covered the reminder of the attack.

As if two strings pulled the others off the sofa at the same time, they jumped up and dropped on either side of her, wrapping their arms around her and crying with her.

They remained there for several minutes. When all their faces had been wiped and hankies tucked away, Helen and Linda moved back to the sofa.

Esther wasn't sure if all the tears were for her, or if each one cried for the things they'd lost.

Helen leaned back and glanced around the room. "I've come to realize this is a healing house. Drew's sister came here after suffering a very bad first marriage. She found healing and love here. Drew and I fell in love and are now raising our family here." She turned toward Linda. "You and your brother and sister found a place of refuge here." Helen grinned. "And maybe someone who really cares for you."

Linda blushed again, then looked at Esther. "I wonder what this house holds for you."

Esther's arm itched again. She'd found friendship and support here. Suddenly, the marshal's—no—Colin's face popped into her mind. What else *did* the house hold for her?

CHAPTER FOURTEEN

Colin rode to the barn in back of the Hollingsworths' house, still thinking about what a couple of miners told him earlier when he'd made his rounds looking for information on the Millers or Confederate sympathizers.

While he dismounted, Dougal came out of the barn and glared at him. "Did you really have to put Linda through that this morning? It took her half an hour to quit crying. I hope you got what you wanted."

Colin's stomach ached, and had since he left the kitchen. Sometimes he wondered if he was really cut out to be a lawman. The only thing really driving him to keep the badge was the support it gave him while he searched for the Millers. Once he found them and they were dead or back in prison, he might give it back. A hollow chuckle almost burst out his lips at the irony of it. Jessie left him because he refused to give up the badge, and the only reason he kept it was because of her.

He didn't want to fight with his brother, but there was a job to be done. His gut twisted a little more. "How's she doing now?"

"Do you really want to know, or is it just guilt asking?"

Colin gripped his reins tighter. "I really want to know. I don't want to hurt her or you."

Dougal shrugged. "Better, I guess. Pippa told me to go out and let Linda be for a while. I hope to see her at noon."

"I need to get the saddlebags from my room. I'll be gone for a few days. Tuck's got a prisoner I have to take to Denver. On the way back, thought I'd check out some of the nearby towns. See what information I might come across."

Dougal retreated to the barn.

Before Colin reached the house, a buggy rode into the yard.

Drew pulled the horse to a halt. "Forgot a book I needed, so I thought I'd come and eat with Helen." He climbed down. Together the two of them went into the house.

In the kitchen, Pippa clanged pots on the stove, but stopped and scowled at Colin for a moment. Drew cleared his throat.

"I'll be staying for lunch."

She nodded and turned back to the stove.

Colin slipped out into the hall with Drew on his tail. Suddenly they were hit with crying from two directions, down the hall and up the stairs. Drew quickly moved toward the parlor and peeked around the corner. He jerked back and motioned Colin upstairs.

When they reached the top, Drew waved him into the nursery. "The women are fine. They're having some kind of crying party. The babies need us more."

He stripped off his coat and grabbed the baby on the left.

Colin shrugged and took the one on the right. It'd been several years since he had dealt with a baby this small, but he'd helped Jessie with Matty when he'd been home. Which, as he thought about it, hadn't been a lot of time.

A few minutes later, Colin sat in one chair rocking with a baby on his shoulder all clean and dry while Drew sat in the other chair doing the same thing.

Davey came into the nursery, carrying a cloth bag. "Play here?"

Colin nodded. "Sure, Davey. What have you got there in there?"

The boy plopped his bottom on the rug and upended the bag. Wooden horses fell out. He grabbed one in each hand and ran to Drew. "Baby wanna play?"

"Sorry, Davey. Sarah and Andy are still too young to play with you." Drew smiled at the boy.

Colin felt sorry for the little fellow when his lips drooped, but the boy never complained. "Tell you what, Davey. If Drew will hold both of the babies, I'll read you a story."

The kid's grin almost split his face. "Really? Me like stories."

"Go get a book while I give this baby to his papa."

Davey's head bobbed, then he raced out of the room.

Drew wrapped his arm around the second twin. "Don't want to get your ears blown out if they decide they're hungry?"

Colin grinned. "Just trying to help out."

Esther climbed the stairs. Pippa said lunch was ready, and Drew would be eating with them. She figured he was in the nursery with the babies since he wasn't in the parlor with Helen.

She held back a giggle. Of course, he might have seen them all crying and gone upstairs out of self-defense. But the sharing, both the secrets and the tears, left her feeling drained and good. She now had women she could share her thoughts with, women who understood what she'd gone through, women who cared.

She neared the nursery and heard Davey jabbering away, then she stopped when she heard another voice. Colin was in there with him. She edged to the open door and peeked in. Drew sat in one rocking chair making funny faces at his children. But it was the other chair which really caught her attention.

Davey sat on the marshal's lap, resting back against the man's chest with his favorite storybook in his hands. She'd read the book to him so many times, Davey knew all the words by memory. But this time he recited only the parts of the little boy while the marshal read the parts of the animals, making his voice change with each creature.

She would've laughed at the way Colin sounded, if it didn't hurt so much since Davey didn't have a father to share that with. *Before those men came, this was what I thought my husband and child would look like.* She shook her head a bit. *Not in looks, but in love. It's how Papa loved me. Colin would make a good father for Davey.* She rubbed her clenched fist over the left side of her chest. *No, he'd make a good husband...for some woman.*

"Lunch ready?" Drew's voice pulled her out of her thoughts.

Esther felt heat rise in her cheeks. "It's why I came upstairs. Time to eat." She helped Drew put the babies back in their beds, thankful they'd gone back to sleep.

As they left the nursery, Davey skipped along the hall, jabbering about the story they'd been reading.

All at once the heel of her shoe caught in the hem of her skirt. Falling, she reached out her hands to grab anything that would keep her from hurting herself. Her fingers clamped onto something hard and warm. An arm wrapped itself around her waist.

"Careful there, Essie. Wouldn't want you to get hurt." Colin pulled her against his chest.

Her head popped up as a warmth she'd never felt before wove its way around her insides. She looked up at him, then whispered, "Do you always grab women to save them from danger?"

A grin spread across his face as if he also remembered the moments in the livery when they first met. "Only if I can hold them in my arms for a bit."

Esther stared at him for a few seconds longer. He stared back, wrapping her a bit closer in his arms. She gave herself a mental shake and pulled away. "Uh, thank you."

She was handling this all wrong. Instead of stepping back after he helped her, she'd stayed wrapped in that cocoon of warmth. She kept her eyes on the steps all the way down the stairs.

But she couldn't get the look he gave her out of her mind.

And it'd felt good to have him hold her, maybe too good.

Ray Miller huddled in the dim corner of the saloon and mumbled curses as he listened to a couple of dusty miners talking about how the law was asking around, seeing if anyone had seen men who looked like him and his boys. He finished his drink and made his way to a building in the better part of town, checking on the whereabouts of the law along the way.

Ray slipped out of the alley behind Ed Small's barbershop and moved around to the front of the shop. He glanced in the window. There weren't any customers inside. He opened the door just a bit, reached up, and held the bell still so no would know he entered. Once inside, he slipped his gun out of the holster at his side.

Small stepped into the room, toting a jar. When he spotted Ray, the barber's face turned as pale as a mourning widow. He dropped the jar he was holding. The glass shattered. The smell of bay rum filled the air as the contents oozed onto the floor.

Ray snickered. "Good to see you. It's been a while."

"H—how'd you know where I—I'd gone?" Small tried to swallow but his Adam's apple just bobbed around like a dance hall gal's skirt. "Wh—wh—what do you want?" Spittle shot from the barber's stuttering mouth.

Poor man's all afraid. And he had reason to be. The hairs of Ray's mustache rubbed across his teeth and gums as he stretched his lips wide in a gleeful grin. This was the way he liked the people he dealt with—scared and eager to please. "Last time I saw you, you was right accommodating, moving your family to the place I told you to go. But then you did wrong and moved again." He let his grin drop into a frown. "You knew I was coming, but you took off anyway. Not good. Not good at all."

"M-m-mister M-m-miller—" The barber's hands shook at his sides.

"Shut up. I just wanted you to know I've found you and got an eye on you." Ray snickered again at the way the barber's face turned even paler. *How pale could a man get before he passed out?* His eyes flickered around the shop. "Seem to be doing mighty good, what with this shop and the boardinghouse." Then he turned his eyes on the barber. "Take you long to clean the mess in the room off the kitchen?"

The puny man shivered in his pants. "You were in my house?"

"Yep. See how easy it is to visit you? How's the pretty daughter of yours doing?"

"What do you want from me?"

Ray hadn't had this much fun in a long while. He pulled a sack he'd tucked in his back pocket. "Well, since you asked, you can dump all your cash in here." He looked around the room again. "Get another bag and load it with anything you have to eat and any liquor you got." He waved his gun for emphasis. "And don't tell me you ain't got any. I can smell it on your breath."

A few minutes later, Ray grabbed the bags the scared little man had filled and started for the door. With another of those mouth-tickling grins, he looked back at Small. "Just remember, if you go to the law about our little meeting, I'll know. And no matter where you try to hide that girl of yours, I'll find her and take her back as a gift for my boys."

He slipped out the front door as sweat popped out on the barber's face.

As the door snapped shut behind Ray, he bit back his laughter so he wouldn't draw any attention to himself, but he hadn't enjoyed anything like that in a long time. Now all he needed was a plan to get the law off his trail so he could get that boy.

CHAPTER FIFTEEN

Sunday morning broke with a clear blue sky. Esther shifted in her bed. She couldn't keep the smile from her face. It came all the way from her heart. Today, she and Davey would go to church.

She jumped out of bed and touched her new robe hanging on the end of the bed. Using some of the money Aunt Bonny had left her, she'd gone to the mercantile. Wanda had helped her buy new clothes for Davey and herself. Not just items to replace the things which had been patched so much they couldn't be patched any more. No, this time she was able to buy Davey three sets of pants and shirts, new underthings, and a pair of shoes.

Moving across the bedroom, she opened the door to the wardrobe and looked at her new dresses—store-bought ones, not dresses that had been remade from the cast-offs Tina no longer wanted. No, these were new, in colors which flattered Esther. She pulled out the one she'd bought to wear to church. It was a lovely green-sprigged cotton dress. She'd bought a paisley shawl to wear with it and black buttoned boots along with fine stockings.

Using her brush and hairpins, she styled her hair a little differently today with a few loose curls framing her face. How she wished she had her natural hair color back. Patience, she told herself, patience. She'd have to wait until the walnut dye lightened enough to let her natural hair color show again. It was another good thing about leaving Uncle Ed's house. Soon she'd look like she had before she'd gone to live with him.

After she washed and dressed, she woke Davey. His eyes grew wide when he saw her.

"You pretty, Mama."

She hugged and kissed him, then ruffled his hair. "And you're going to look quite handsome today, too. Hurry and take off your nightshirt so you can get dressed. We need to eat breakfast, then we'll go to church."

His tongue slipped out between his lips as he struggled to button one of his new shirts. When he finished, his grin lit his face. "Mama, Unca Collie go to church?"

Esther bit her tongue and tried to keep from laughing, not at her son's name for the marshal, but at the memory of the first time he used it. The poor man's face turned several shades of red, then he tried to get Davey to say it right, all the while explaining that a collie was a dog. But her son was very, very stubborn. And once he chose a name for someone—it was the name they were stuck with.

"I'm not sure he'll be going." She brushed his hair, then nudged him to the door. They didn't need to check on the babies. Helen said she and Drew would take care of them. In fact, Helen said Sunday was Esther's day off.

In the kitchen, Linda had laid out cinnamon rolls and had a pot of coffee on the stove. The two MacPherson brothers sat at the table, each nursing a cup of coffee. A plate with crumbs and tiny chunks of icing sat before both of them.

"Unca Dewey. Unca Collie." Davey ran to the table and crawled onto the marshal's lap.

"Colin. My name is Colin."

"I know, Uncle Collie."

Dougal didn't even try to hide his grin. He did swallow his chuckles, although not very well. Esther couldn't blame him. She bit back her laughter as well.

Even though she kept her eyes lowered for a moment, she raised them just to see how upset Colin was with Davey.

He sat with his fists resting on his hips and stared at the ceiling, then looked at her. He caught her grin and returned it. They both laughed until their eyes met and held. Slowly the laughter ended.

She cleared her throat and lifted a cinnamon roll onto a small plate. She set it on the table a little ways from the marshal. "Come on, son. You need to eat so we'll be ready for church."

Davey leaned his head back against the marshal's chest and looked at him. "Unca Collie, go church with us?"

She tightened her fingers on the back of the chair—not because of the question, but because of the way the marshal looked. His face grew harder as he glared at something just beyond his brother's head. Ragged breaths dragged across his lips. She looked at Dougal for an answer to what was happening.

Sorrow dug deep lines in Dougal's usually jolly face. He glanced at her and gave a tiny shake of the head.

"Ow, Unca Collie. Too tight."

"Sorry." The marshal lifted Davey out of his lap and set him on the chair next to him. "I've got to go take care of something." He grabbed his hat from the hook at the back door and rushed out of the house without another word.

"Unca Collie, Unca Collie." Davey's wails filled the air. He scrambled off the chair and chased after his new friend, but the door closed before he could get to him.

"Hey, fella." Dougal lifted Davey in his arms before Esther could get to him. "We need to finish our breakfast so we can get to church. I've been planning on you sitting with me."

Davey swiped at a couple of tears with the back of his hands. Esther handed Dougal a napkin so he could finish the job for her son.

"If it's all right with your mama, I thought you could ride up front on my horse." Dougal raised his eyebrow in question to her.

As confused as she was at what just happened with Colin, she was just as thankful to Dougal for cheering her son. She nodded.

Dougal motioned for her to sit and kept his voice low. "You'll have to excuse my big brother. It's not my place to tell you what all's happened to him. Let's just say I'm surprised he's taken to this little guy like he has."

He lightly rubbed Davey's hair while pained sorrow filled his face again. "As far as church, he stopped going several years ago. I don't know if he'll ever go back."

Before she could ask any questions, Jack burst out of his bedroom. "Yippee, we got cinnamon rolls. It's what I miss most 'bout not living 'bove the bak'ry." He grabbed a plate, dug out a roll from the pan, and bowed his head for a moment, then downed the roll in three bites.

Esther grinned at the idea of Davey doing that in about ten years, but the thought was pushed away when she remembered the way the marshal looked holding her son. What had hurt him so deeply? More importantly, if he could turn so cold so quickly, could he hurt Davey? She knew the marshal wouldn't hit Davey. But with the cruel words her uncle had spoken to her through the years, the hateful glares, the shutting her off from a sense of family, she knew there were other ways to hurt a child. And she'd never allow her son to be treated that way. Not now—now that she had the means to support him and not be at someone else's mercy.

Davey came first with her. Still something in her wanted—no—needed to know what caused the look in Colin's eyes. Would he ever open up enough to tell her?

Colin stood in the back of the barn while the others left for the morning church service. He'd helped where he could by hitching the horse to the carriage and saddling Kerr's and Dougal's horses. He told them he'd stay and watch the house, but in truth it was just an excuse, and Dougal knew it. His brother had been with him when Matty's broken body had been pulled from the wreckage, cold and lifeless. Dougal had heard the words he'd spoken, curses against those who'd done the horrible crime, curses against God who allowed it to happen, vowing never to enter a church to worship such a God again.

Colin had made another vow that day, a vow he'd repeated over his son's grave a few days later, a vow he was still trying to fulfill, a vow he didn't think he could complete when the Miller boys went to prison, but now he could. He just had to find them. He could feel their presences somewhere nearby, but he didn't know what they were searching for.

With nothing better to do for the moment, he grabbed the pitchfork to muck out the stalls. The door creaked open. He reached for his gun, but he hadn't put it on this morning yet. And being the blockhead that he'd been earlier, he'd left it in the house when he'd rushed out, rushed away from the boy, rushed away from the memories.

He gripped the pitchfork and raised it higher. He wouldn't put it past one of the Millers to come after him, if they knew he was unarmed and alone.

The door opened wider. Adam Lone Eagle, wearing a buckskin shirt and dusty boots, chuckled and stepped into the opening. "If I'd wanted to attack you, you wouldn't have had a chance. Put that thing down and let's go have some coffee."

Feeling a bit foolish for being caught unawares, Colin rested the pitchfork against the barn wall and followed the man into the house.

A few minutes later, they sat at the table with coffee in front of them. Colin looked at the pan someone'd left covered in the middle of the table, but he didn't think he could swallow anything. Adam didn't seem to have any trouble though. He lifted the cloth and dug out three of the last four rolls. "Don't care about the new folks using the same recipe for these, Linda still makes 'em better."

Colin tapped his fingers on the table while he waited for the other man to finish. He figured Adam must have some information to share and would when he was ready.

Once the last of the rolls had gone down the man's throat along with two cups of coffee, Adam wiped his mouth and leaned back in his chair. "Thought you might want to know I spotted those same hoofprints leading out of town a couple of days ago."

Colin shoved back his chair as he stood. "Let's go."

"Simmer down." Adam waved his hand back to the chair Colin had shoved back. "I wouldn't have come here if I'd just seen them. I tracked them heading south for a while most of yesterday. By the way, the man was by himself, and he knows how to hide his tracks when he wants." He stood. "Thought you'd want to know the man's still nearby and coming into town." He flicked the brim of his hat. "See you later."

After Adam left, Colin hurried up the stairs, two steps at a time. He grabbed his holster and checked to make sure the gun was loaded, not that he thought it wasn't. Out of habit, he checked every time he put it on. Taking his canteen and saddlebags, he went to the kitchen, grabbed some cookies out of the jar, and filled his canteen from the pump at the dry sink. He left behind the smell of roast and potatoes cooking in the oven and headed to the barn.

It might be stupid and useless, but he needed to ride around town and the nearby area. If Miller came into town after what he had done to the miners, maybe he'd left some other tracks somewhere. Maybe he was meeting someone in town.

Esther spotted her uncle and Tina arrive at the small church building. Uncle Ed started toward her when the man who led the songs asked the congregation to rise. Her uncle shook his head and motioned his daughter into a pew across the aisle and one row back. At least with them behind her, she'd be able to worship for the first time in a long time. Partway through the service, the feeling of someone watching her made the hairs on the back of her neck rise.

She lowered her head and peeked backwards. Uncle Ed sat in the pew with his chin on his chest. Tina had her eyes on a young man in a nice suit sitting with his parents in front of her.

Davey grew tired and laid his head against Jack who sat next to him. She lifted her son so he straddled her lap and rested his face against her shoulder. After a few minutes he lifted his hand and waved at someone behind them. She pulled his hand to his side. He got close to her ear. "Man waved to me. Play hide-an-seek 'gain?"

Her head jerked around, but all she saw was the door to the outside closing and a couple of old women behind her frowning and wagging their fingers at her.

She set Davey on the floor when they rose for the final song and the closing prayer, but her mind was on the man who'd been at the back of the building. Had he come to worship? If so, why did he leave so early?

She realized there was someone she could ask about the man. The preacher stood at the back door and greeted the people as they left. She held Davey's hand and held back until almost everyone had gone out, then she approached him.

"Hello, Sister Sanders, uh, Sister O'Brien. I'm happy to see you here today."

Word about her had spread, but she didn't have time to deal with it right now. She nodded to the older gentleman. "I'm happy to be here. Could I ask you something?"

He smiled. "I'm always happy to answer questions. Was there something in the sermon you didn't understand?"

"No, no, nothing like that. I mean I enjoyed what you said very much. Except close to the end, I got distracted. Did you notice a man leave just before you finished?"

He looked a little disappointed she wasn't asking about the sermon, but then he seemed to remember something. "Yes, I do believe there was an older man with a limp who came in late. He stood at the back even though there were places to sit closer to the front, but then not everyone likes to sit so close to a preacher, especially if they aren't used to coming. But I've seen him around town several times. Maybe he was just checking us out and will come back again."

So it wasn't just her imagination. There was a man in town, and she'd seen him twice—no, really she'd seen him only once. Davey had seen him twice. But what was it about the man that bothered her? Who was he? And what did he want?

Ray Miller saw the deputy US marshal on the road ahead and forced his horse off the road, taking a back trail he'd found a few days earlier. Ray cursed. Coming to town today hadn't been the smartest move he'd ever made, but he'd come anyway. During the night, Harve had died, followed by Jake about sunrise. That only left Blake, who was near worthless.

He spit out the bad taste in his mouth. But none of that mattered. Soon he'd have a new boy, one he'd train in his own image.

An hour later, he passed close to a shack where a couple of old miners lived. He'd come across them a few times before. They hadn't offended him much, so he'd let them be. No sense killing unless he had a need. Besides, they were a gossipy group, and it was kinda nice to find out what was going on without having to sneak into town to find out the latest news.

He drew nearer. The air carried a smell he couldn't mistake. Death rode the wind. He pulled out his gun, keeping his finger on the trigger and reined his horse off the trail. Coming up to the back side of the cabin, he checked things over. No animals in the lean-to, no smoke from the chimney, no movement of any kind. Just that stink.

He dismounted and tied the reins to a branch of a nearby bush, a scrawny thing, but it did the job. Slipping around the side, he ducked under the hole where a window should've been and peeked in the open door. The miners lay dead on the dirt floor. The place had been ransacked. Somebody must have thought the miners had found a rich vein and killed them for it. He shrugged. Cards were scattered in the dirt. Maybe someone didn't like the way the miners played poker. Whatever the reason, the men were dead.

An idea slipped into Ray's head and took root. The perfect way to get the marshal off his trail had just presented itself to him, almost as if it was meant to be. He chuckled at the thought.

He mounted and rode hard to find a wagon. He had to get matters taken care of before anyone else found the miners.

CHAPTER SIXTEEN

The night's darkness surrounded Esther while she sat on the wooden swing hanging from the covered back porch. Davey was asleep, but she felt too restless to crawl into bed, knowing she wouldn't be able to sleep. A nightmare had woken her from the nap she'd taken during the afternoon. Not a bad one, not one which caused her to wake screaming, not the one where two men had destroyed the life she'd had before. No, this nightmare had some unknown creature trying to get her. The creature slipped around her, playing with her, tormenting her, but never really harming her. It was just an evil presence that wouldn't leave her alone.

And now with the rest of the household in bed, the unrest in her spirit kept her from sleep, so she sat out here by herself.

The sound of horse's hooves striking the ground thudded in the night air. The barn door creaked open. Kerr called out, then held a lantern nudging the darkness to the side. The marshal had returned. He got off his horse and led the animal into the barn. A few minutes later, he came back through the door and walked to the house.

Esther figured if she kept real still, he'd go inside. But she'd forgotten Kerr knew she was sitting out here and probably told the marshal since he stopped at the top of the stairs and looked toward the end of the porch where she sat.

"Mind if I join you?" He didn't move. He seemed to be waiting for her answer. It'd be so easy not to give him permission, but that seemed a bit childish. She wasn't afraid of him, not really. He'd shown kindness to Davey, and that went a long way in making her trust him. It was just…just that he was a man. She could almost hear Aunt Bonny's voice in her ear. *Do you really want to live the rest of your life afraid to sit near a man, to shove all of them aside because of what two horrid men had done? Do you want to take the chance Davey will see how you aren't sure you trust men? How might it affect him as he grows?*

He seemed to know she was debating his question, so he asked another. "Is it me or the badge? You don't seem to have any problem being around my brother."

Esther clamped her teeth over her bottom lip to keep from laughing. He sounded just like a little boy who was upset that something was being kept from him.

But his question struck a nerve in her as well. "Maybe a little of both—you and the badge. Bad memories about bad times are connected with the badge. You…I'm just not sure about." She let out a small sigh and decided to take a chance. "The swing's big enough for two, even three."

He made a noise, a tired sound that held a bit of humor. "Thanks, but no. The railing's fine enough for me." He took a few steps nearer, then dropped something on the porch, something metal, maybe a canteen since it sloshed. "I want to apologize for this morning, for leaving like I did."

"It's fine. Your brother made your excuses."

He made another noise, only this time it sounded somewhere between a grunt and a snort with a bark of laughter thrown in. "Yeah, he's been making excuses for me for a long time. Have to thank him for it sometime."

"Well then, why don't you go ahead and make your own apology?"

"How's Davey? I mean, did I upset him too much?"

"For a moment, but Dougal offered to let Davey ride in front of him on his horse. Then everything else was forgotten."

"I saw Dougal put the boy on the saddle. I was a mite surprised you let him do it, but I understand now."

"You saw?"

"Yeah, I was in the barn." Before he could say anything else, his stomach growled long and deep.

"Have you had anything to eat today? As I recall you left before you'd eaten breakfast." She touched the napkin-wrapped cookies in her lap. She hadn't been hungry when she came out, but she wasn't sure how long she'd stay, or if Kerr would stop by as he made his rounds during the night.

"Some. I always keep a bit of jerky in my saddlebags, just in case I'm out longer than I'd planned." His stomach growled again.

She lifted the white napkin which could barely be seen against the night's darkness. "Here, take these. It's only a couple of cookies, just in case I got hungry. But I think you are hungrier than I am tonight. Besides, I had supper."

He hesitated.

"Go on. No sense in your stomach waking the whole house."

Colin reached for the napkin. Her husky voice soothed him, brought peace to the troubles battling within his mind and heart. His hand glided over hers when he took the cookies. He heard her gasp, a tiny one, but still there. His gut twisted, but it wasn't from hunger this time.

How long had it been since a woman had showed concern for his comfort? It'd been a long time, too long since he'd let anyone get this close. This was too dangerous, especially with Ray Miller somewhere close by.

He shoved the two small cookies in his mouth, but it was harder to shove her care, her concern aside. He could fill his belly, but nothing would fill the hole in his heart until justice was done.

Then what? The question erupted into his thoughts, followed by a vision of Esther and Davey laughing and hugging each other. He wanted to join them, share—

The chains on the swing rattled when Esther shifted on the seat.

Colin swallowed the last of the cookies down his suddenly dry throat, then grabbed his canteen. He pulled out the cork and drank it dry. "Thanks, that'll hold me 'til breakfast."

The swing's chains rattled again as she rose. "It's time for me to go inside. I don't want Davey to wake and not be able to find me."

He stood. Only he didn't realize how close it'd put him to her. She brushed against him and jerked back. He put out his arm to keep her from falling. All at once she was leaning against him. Sweet and soft, and smelling like some kind of flowers. A nameless need called out to him, or rather, a need he wouldn't name. He lowered his head and tightened his hold on her. His eyes rested on the dim shadow of her lips.

Suddenly she trembled and made a small sound deep in her throat, not a sound of pleasure, but one of panic.

He loosened his arm. *Stupid. Stupid. Stupid.*

She took a step back, then moved farther away. "I, uh, I need to go in."

And without another word, she slipped inside the house.

Colin dropped onto the swing and covered his face with his hands. What was he doing? Esther needed a man who'd stand with her, one who'd show her how good life could be between a man and a woman. And as long as he wore his star, he wasn't that man.

He gathered his canteen and went to his room. Maybe he'd get through the night without the Millers disturbing his sleep, but he wasn't sure about Esther.

"Mama, Mama, wake up. Me hungry."

Esther lifted one eyelid and peered into the darkness. Davey sat cross-legged next to her on the bed in his nightshirt, holding onto her arm.

"Mama, Mama. Hear me? Wake up."

She slipped her arm out of his grasp and wrapped it around him, then pulled him back on the bed beside her. Maybe he'd fall back asleep if she hugged him long enough.

She was so tired. But then she hadn't gotten to sleep until late into the night, or early in the morning, whichever way one looked at it. The last time she remembered the clock in the parlor chiming, it had struck three times. The scene on the back porch with the marshal kept running through her mind. The feel of his hands on her, the warmth of his breath, the closeness of his lips to hers. For the first time in years, she wanted a man's arms around her, wanted him to hold her close. But then terror had roared to life. She'd never been kissed before. Not really.

What those men had done…no, she wouldn't think of about it. But she did wonder how it'd feel to have a man gently kiss her. And for a moment it almost happened. He wouldn't have taken what she hadn't been ready to give. Just a kiss. A simple, little kiss. She didn't know how many times she'd slammed her fist against the feather mattress every time she got to that point.

Davey wiggled. "Me still hungry. Get up?"

She surrendered and let him up. "Yes dear, let's go and see what we can find in the kitchen. But you must be very quiet so we don't wake anyone else."

"Me be quiet." He didn't give her a chance to get out of bed. Instead he crawled over her and slid to the floor. She followed him, although she didn't have to slide. Soon both of them were washed and dressed for the day. She held his hand, and they left their room. On the way to the stairs, she looked over her shoulder. The marshal's door was closed. She hoped he was still fast asleep, and they could finish their breakfast and get back to the babies before he woke up.

She tightened her grip on Davey's hand and placed her hand on the stair railing as they made their way downstairs. Once there, they headed for the kitchen. She breathed a sigh of relief when she saw light under the closed kitchen door. The smell of coffee filled the air. Linda must be up early, too.

Esther opened the door. She needed someone to talk to, and Linda seemed just the person. A cup of coffee and a listening ear would help her get things straight about what happened on the porch last night. After all, Linda had been hurt like she had and gone on to get engaged, even if she hadn't married the man. Surely she'd kissed him at some point while they were courting.

Davey ran in front of her into the kitchen. "Unca Collie, you come back."

Esther wanted to pull back out of the room, but the marshal had already seen her. He nodded to her and let Davey climb on his leg. No one else was in the room so it must have been earlier than she thought when they woke.

"There's coffee if you want some. It's not as good as Linda's, but it's drinkable." His eyes followed her as she crossed the room, eyes that seemed a little bloodshot, like he hadn't had enough sleep. She wondered if hers looked the same.

"Thanks, but I need to get Davey something to eat first." She took out a loaf of bread Pippa had baked on Saturday and sliced off a piece, then smeared it with some jam from a jar on the counter. She folded it so Davey wouldn't make a mess with it.

"Me hungry." Davey glanced at the marshal. "You hungry?"

Esther glanced at Colin. "I can make you something for breakfast, if you like."

"No thanks, the coffee's fine for now."

She nodded and set a small plate with the bread and jam on the table. "You need to get into a chair to eat, Davey."

He was hungry enough to scamper down from the marshal's lap and to the chair. Without any prompting, he bowed his head and clasped his hands together in front of him. "God in Heben, tank You for this food. Tank You for Mama. Tank You for Unca Collie. Tank you for Unca Dewey. Jesus name. Amen."

When he finished, he got on his knees, grabbed the jam sandwich, and took a bite. Jam smeared his cheek as he grinned. "Ood."

She set a metal cup half-filled with water near his plate. "No talking with food in your mouth, young man."

He struggled to get the bite swallowed. "Good."

Esther got herself a cup of coffee, took a small sip, then sat across the table from Davey, but not quite in front of the marshal. A mistake she realized almost immediately. The scrape of his boot heels echoed around the room when he stretched his legs out under the table. They rested just a few inches from hers.

Her head popped up from where she'd been staring at her coffee. The marshal's hands gripped his cup, but his eyes were staring at her. One side of his mouth rose just the slightest bit.

A ripple of excitement worked its way through her. Was he thinking about last night? Heat filled her cheeks. "What, uh, do you...oh, never mind."

"All done." Davey grinned at her and grabbed his cup of water.

She pulled her eyes away from the marshal's and grabbed a cloth, then wiped Davey's face. Well, she tried. Little boys don't like someone washing their faces. Heat returned to her cheeks when she thought about stroking the marshal's cheek like she was Davey's.

When she was finished, Davey looked at the marshal. "You 'n' Unca Dewey play hide-an'-seek wi' me and man?"

The marshal's whole body tensed, then he jerked his head around and glared at her. "What man?"

Her body tightened in response. "He's just an old gray-haired man with a limp we saw a while back at the mercantile. He, uh, he played a game of hide-and-seek with Davey while I was visiting with some friends."

Her stomach felt like it was going to give back the coffee she'd just swallowed when she remembered the look the old man gave her as he left the store. "Davey probably said something about it because he saw him at church yesterday. We wouldn't have even noticed him except I didn't want him to bother Jack who was sitting next to him. So I set my son on my lap and rested his head against my shoulder. That's when he saw the old man. I asked the preacher about him and he said he's seen him several times around town."

"Did he try to take Davey out of the store?"

"Of course not. I won't let anyone take Davey from me."

"I didn't mean it that way." The marshal dropped his head a bit as if he was thinking through some problem. All at once his head snapped up and he looked at her again. "You said Jack was sitting next to you?"

"He was after I took Davey in my lap. Dougal was on the other side of him." Something was going on, and she feared it concerned Davey. A hard shudder gripped her body. She had to know what was going on. To protect her son, she needed to know what this was all about.

"You haven't seen him any other time?"

"No."

"Me seed him."

They both looked at Davey.

The marshal spoke first. "Where was he when you saw him?"

"On grass by road."

The marshal gripped the handle of his cup. His nostrils flared and the vein in his temple throbbed. Yet he kept his voice low and even. "When did you see the man by the road?"

As if sensing the anger in the marshal, Davey pulled closer to his mother and grabbed her apron. "When mama said me go to bed."

"What was the man doing?"

Davey shrugged his shoulder. "Sit on horse." He flung his hands outward. "Rode 'way."

The marshal stood and touched Davey on his head, then smiled. "If you see him again, will you tell me, son?"

All at once he looked like someone'd punched him hard in the gut. His face lost its color. He turned on the heel of his boot and went outside.

Esther felt the same feeling in her middle. No one'd ever called Davey "son." Not Uncle Ed. Not Uncle Will. Not even Dougal. Why this man? And why did him saying the word to Davey shake Colin so badly?

She scratched her arm. There was one more man who'd called Davey that. The man in the store—and at church and sitting on his horse outside the house. Was he following them? What did he want?

CHAPTER SEVENTEEN

Colin raced to the barn through the pre-dawn dimness. The word burned in his mind. He didn't have a son, not anymore. Matty was dead, and he hadn't found his killers. But he would.

As he grabbed the barn door, it moved. Dougal stepped out. "Where's the stampede?"

"Ray Miller's been watching the house."

"You sure it's him?"

Yes, it's him. Choking fear clamped around Colin's chest, his heart. Nobody was safe when Miller was after someone. What if he got past Dougal and Kerr? Cold sweat broke out on his back and face. Miller would show no mercy to Esther and Davey. No. Colin pounded his fist against his leg. Never again would the murderous outlaw get his hands on a woman and boy he loved.

He took a step back, as if to get away from the thought. He refused to love them. It hurt too much when love died. Or when the ones you loved died. Giving his head a quick shake, he turned to Dougal. "She described him, although she doesn't know who he is."

Dougal grabbed a lantern in the barn and lit it. The two of them walked to the front of the house and crossed the road.

Colin bit back the words screaming to jump out of his mouth. In the dirt across from the house were the same hoofprints they'd followed from the dead miners' shack to the stage station shortly after he'd come to town.

The double notch showed the horse had moved back and forth several times. Miller had been watching the house for quite a while. He came from the main part of town and headed back the same way. The trail would be lost in all the traffic, but maybe Adam Lone Eagle could find it.

Colin waved for his brother to follow him, and they hurried to the barn. "Watch the house. I've got to see the sheriff, then try to find Lone Eagle."

As he rode away, questions pounded in his head. Why had Miller changed the way he did things? He'd always just taken what he wanted and killed any witnesses who could identify him.

Colin's gut twisted. What had changed? More importantly for those in the house, who was Miller after? He went back over the possibilities. The baby for ransom? Didn't make sense. Drew's sister had a lot of money, but would it be enough to bring Miller to Colorado? Besides, the baby hadn't been born when Ray broke his boys out of prison. Same thing with the money and diamonds Bonny Small left Esther. Which only left the housekeeper's brother.

Could one of the Millers be Jack's pa?

Memories of the way Dougal acted with Linda popped into Colin's mind. He was pretty sure his brother was courting the girl. She just didn't know it. And that made it even more important to find Miller. If what Colin figured was right, then Miller could kill the woman Dougal loved.

Esther put the twins down for their afternoon nap, then read two stories to Davey before he fell asleep. She kissed his cheek, then went to find Linda. She couldn't get the feelings that had swamped her last night out of her mind.

She entered the kitchen as the girls who came in each day to help clean and do the laundry left. Linda closed the door and turned to Esther.

"Tea sound good?' Linda filled the kettle and put it on the stove.

Esther nodded. She got the cups and saucers from the shelf. The roast Pippa had in the oven, along with the gingerbread for dessert, filled the room with memories of times with her parents.

They sat at the table as they waited for the tea to steep.

Esther drew circles on the table with her fingertip. She couldn't keep her thoughts to herself any longer. "Linda, could I ask you something?"

The smile on Linda's face drooped into a frown. "Sounds serious."

Esther nodded. "I understand if you don't want to talk about this."

"When I was attacked?"

"Yes and no." Esther shrugged. "No, not about when it happened. Later, when you started seeing that cowboy. Did he kiss you? How did it make you feel when he touched you?" The last part came out in a whispered rush.

Before she said anything, Linda poured them each a cup. The steam rose in the air and billowed into a thin cloud between them. Next, she spooned some sugar into her cup and stirred and stirred and stirred. At last she let go of the spoon and folded her hands in front of her on the table.

"So many thoughts and memories just jumped into my head, some good, some not. Before I answer your questions, let me ask you some things. Why do you want to know? Are you still haunted by nightmares? Are you still scared about what some man may think of you? Or is this about one man in particular?"

Esther had been stirring her tea too, even though she hadn't put any sugar in hers. "No, no, no. Nothing about the first things you asked about."

She put her spoon on the saucer by the cup. "Aunt Bonny helped me after it happened, helped me find peace with the attack and the loss of my parents."

Linda nodded. "I understand. Drew's sister helped me. She'd had a bad marriage and understood a lot of what I felt."

Esther shrugged, then lifted her spoon again. "We just never talked about how I might feel if ever a man liked me enough to kiss me."

"And do you now? Like a man enough to want him to kiss you? Has Colin tried?" Pink tinted the skin on Linda's cheeks. "I'm sorry. I heard you both on the porch last night." She lifted her hands, palms up. "I didn't hear what you were saying, not that I tried to listen or anything. It's just with you both out there last night, and now you're asking these questions, I guess I put things together. Besides, Kerr has a girl and, uh, and Dougal…well—"

Linda turned an even brighter shade of pink. "Let's just say, with the right man, kisses can be very enjoyable, and thoughts of the past don't even come to mind. Dougal knows what happened to me, and he's been very understanding and gentle. He didn't try to force anything. He gave me time to get comfortable just being around him, and then his little touches. I don't know how much of it's the MacPherson upbringing and how much of it's Dougal, but it's really given me hope about the future."

A tiny bit of peace nudged its way into Esther's heart with Linda's words.

Linda lifted her cup and stared at the tea for a moment. "Have you told Colin about…what happened to you?" She set the cup on the table and swallowed hard. Moisture floated in her eyes. "Because if you haven't, you need to. It'll be worse if he finds out later, even if you tell him yourself. Trust will be broken, and not all men will stay around to repair it. They feel betrayed and will abandon you."

Esther laid her hand on Linda's. "I sorry you went through that. And, yes to your question. Colin knows what happened to me. My cousin Tina spewed it out the night Aunt Bonny died. I'm not sure Colin believed her, but I told him it was true."

"Good. If he knows the whole truth, nothing can come back and hurt you."

The arm started itching again. Esther pulled her arm back and rubbed the sleeve covering it. She'd told Colin about the attack, but she hadn't told him everything. She rubbed her arm again. She couldn't tell him or anyone everything, mainly because she didn't remember it all. Even now it was a blur, a blur filled with pain and fear and loss.

Linda let out a small sigh, but it was a happy sound. "I hope you find as much joy with a MacPherson man as I have."

All at once, the nerves in Esther's chest loosened. Peace flooded in and wrapped around her heart. She suspected a lot of Colin was the MacPherson upbringing, but she looked forward to getting to know more about the man himself.

A few days later while she and Davey finished breakfast, Esther felt happier than she had in longer than she could remember. For the first time in her life, she was enjoying the attention of a man. Each day, Colin went out to do whatever a marshal did, but he usually returned before she went to bed. On the nights he'd been back in time for supper, they sat on the back porch swing. A time or two he'd brushed her cheek when it was time to go inside. She just wished he'd made it back earlier the night before, so they could've sat on the swing.

Heavy footsteps sounded in the hall.

She felt her smile grow wider when Colin walked into the kitchen.

Davey wiggled in his seat. A grin spread across his face. "Unca Collie. Sit by me. Sit by me."

Colin stepped to the table and ruffled her son's hair, but kept his eyes on Esther. "Sorry, I don't have time this morning. I have to get to Nevada City, follow up a few leads. I'll probably be gone a few days."

Fear and sadness battled in Esther, fear for Colin and sadness for herself since they wouldn't share the swing that night. She tried to smile because she didn't think she could say anything like "good-bye" right now.

Colin seemed to realize her struggle because he gave her a quick nod and used his other hand to lightly squeeze her shoulder.

"Drew said to fix you enough food for a couple of days." Pippa held out a canvas bag as well as a canteen.

"Thanks, ma'am." Colin took the food and water.

Esther looked at the bag. How she wished she could have fixed it for him, so he could think about her every time he ate.

Drew entered the kitchen and walked to Colin. "I hear you're going to be gone a couple of days. Take care."

While the two men shook hands, someone tapped on the kitchen's back door. Esther went to see who was there, since Dougal kept his arm wrapped around Linda, and she didn't try to make him take it away.

When Esther opened the door, all the relaxation and peace that had been oozing through her body and mind for the last few days fled. The blood in her head pounded. She wanted to grab Davey and run away to some place where no one would ever find them again. But her feet wouldn't move.

The town deputy stood at the door just like he had when he took her to jail before.

All at once something nudged her aside. A scream filled the air.

"No! No! No! My Mama. Can't take her." Redness from anger or fear, or both, colored Davey's face. He shoved the young man's legs, almost pushing him over.

No matter how she felt, she couldn't let Davey act that way. She grabbed her son to her chest, even as he fought her, fought to get to the man he feared would take his mother away again. She cried out when his leather shoes kicked her two or three times.

Her arms collapsed around nothingness when Colin pulled her kicking son from her arms and held him with one arm around Davey's chest and the other keeping his booted feet from hitting anyone, especially him.

Colin held him close until the boy stopped screaming and grew still.

"Unca Collie, don't let him take Mama. Ple-e-e-ase don't let dep'ty take Mama."

Turning his back on the deputy, Colin glanced at Esther and tipped his chin toward the table. "Sit."

It was the way Davey said please which cut at Colin. It was said the same way Matty had screamed it from their front porch when he'd ridden out that last time, planning to come back when his job was done. Only it was never done, and Matty was dead. He couldn't change things for his boy. But he could help Davey.

Colin waited for Esther to sit. He figured she'd have bruises on her legs from where Davey's boots had kicked her, even though the boy wasn't trying to hurt his mother. The little fella was just scared.

Once Esther sat, he put Davey in her arms, then turned back to the deputy. "Let's go outside."

"Sorry for the ruckus, ma'am." The deputy tipped his hat and scurried out. He crossed the porch and walked several feet from the house. He turned around to face

Colin. "I meant what I said in there. I didn't mean to cause a problem. Tuck said to get you pronto, and Kerr told me you were probably in the kitchen."

Colin jerked his head in a quick nod. He understood the way the deputy felt. Davey's reaction shook him, too. By the time they got to the barn, Kerr had his horse saddled along with a rifle in the scabbard on the side.

Colin took the reins, nodded his thanks to his cousin, and mounted. He couldn't help but glance back at the house. Esther stood at the door. The sad look on her face pulled at him. In some ways he wished he could just grab her and Davey, run away, and start a new life somewhere without all the pain of the past. Instead, he gripped the reins tighter and headed out, taking one last look at Esther before he rounded to the front of the house and out on the road.

He hadn't asked the deputy what Tuck wanted. As far as Colin was concerned, there was only one thing the sheriff wanted him for. The Millers had killed someone else, and they needed to go after the murderers.

It didn't take them long to get to the sheriff's office. As soon as they arrived, Colin dismounted, slung the reins across the hitching post, and thudded across the boardwalk, then slung open the door. Tuck set his rifle on the desk next to a box of shells.

"Trent, go out back and fill those." Tuck waved to two canteens hanging from hooks on the back wall."

The deputy hurried to do what the sheriff said.

Tuck slid shells into the rifle. "Adam Lone Eagle came in a little while ago. Found something we'll wanna go check out. But first, we need to get to the undertaker's place." Grabbing his hat and rifle, he headed outside.

Colin stayed on his heels. "What's at the undertaker's?"

Tuck's face hardened. "Jake Miller and three bodies."

"Others are Ray and his boys?" Colin picked up his speed. He had to see with his own eyes that all the Millers were dead and couldn't hurt anyone else. He was just sorry he wasn't the one to get the revenge for Jessie and Matty.

"Adam said Harve and Jake's bodies was lying outside a burned-out cabin. Couldn't tell who the others were for sure. Thought you'd want to check out the bodies 'fore we head out to where they were hiding out."

Colin gave a quick nod.

The sound of their boots echoed on the wooden planks of the boardwalk as they made their way to the undertaker's place. Something didn't seem right. Tuck should have been able to identify Ray Miller at least, even if it had been years since he'd seen the man. Blake might have been a bit harder since there probably weren't any wanted posters out on him yet.

They opened the door to the undertaker's place. A smell that didn't belong filled the air. Faint at first, but growing stronger with each step they took. He'd smelled it a few times before, and he'd always had to force himself to keep from gagging.

As they headed for the back where the man did his work, the undertaker stepped out and pulled a kerchief from his face. His face was pale and streaked with black marks.

"These two aren't bad." He shook his head and wiped his face. "But those other two. Hate to deal with burned bodies."

Colin pushed past the undertaker and hurried into his workroom, even though the stench was stronger there. He slung his arm across his face. The smell of the soap the Chinese laundry used covered some of the smell of burnt flesh.

He moved from one pine box to the next. In the first two, he recognized Jake, then Harve. Both skinnier than their last wanted poster, but there was no denying it was them. The other two boxes were a different matter. Those bodies were burned beyond recognition. He stared at them, one by one, and tried to see the face and body size of the men he'd been hunting.

Much as he wanted, he couldn't be sure in his own heart and mind that Ray Miller and all his sons lay in those boxes.

He turned and joined the men in the office area.

Tuck eyed him. "Well?"

"Jake and Harve for sure. The others could be them. Might not be." Colin shook his head in disgust.

The undertaker stepped to a desk in the corner and pulled out a lidless box. "Don't know if this will help any or not, but this is what I found on the bodies."

Tuck took it and looked inside, but didn't touch any of it.

Colin came up beside him. "See anything that can help?"

"Nah, most of it's too burned to be of any use." Tuck set the box on the desk and looked at the undertaker. "What can you tell us 'bout the bodies, the burned ones?"

The undertaker pulled a piece of paper from his pocket and studied it for a moment. "All of them seemed underweight, but the same thing could be said for a lot of men around here who live outside of town." He shrugged, then looked at his notes. "Oh, one of 'em had a little graying hair. Looks like something fell on the back of his head and protected part of his scalp from the fire. The other one..." He shrugged. "Couldn't tell much."

"Thanks." Colin tapped Tuck on the shoulder. "Let's get out of here. We need to get to their cabin."

When they turned to leave, the undertaker called out. "Can I bury 'em now? And if so, what names do I put on 'em?"

Colin wanted to tell him to keep them there until they made sure it was all the Millers. But he knew it couldn't happen, so he made his way outside and let Tuck handle the matter.

A thought struck him while he waited for Tuck. He walked across the street to the mercantile. The memory of those footprints in front of the Hollingsworths' house still bothered him. After talking with the storeowner and a little money changing hands, he arranged for the delivery boy to take a message to Dougal. His brother needed to know they needed to continue to stand guard no matter what rumors they heard floating around town about the death of the Millers.

A bit later, with canteens tied to their saddles and rifles in scabbards, Colin rode out of town with Tuck and Adam, hopefully to find proof Ray Miller and all his sons were dead. But at least for now, Colin felt better that Dougal and Kerr remained to guard the house and those within.

Ray Miller hid behind a mound of rocks and held back a hoot as he sat on his horse and watched the undertaker's helpers bury four pine boxes. He'd wait until the gravediggers left. Be interesting to see his name on a grave marker before he died. If it worked out like he planned, he'd have the freedom to do what needed to be done. Then he could leave this dry, rotten place and start a new life.

An hour later, he guided his horse to the fresh mounds of dirt. He gazed at the names scrawled on the wooden markers. Ray Miller. Jake Miller. Harve Miller. Blake Miller.

He let out a belly laugh, then kicked his horse—a new one—in the sides and left town. If he'd had Blake with him, he might've chanced grabbing the boy. But with those two guards hanging around, there were too many people in the house to try it on his own. Besides he had a plan to get rid of the lawman named MacPherson and the gal he was sweet on. One that would put them out of the way for good. He'd just bide his time for now. But soon he'd have the boy.

CHAPTER EIGHTEEN

Colin was thankful the wind had cleared most of the stench of charred flesh away when Adam Lone Eagle led them to the clearing where the burned-out cabin lay. All three of them dismounted. Adam showed them where he'd found Harve's and Jake's bodies, then stood outside the ruins of the cabin.

"All I took was the bodies. Don't know if anything else can be salvaged."

Colin moved past Adam and stepped into the burned, wooden mass. He kicked aside a few crumbling boards and headed to the overturned stove. If what the undertaker said about the gray hair on one of the dead men was right, this would be where Ray would've been. "Adam, is this where you found one of the bodies?"

Adam stepped toward several burned chunks of wood. "Not quite. I moved the stove to get him out." He moved a foot or two farther and pointed to another area. "There's where the body was."

Colin searched the area but didn't find anything.

"Hey, over here." Tuck was rummaging through something in the far corner. He stood, holding a metal box in one hand and a chain dangling from his other. "Figured if this happened at night when the men were asleep, there might be something by the bed. I was right."

Crunching through the debris, Colin and Adam moved to Tuck's side. The sheriff handed Colin the chain with a damaged watch attached.

Colin looked at the back. Something was scratched on the back. He rubbed the watch against his pants leg, then looked at it again. The letters R and M had been carved into the metal with the point of a knife or something, nothing like what a jeweler or a watchmaker would do. "Might have been Ray Miller's. What else you got?"

"Most of it burned from the heat, but there's this." Tuck held up a knife. "It's got the initials JN carved into it.

"Jack Nelson. Linda's younger brother. He threw his knife at one of the men who broke into the Hollingsworths' place." Colin took the knife and examined it. Was this enough proof Ray Miller and his sons were dead?

Tuck looked around the burned-out shell again. "Figure the cabin caught on fire somehow, a lamp knocked over, maybe a spark from the stove. With Jake's body outside, the old man must have gotten him out, then went back in to help Harve, and the roof must have collapsed and trapped them inside."

Adam pointed to the corral where four horses stood. "One of them has the double notch on his shoe."

Colin stepped over the burned wood and headed for the corral. He had to see it for himself. He lifted the horse's leg and examined the mark, then sighed deeply. This was the horse they'd been chasing for weeks.

Tuck came over. "His horse?"

"Adam's right." Colin dropped the hoof. "It's Miller's."

Tuck let out a sigh like Colin had. "So I guess the gang's finally dead." Tuck rubbed his leg, the one Ray Miller had shot. "Might as well get on back to town."

Colin left with the other two, but he turned and took a last look at the burned-down cabin. Was it really that easy to end this all? A fire. Four dead men. And justice was paid? He shook his head. The others might agree, but his gut told him there was no way an overturned lamp marked paid to the debt Ray Miller and his sons owed.

All at once, Esther's face floated into his mind and pushed out the thoughts of Ray Miller and his murderous sons. He still had some time in Central City. Who knew what he'd find.

When night settled around them, Esther brushed a lock of hair off Davey's face as he slept. He'd been upset all morning after the deputy came to the door and Colin left with him. No matter what she said, her son thought Colin was going to be taken to jail like she'd been. Thankfully, Dougal had offered to take Davey for a ride on his horse. Oh, how her son loved horses.

Sleep hadn't come easy tonight for him, since he was still excited about the ride he'd taken with Unca Dewy on his horse. It was only back and forth in front of the house. So at bedtime, she let him talk out his excitement. Then, she told him two stories about horses and cowboys before he finally drifted off to sleep, hugging one of his beloved wooden horses.

She opened the back door and stepped onto the porch, planning to sit awhile on the swing. Maybe Colin would join her. She liked him and had gotten used to him being near her. Comfortable with him was how she'd put it, and she hadn't been able to help it. She liked to sit with him on the swing in the evening. They talked about so many different things.

She stopped when she heard giggling and turned her head to the left. The full moon shone its light on Dougal and Linda sitting on the swing.

Dougal raised his voice. "Yes, right there is the North Star." He paused a moment as if he'd just seen someone else on the porch. "Oh, good evening, Star. Just teaching Linda about what all is in the sky at night."

Linda giggled again, and this time Esther joined in.

"That's wonderful, Unca Dewy. Only problem, the North Star's behind you, over your left shoulder."

"Uh, uh, uh. Remember only Davey calls me that."

"Well then, don't act like a schoolboy caught stealing a kiss from a pigtailed girl behind the schoolhouse. Carry on with your courting. I'm just going to take a walk to the bench by the roses. Be back in a little while." Esther bit back a chuckle while the two on the swing giggled again, and the chains rattled.

She walked near the barn until something moved in the shadows. Her breath came out in a burst when she recognized Kerr. He lifted his hand in greeting. She returned the wave and continued her stroll until she got to the roses lining the end of the property. Helen had told her that Sarah, Drew's sister, had planted them shortly after she'd moved here. Later Drew had a bench built so his sister could still enjoy the fragrance when she came to visit.

Esther touched one of the velvety-soft petals and wished someone loved her enough to do something nice like that for her. It wasn't the need to have roses of her own. If roses were all she wanted, she could buy a field full of rosebushes with the money her great-uncles left her. No, it was the desire, or rather the deep need, to have someone who loved her enough to do it.

Colin's face flashed into her thoughts. She bit her lips to keep from smiling. He'd be nice. She touched another rose and thought she'd come far enough from what happened in the past to be ready to start seeing a man. If that man was Colin. Other than Dougal, who felt like a brother, Colin was the first man to have caught her interest, who she felt like getting to know, who didn't bother her if he brushed against her. And he knew about Davey—knew and accepted him.

She slipped onto the bench and bowed her head. *Dear Father in Heaven, thank You for the wonderful way You take care of Davey and me. You know our every need and You provide for them all. Please, help me to know what I should do with Colin, if he is someone You want in my life. Please just help me know.*

Someone cleared his voice nearby.

Esther's head jerked up.

Colin stood at the end of the bench. "Thought I might join you out here, if you don't mind? The swing seems occupied."

"Please sit." Her breath came a little faster. She scooted to the side. "I didn't know you were back."

"I got back a few minutes ago." He pulled off his hat and sat. "And had some thinking to do, but I wanted to see you tonight."

A thought shot through her head, a thought that sent a pain to the middle of her chest. "Are you thinking about leaving town? Have you been assigned somewhere else?" She could barely see his head moving from side to side in the pale moonlight while his fingers toyed with his badge.

"Not yet. But it seems I finished what I came here for, and now I'm trying to decide if I want to keep my star."

"Why wouldn't you keep it? You're good at your job, aren't you?"

He bent forward and rested his elbows against his knees. In the dim moonlight, she could just make out his head bowing, as if the weight of all the problems of the people of the territory rested on his shoulder. "Some say so, but lately I'm thinking the cost of the job is too high?"

Something bad was coming. She could feel it. Her arm itched again. She wanted to leave, but couldn't. "Why now? Why would you think about giving up your badge now?"

He sucked in a chestful of air. Ever so slowly, the air seeped out of his mouth. He straightened for a moment, then leaned against the back of the bench and stared at the stars. "Years ago—a lifetime it seems—my wife wanted me to stop being a marshal."

Wife? You're married? Cold chills wrapped themselves around her as her stomach threatened to empty. Trust, hope, and maybe just a little love twisted together, strangling one another. Pain filled her heart. She needed to get out of there before she broke down in front of this man.

"But I told Jessie I couldn't do it, so she took our son Matty and left me. Planned to go back to her parents, but they never made it." He rubbed his hand across his face as if to wipe away the loss and pain. "The Miller gang attacked the stagecoach. They forced it off the road, and it went over a cliff. Everyone was killed."

"How horrible!" She knew the pain of losing her parents, but to have lost a mate and son. She bit her lip as she thought of the pain he must have gone through.

He wrapped his fingers around her hand, rubbing his thumb over her knuckles.

As they sat in silence, Esther hoped her presence gave him some comfort.

Colin sucked in a deep breath, then let it out. "They went to prison for bank robbery but escaped. So I followed them here. I needed to make them pay. For Matty. For Jessie." He gripped her hand tighter. "For not being there when they needed me."

Vengeance or justice? She wondered which one still drove him. "What will you do when you find them?

"That's just it. I've no say in the matter. It's where I went today with the sheriff. They're all dead. They died in a cabin fire." He let go of her hand. "A stupid cabin fire."

He slammed his balled-up fist against his leg. "Jessie and Matty didn't get any justice. The murderers killed them, and they never paid for it."

Esther wanted to run back to the house as fast as she could, to get away from Colin and the pain that poured out of him. But she couldn't walk away and leave Colin this way. So she sat with him for a minute, or ten, or sixty. She wasn't sure.

When he relaxed a bit, she couldn't help but ask, "What would you do if you weren't a marshal?"

He was silent for a moment, but slowly his fist uncurled and lay loose on top of his leg. "Not sure. I've been a lawman since I was eighteen." He raised his arm.

She thought he was going to rest his arm along the back of the bench, so close to her.

Instead he ran his fingers through his hair with his other hand. "It's all I really know." After a moment or two, he raised his head again and stared at the night sky. The waning moon shed a little light on his face. "Been thinking about heading to the family ranch Dougal's told me about. Never met my grandda and granny."

Esther clamped her fingers together. Longing for her own grandparents, who'd lived with them until they died when she was about thirteen, filled her chest. It seemed like everyone she loved or grew close to died. Everyone, except Davey.

And now Colin was leaving. Would she ever see him again?

Her fingers twisted together.

She closed her eyes and let out a shuddering breath.

Colin shifted beside her. Warm fingers covered her hands. "Nothing's decided yet. Just thinking of possibilities." He stood and held out his hand. "Getting late. Best we get inside."

She nodded.

They headed for the house when a soft whistle floated on the night air. Colin waved his hand. Kerr's chuckle drifted back to them.

When they reached their bedrooms, Colin lifted her hand and kissed it. "Good night."

"G-good night." Her voice barely passed through her lips. No one'd ever done that before. Without looking at him, she slipped into her room and leaned against the closed door.

What hope was there for her and Colin? He still loved his dead wife, and she was nothing but damaged goods. *Oh, God, why did You let me feel something for Colin, only to take him away? Why, God, why?*

Three days later, after following leads about any Confederates looking for easy gold, Colin walked into the sheriff's office. The building still smelled like burnt coffee and stale bodies. Maybe someday he'd come in here and the smell would be gone. "Morning, Tuck. Got a minute?"

"Sure. Want some coffee?"

Colin shook his head. "Not right now, just finished breakfast at Drew's house." He patted his middle. "Miss Pippa sets a fine table."

Tuck filled his cup and sat back in his chair, then pointed to the straight-backed wooden one across from his desk. "What's on your mind?"

Colin pulled his hat from his head and dropped onto the chair. "Been thinking about the future. What I want to do."

"Thinking about leaving the Marshals?" Tuck waited a moment while he looked over the rim of his cup. "I'd take you on as a deputy, if you say the word." Tuck eased back in his chair. "'Course you might be raring to get into the war."

Colin shook his head. He felt all wrung out and needed to get away from the killing for a while. Esther's face popped into his thoughts. The one thing he knew was that if he wanted a woman in his life, he'd need a job where she wouldn't worry about him.

"I already made one—well, two—decisions. I'm not going into the Army, and I've already sent my badge and a letter of resignation to the US Marshal in Denver."

Colin shut his eyes for a moment. The star had served its purpose. Miller was dead. But if that was the case, why did he still have such an empty hole in his gut?

Tuck's mug thudded on his desk. "Well then, can I offer you a job here?"

Colin opened his eyes to see if the bottom was going to bust out of this one. He grinned when the sludge didn't ooze out.

"Now think about it for a minute before you say anything." Tuck grinned from ear to ear. "Wife wants me to retire in the not-too-distant future. You've got experience with the law. If you became my deputy, then say, first part of next year, I'd retire. The town could hire you as the new sheriff. It'd sure take a weight off my mind. I couldn't leave the town protected with the likes of young Trent Ellis. You saw the mess he made with arresting Miss Essie."

Tuck rolled his eyes. "The boy'd have this town in such an uproar. No, we need an experienced man like you."

Colin shook his head and stood. "Thanks for the invite, but I think I'll stay away from wearing a star for a while. If I feel the need to do it again, I'll stop by and tell you."

The man's face fell. Colin felt sorry for him. His wife must be putting pressure on him. Just like Jessie had.

With the older children at school, Helen and the little ones napping, and the men outside doing something or other, now was the time to talk to Linda. Esther entered the kitchen. She was ready to do something, but she'd need help.

Linda glanced at her and grinned. "You look like you are ready to burst. Want to talk about it?"

"I like Colin." Esther nibbled on the nail of her little finger, something she hadn't done since she was a little girl.

"And it scares you."

"At first. But not now." She dropped her hand and gripped her skirt. "I want to spend time with him, get to know him better." She held her breath for a moment, then let it out. "I thought with as close as you and Dougal have gotten, we could all have a picnic."

Linda giggled. "Wonderful idea, but I've got an idea of something else, too. Let me talk to Dougal first."

Esther nodded slowly at the look on Linda's face.

A few nights later, after spending several days fixing a few things for Drew around his house, Colin sat at the Golden Nugget Café and swallowed the last of his pie. He was glad Dougal had suggested that the two of them invite Linda and Esther out for supper.

His feelings for her were changing, but he hadn't had a chance to really talk with her since the night he'd come back from the burned-out cabin.

Dougal nudged him with his boot under the table. "Lady's asked you a question."

Colin felt the heat rise up his neck and across his cheeks. He looked at Esther, then Linda. "Sorry, I guess I was woolgathering for a moment. What were you asking?"

"Where do you think would be a good place to go for a picnic?" Linda seemed to be the one who'd tried to get his attention while he was thinking about Esther. Dougal grinned at him with a look in his eye that as the older brother he'd come to fear.

"I know just the place for it." Dougal's grin grew wider. "My, uh, our cousin Jason has the prettiest spot for it. Got a great pond for fishing. Matter of fact, the first

time I saw Drew's sister was when she pulled a big ole
catfish from the pond."

A little while later, with all the plans made, Colin
dropped the shawl over Esther's shoulders while Dougal
did the same for Linda. It'd been a good supper. Maybe
when they got back to the house, Esther would like to sit
out on the swing with him.

Colin held the restaurant door open as the ladies and
Dougal passed through.

Once outside on the boardwalk, they partnered up.
Linda slipped her hand into the bend of Dougal's elbow.
They whispered something to each other, then smiled at
whatever they shared.

Colin nudged his elbow slightly out to the side nearest
Esther. She took the invitation and rested her hand
against his arm. He tucked his arm a little closer to his
side. Stirrings started deep inside him. Stirrings that were
growing every day. He pulled his elbow even closer to his
side. Esther smiled and glanced at him. The tug on his
lips joined with the glow in her eyes. Maybe life could
start again. The stirrings wrapped tighter around his heart.
It'd be good to have a family again. A woman to
welcome him home, a son to see into manhood.

He reached over with his other hand and rested it on
top of her fingers that nestled in the crook of his elbow.
Maybe someday he'd take her out to his grandparents'
ranch. For the first time in years, the future seemed to
have meaning. Maybe for the first time, he could see
what Jessie wanted him to get away from. And to stay
home for.

As they crossed the area between the buildings, shots
rang out. Dougal and Linda tumbled to the ground.

Colin yanked his arm out of Esther's hold and shoved
her to the ground. "Stay there."

He drew his gun from his holster and edged around the
corner to see who was in the alley. He spotted a man in
the shadows, a rifle in his hands. He aimed at him, but

before he got the shot off, Esther screamed. He looked back at her. She lay slumped on the boardwalk. The shot hadn't come from the alley. He switched around and tried to see where the shot came from. Nothing. He looked down the alley. Nothing again.

Linda crawled to her knees and tugged on Dougal's arm, trying to get him to cover. Colin stayed low and went to help her. More shots rang out. One caused Dougal's body to jerk. He was hit again. More shots. Linda screamed and fell to the ground.

The next one hit Colin. A blast of pain spread through his chest. It ripped his breath away. The ground reached out and grabbed him. Darkness grew thicker. Blackness covered him like one of his mama's quilts.

Through the darkness and pain, shadows moved through the alley and stood over them.

"And they thought a fire could kill Ray Miller. Now let's go get that boy."

CHAPTER NINETEEN

Darkness surrounded Colin. Weights crushed down on his chest, his eyes. Heat burned through him. Colin tried to claw his way out of the crushing cave-in around him, but he was trapped—trapped and dying. Dying, if he couldn't find a way out.

Light touched him. No, not light, a cool brush against his arm, but it caused warmth to spread to his insides. A voice floated over him, a sound as light and delicate as an angel's wing, but with a husky, grieving note. Was this how one died? Though still soft, the voice grew clearer, pleading, begging. The voice drifted away as the heat grew hotter. Heat so hot that it stole away his thoughts.

Moments later, an eternity later, damp coolness floated onto his head. Darkness still surrounded him, but the heat wasn't as blazing hot. Voices floated over him again, but it wasn't the one from before. No, these were men talking. Words that finally made sense—sheriff, Blake, Ray Miller, not dead.

Colin pushed and shoved the weight from his eyes. At last, one eyelid opened. Bright light blinded him. His eye shut. He sucked in a deep breath, but the pain ripped his strength away. Agony jerked him back into its hold.

Esther sat in the comfortable chair that Drew had brought into Colin's room. Her head pounded. She brushed her hand against the bandage Doc had wrapped around her head covering flesh wound on the side of her head. A wound caused by the men who attacked them. "Are you sure Dougal and Linda are doing all right?"

A man named Thorn sat in the straight-backed chair next to the bed—another MacPherson, and Drew's brother-in-law. A slight smile graced his lips at her question. He nodded. "Almost as well as you're doing. Doc says Dougal can get out of bed in a few days, and Linda's already sitting at his side, feeding him chicken broth, which he hates but will eat because she spoons it between his lips."

She let out a small sigh. She knew the three of them hadn't been hurt as badly as Colin. But sometimes the memories of those few moments near the alley roared back to life, and she had to be reassured everyone had survived. Dougal had been shot in the chest, but the bullet had passed through with very little damage. The ones to his leg and arm had done more. Linda had been grazed in the side and cracked a rib, but was able to sit with Dougal. Like she sat with Colin, staying very still in the chair so the pain in her head would be bearable.

Esther tried to swallow the moans when boots thumped on the stairs. Moments later, the sheriff and two other men stood at the open door. They'd already removed their hats, but they nodded to her, then gave a nod to Thorn.

The sheriff looked back at her. "We need to do some palavering. Could you leave us for a bit?"

Esther wanted to say she wouldn't leave, but one of the men was already helping her from the chair. He led her to the door. Once she was in the hall, the door closed behind her. Helen peeked out the nursery door and waved her in.

As soon as Esther entered the room, Davey ran to her and grabbed her hand. The sounds of his cries, when they were first brought back to the house, still echoed in her head.

Helen motioned to a comfortable-looking high-backed chair someone'd brought to the nursery, one that didn't rock. "Let's sit in here while the men make their plans."

Esther moved carefully and lowered herself onto the chair. She didn't want to start her head spinning again. Davey curled at her feet and fell asleep. *Poor little fellow. This has been so hard on him.*

She wished she could rest her hand on his head, feel his soft hair, but there was no way she could reach down that far. Just thinking about it made her head swim. Gripping the arms of the chair, she looked at Helen. "What plans? Shouldn't the sheriff be leading a posse to catch the men who shot us?" She wanted to scream out the words, but the babies were sleeping and she didn't want to frighten Davey, so she kept her voice low.

"Esther, lean back and rest your head. I'll tell you what's going on." Helen waited for a moment, then continued. "That awful outlaw gang is still alive, at least some of them are. It isn't safe here for the four of you right now. In a few days, when Colin is better and ready to travel, the MacPherson clan is gathering here, the ones from the main ranch, the ones from Jason's ranch and even the Denver MacPhersons. With a gathering so large, no one spying on us will know if there're a few extra when they leave."

It took Esther a minute or two to think about what Helen said, but then she had a few questions of her own. "But what about when those outlaws—the Millers aren't they called? Well, who will protect the ones left here when the MacPhersons all leave? Won't you and the babies be in danger?"

"That's all taken care of. Drew, the twins, and I will go to Denver with the MacPhersons who live there.

We're taking Nancy to help with the twins. Pippa's going with us but will stay with her daughter. A couple of the clan will stay here to look like we're still here. After a few days, they'll drift away, too. It's a perfect plan to protect you and the others while you, Linda, and the men heal, and no one gets hurt. This will give the law time to hunt down the Miller gang."

Esther drew in a breath. Someone was trying to tear her life apart again. Only this time, she wasn't going to let them. She had a son to protect and a man she might love. She needed time for both.

The darkness lifted a bit. Voices filled the air. Not the delicate angel-wing voice. No, he recognized Tuck's sound, then there were three more—all with a light Scottish accent, a little like his pa's.

At last, he forced his eyes open just a slit. He could see the men. They stood or sat around the room. Tuck sat in a stuffed chair across the room. A man he didn't know sat in a wooden chair next to the bed, and two more stood by the door.

Tuck pounded his fist on his leg. "Adam couldn't pick up their trail. So all we know is the Millers are still out there somewhere, waiting to attack." He hit his leg again. "We don't even know who it is they're after."

"Millers?" The word came out dry and scratchy, just the way Colin's throat felt.

The man in the wooden chair turned his head toward the bed and poured a little water into a glass.

Colin gritted his teeth when the stranger raised his head a little from the pillow, but the water that slipped past his lips and down his throat was the sweetest he'd ever had. Once he was back on the pillows, he asked again, "Millers?"

"Good to see you're back with us again." Tuck grinned. "These here are three of your MacPherson cousins." He pointed first to the man who'd helped him with the water. "Thorn." Then to the other two. "Jason and Daniel. Kerr's still outside watching over things."

Colin wanted to greet his new family the MacPherson way, but the effort was too much. If he wanted to be a part of whatever was going on, he'd need to keep still and listen.

The grin dropped from Tuck's lips. His face grew serious again. "Seems Ray Miller and his boy fooled us. Don't know whose bodies were in the burned-out shack, but it was Miller and his son who shot you and Dougal, along with the ladies."

The sheriff's face lost its color, then flushed red. "I saw 'em, but they were gone before I could get a shot off. Just wasn't expecting to see 'em again, not this side of the Judgment Day."

Colin tried to take it all in while he fought to stay awake. Weariness tugged at him.

"We still don't know who he's after." The man in the chair by the bed stood and paced. "With what Drew said about them trying to break in to this house, then shooting all four of you, we've come up with a plan to keep you all safe. We're going to set a trap for them. The thing is…well, we've got to have your funeral."

Ray Miller clasped his hand over his mouth to cover the cursed cough. Ever since that kid hit him with his knife, his chest had gotten worse and worse. Which meant it was more important than ever to get what he came for.

He cursed again as he thought how his last plan had failed. First, the sheriff saw him and Blake shooting the marshal and his bunch. Then, when they hightailed it to that big fancy house, there'd been another MacPherson standing guard. He'd gotten off a couple of shots. One nicked Blake in the side. Now more of those

MacPhersons arrived each day. Whole place had more guards than a bank filled with gold.

The setting sun cast long shadows. Ray slipped around the back of Ed Small's shop. He'd watched the place for just such a moment as this. The barber had started to leave, then must have remembered something, 'cause the weasel hurried back inside.

Carrying a wicked-looking knife in one hand, Ray tested the doorknob with the other. The foolish man hadn't locked the door. He swallowed a chuckle. Must have planned on visitors. Well, he wouldn't want to disappoint the man.

The door swung inward. Ed Small stood before him, clutching a bag to his chest. The man's face turned white, just like a ghost.

"I-I-I heard you were d-d-dead."

This time, Ray let out his chuckle. "Well, now, as you can see, I'm living and breathing." Another chuckle cackled out. "Or else I'm a ghost come back to haunt ya." He wiggled the knife back and forth a couple of times. "Nah, this thing is too heavy for me to be a ghost. I must be real."

He flicked the knife toward the bag. "You won't be sneaking out of town by any chance, would ya?"

"No. No. No. Just taking some work home with me. Inventories and bills and such." The man never was a good liar. And even more so when he was scared. And the man was scared now.

Ray wiggled his knife in front of Small's chest. "Open 'er up. Let's have a look-see."

Small's Adam's apple bobbed like a little kid needing to get to the outhouse real, real bad. The man opened the case and flicked through the papers, showing Ray the papers in the bag—just papers, no money. Seemed to be telling the truth this time.

"Close it. And I'll tell you what you're gonna do."

A little bit later, Ray slipped out the back of Small's place, got on his horse, and left town. For now.

Colin still found it hard to stand for long, so he rested his forearm on the wall while he stood near the window in Dougal's room, the one which looked out over the road in front of the house. Buggies and carriages had been coming all day, along with men on horses. Children played in the yard, quietly as would befit a place of mourning.

Dougal had said MacPhersons would come from far and near. Word had spread that two of their own had died, and they all came to see the brothers off. He'd just never seen so many MacPhersons all in one place before, even when his family back in Missouri got together with his five sisters and their families.

"Kinda seems strange to look at all the people who're coming to say their good-byes to us." Dougal sat on his bed, propped on several pillows. "But it seemed a good way to get us and the girls out of here without the Millers following us and picking off some of the family. With Drew and his family going with the Denver MacPhersons and some of the others heading west, the Millers won't be able to follow all of us. Not if there's just Ray and Blake left."

Colin let out a sigh and rubbed his fist against his chest where the gunshot wound was still healing. Doc told him he was lucky to be alive, since the bullet had to be dug out, and it'd made a mess with where it'd gone. And now the doc said to take it easy for a while. But it wasn't what Colin wanted to do. All he wanted to do was find Ray Miller and his son, then bring them to justice and protect what was his.

Another wagon arrived, and a couple with a few more children got out.

Suddenly something—or rather, someone—caught his eye. "What in the—?" he turned from the window. "You won't believe who just arrived."

Dougal grunted as he climbed off the bed. "Who?"

"Ed Small and his daughter."

Dougal let out a small growl. "What do they want?"

"I don't know, but I'm gonna find out." Colin stumbled toward the door.

"You can't do that. You're dead, remember?"

Colin stopped and dropped his head to his chest. "I don't like being dead."

His brother chuckled. "Stop whining. Just be thankful we have a place we can hide Linda, Esther, and the boys until we can track down the Millers."

Colin dropped on the chair by the door and shook his head. "I just wish we knew for sure which of the boys they wanted."

Esther's head pounded as she carried a plate of sandwiches up the back stairs. The parlor was filled with MacPhersons all talking about how wonderful Colin and Dougal had been and how terrible that their lives were cut so short. It made the skin on the back of her neck crawl and her arm itch. She'd stayed out of sight, especially after she saw Tina and her father arrive. According to Drew, everyone would be leaving within the hour, some going home to Denver and some heading to the MacPherson ranch with a stop on the way at their cousin Jason's place. Davey was so excited to be going to the ranch, but then he'd never known anything but town living.

At Dougal's door, she stopped and knocked the way Drew told her to do. The lock clicked, and the door opened. Colin stood on the other side, looking better than he had since he'd been shot.

Behind her, someone gasped.

Colin groaned and pushed her out of the way. He aimed his gun past her shoulder. "Get in here, Esther."

Balancing the plate of food, she hurried inside and set the sandwiches on the dresser. She turned around while Colin waved his gun, directing someone into the room.

Uncle Ed and Tina slunk into the room with Colin's gun still pointed at them.

Colin kept his pistol on the two while he closed the door. The clicking of the lock being slid into place echoed in the room. He couldn't keep the spark of anger out of his heart and wondered if the Smalls felt as trapped as Esther had when the two of them had made false accusations. A grin tugged on his face. He wondered how these folks felt meeting dead men.

"Don't shoot us." Sweat popped out on the small man's pale face. "I'm only doing this to protect my daughter."

"Doing what?" Dougal's voice sounded from the other side of the room.

Ed Small's head whipped around. His eyes grew wider when he saw another "dead MacPherson." He swallowed. At least he tried. By the way his Adam's apple was having trouble moving, he must have had a really dry throat. "We'd just come to pay our respects."

Colin narrowed his eyes as he stared at the man. "Upstairs? Did you think those pine boxes were just for show?"

Dougal snickered across the room.

Colin raised his eyes to him, and his cousin shrugged but kept the rest of his sounds locked inside his throat.

"That's just it. The, uh, the man who sent me here wanted to make sure you two were dead and in those boxes, but they weren't opened for viewing." Small tugged at his collar.

Colin waved his gun at the two, then to the bed. "Sit so we can finish our talk."

Tina's face turned deathly pale while she kept a death grip on her father's arm, but they obeyed.

"Now, first of all, as you can see, we aren't dead, so there's no need to say any more about it. Second, who sent you on this little errand? And third, why did you agree to do his bidding?"

"It was a, uh, a man I met once, only once, years ago back in Kansas. But I heard back there he was bad, would kill with no reason. I came here today because he said if I didn't, he'd kidnap my daughter and give her to his sons. I couldn't let that happen. I'd do anything to protect her." He wrapped his hand around Tina's hand which was gripping his arm. "He's waiting for me out there somewhere. Said he'd find me when I left here."

"What's the man's name?" Colin was sure he knew the answer, but he needed the barber to confirm so they were all sure who they were after.

"Ray Miller."

Colin and Dougal exchanged glances.

"I don't know what to do now." The barber's voice grew squeaky as he started to stand. "You've got to protect my daughter. I can't let those animals take her."

"Stay seated." Colin nodded to the two on the bed, then moved to Dougal. He dropped his voice so only his cousin could hear. "Believe him?"

Dougal nodded. "With the way he's acting and knowing how he loves Tina, I do."

"Me, too. Think I know how to handle this. Trust me?"

Dougal nodded again.

Colin stepped away from his cousin. "All right, Small. We've got a plan all worked out. If you go along with it, I can assure you your daughter will be protected."

"Anything, I'll do anything just as long as those men don't get my daughter."

"Good. Esther, take Tina to your room and have her put on the clothes you were going to wear. Someone'll bring you something to wear in a few minutes." Colin touched her shoulder with a soft touch. "All right?"

Her lips wobbled a bit, but she nodded. "Whatever you say."

"That's my girl." He tightened his grip just a bit and smiled at her.

Esther smiled back. She moved to the bed but kept a good distance between herself and her uncle. "Come on, Tina. Let's do what Colin said."

"But Papa." Tina wouldn't let go of her father's arm even though Esther tugged on her hand and tried to get the girl to follow her.

At last, Esther glared at her uncle. "Tell her to come with me, or else she'll become someone's mistress. Or worse."

The barber's face paled again, then flushed dark red. "Go, Tina. Do what Esther says."

Without another word, Esther pulled Tina to the door and left.

Colin rubbed his chin. Before this was all over, he'd find out what that little exchange meant. Though he was pretty sure he already knew.

Ray Miller swatted away a couple of pesky flies that seemed to think he'd be a good place to land. He swiped his head for the fourth time in the last half hour. How long was it going to take for the funeral to end? He shoved a dirty, wadded-up handkerchief against his lips to block the sound of his coughing. Now wouldn't be the time to be caught by anyone.

He dropped the cloth from his lips when he saw the boy running around with the other young'uns in the yard. Soon, very soon, he would have what he had come all this way for. The boy was his—his family, his to raise. With

Harve and Jake gone and Blake a spineless sissy, this boy was all he had left, his reason to keep on. Nobody was going to take that away from him. He'd raise the boy, and together their name would send chills into the hearts of all who heard it.

CHAPTER TWENTY

"I don't want to wear those clothes. They're ugly." Tina glared at Esther, pointing to the black clothes on the bed. "Not everyone is wearing black. I want something bright and cheery. Nobody'll notice me in those."

"Well, isn't that the point, to disguise you to get you away from here?" Esther tapped her foot and waited for her cousin to change clothes. "It's what Uncle Ed said. Or was it a lie?"

"Don't you talk about my father like that! He's a good man. He wouldn't lie or do anything wrong."

Esther bit her tongue. Tina didn't know how her father had forced her and Davey to leave the boardinghouse after Aunt Bonny's funeral. And Esther knew the girl wouldn't believe her if she told her.

"Just get dressed if you're going with us. We'll be leaving in about half an hour."

"But I want to stay here. There're two or three men who want to court me. And they are all rich."

Esther couldn't keep her foot from tapping on the floor. "Look, Tina, you heard what your father told Colin. Do you want some men ripping the clothes off your body, then forcing themselves on you over and over? And you're helpless all that time, screaming and begging them to stop. If that's what you want, then wait until we leave and sashay your way out of this house and right into those men's arms."

Tina's face grew pale with Esther's words, but defiance still sat on her shoulder. "All right, I'll wear the horrid dress for Papa."

Suddenly, she turned around and slammed her balled-up fists on her hips. "But what about all my other clothes at the boardinghouse? What will I wear when we get wherever we're going?"

Esther set her teeth on her tongue to keep from saying what she wanted to. She took a deep breath, then let it out a little at a time. When at last she got control, she moved her teeth a fraction so she could answer. "Tina, I don't know anything about your clothes. All I know is lots of people have come to help us get away from a murdering outlaw. So keep your mouth closed, put on those clothes, and wait for someone to come get you."

A knock sounded on the door.

Esther stepped to it and placed her head near the wood. "Who is it?"

"It's Thorn. I've got some clothes for you."

With a twist of her fingers, she unlocked the door and opened it just a few inches.

Thorn stood on the other side with a grin on his face. He shoved a pile of clothes toward her with one hand. "Colin said you'd know what to do with these."

From his other hand, he dropped a heavy bundle that jingled a bit. "And Drew said this was yours. He didn't want to leave it in the house, even in his safe, after everyone left."

As the man left, Esther wanted to slam the door. Dropping everything on the bed, she pushed the bundle aside. She knew what was in it—the double eagles and the jewelry—and understood why Drew gave it back to her. But it was the clothes which riled her. Colin gave her the clothes he'd worn the day they'd met in the livery. She ran her finger over the front of the shirt. It still had the hole from her knife. Well, she'd wear them and see what he said after she made a few alterations.

Another knock sounded on the door. Not waiting for her to answer, the door opened and Linda stuck her head in. She was dressed in black and her hair was powdered to make her look like an old woman. "Need any help? Thorn said we have one more in our group."

Esther waved her friend in. "I need to fix these fast. Can you help?"

Linda eyed the men's clothes, then covered her mouth and tried to hide her giggles. "Colin's?" She giggled even more when Esther nodded. She held the pants in front of her. "We can cinch the waist with a belt and roll up the bottoms, but I don't think we can do anything about the shirt." She touched her thumb and index finger to her chin and thought for a moment. "I know! I have one I'd planned to give to my brother for his birthday. It might be a little tight on you, but it should get you through the day. Then we can alter what we need to when we stop for the night."

Without any agreement from Esther, Linda slipped out of the room and disappeared.

"I can't wear this. It makes me look frumpy." Tina's voice whined around the room. The girl stood by the bed. Her face looked like she'd sucked on a lemon, followed by a sour pickle—a very, very sour pickle. "Why can't someone go back to the boardinghouse and get my clothes? I have a beautiful dark blue dress. It'd work for a funeral outfit. And there's a hat to match it, too."

The door burst open. Linda hurried inside. "Get dressed quick. They're loading the caskets into the wagon right now. Everyone's going to leave in the next few minutes."

"Davey?" Even though Esther knew the plan, she still asked as she tugged off her light-colored dress.

"He and Jack are already disguised. Kerr and a couple other cousins have the little ones in one of the wagons. They'll ride alongside the children's wagon all the way to the ranch." Linda slid the shirt over Esther's shoulder, then buttoned it as Esther fastened the front of the pants and cinched them tight.

While Linda pinned up Esther's hair, Esther worked on an old pair of Jack's shoes. They were a bit tight and too long, but would do, especially since they'd be riding in a wagon. Slightly out of breath after hurrying to slip on a long duster, she looked at her cousin. "Tina, put the sunbonnet on your head and tie it on good so no one'll know who you are."

Tina did what she was told but complained all the time. "I don't want to wear this. It makes me look like an old woman."

"That's the whole point." Esther grabbed her cousin's arm with one hand and her bundle from Drew, along with Colin's shirt with the other, then headed to the door. "Let's get downstairs before everyone gets loaded. We need to stay close to the MacPhersons."

A few moments later, they joined the clan, who were loading into various buggies and wagons. A few of the men mounted on horses. Linda, with a slat bonnet hiding her face, directed them to a farm wagon which'd been altered so that there were two wooden benches running the length of both sides of the wagon bed.

Esther looked around and saw Davey and Jack, along with the other children, sitting in a similar wagon. A stooped man with a limp and leaning heavily on a cane stopped next to her. He bumped into her side. "Sorry, but I think this is the one you are supposed to be in, uh, sir."

Esther couldn't keep her head from jerking sideways when Colin's voice whispered next to her. "Colin?"

"Quiet, now. We can talk once we're on the trail." He nodded toward Tina. "Help me get her on the wagon. We need to leave."

An hour later, and with Tina whining for most of the time, Esther was ready to get out of the wagon and walk alongside, like the pioneers on the Oregon Trail. Only thing different, those pioneers were using oxen which moved much slower than horses, so she wouldn't be able to keep up.

Several times she'd exchanged glances with Gavenia, Thorn's sister. And although the other woman hadn't said anything, she seemed as irritated as Esther with Tina's carrying-on.

A low growl filled the air on the other side of Tina where Colin sat. She snuck a peek at him. His jaw had tightened so much she could almost imagine hearing his teeth grinding together. His eyebrows were drawn together and a deep crease was carved in a line right above them. Poor man, his fingers were intertwined almost as if he had them wrapped around someone's throat.

"Enough." He glared past Esther. "Miss Ernestina, we all are abundantly aware you aren't happy about being taken to the ranch. We all know you aren't happy about not having your clothes or having to wear the ones you have on or your father going to Denver instead of coming to the ranch. And we all know you aren't happy you are going away from your friends and beaus without a single word."

His fingers spread out and clenched his legs just above his knees as if to keep them from grabbing something else. "Well, miss, right now, none of us are happy that you are with us. We hadn't planned on taking you, but we graciously made arrangements when your father begged us to get you out of town. The MacPherson clan is opening their home to you and offering you their protection. Could you please stop your whining and complaining and be quiet until we get to Jason's place? When we get there, you can go into the barn and complain all you want to the cows and horses and pigs. Then, when we leave tomorrow for the next leg of the trip, hopefully you'll have gotten it all out of your system. But if not, then please keep your mouth shut tomorrow, too."

Tina sat a bit straighter and crossed her arms over her chest. "Well, I never—"

Colin continued to glare at her. "No, I doubt your father ever told you to stop anything. But he's not here, and you're going to have to stay with us until he returns, so you'll have to live under our rules. And the number one rule at the main ranch is that you don't complain about anything—no griping, no whining. If the need to do so gets so strong you can't control it, then go out to the barn again and let loose there. The animals listen long, and they won't stop you."

Even though it wasn't a nice thing to do, Esther wanted to applaud what Colin said. She peeked around at the others in the wagon. They were all nodding their heads in agreement. Holding her breath, she glanced at her cousin.

Tina's face flushed bright red. Her mouth opened and closed like a fish lying on the river bank. All at once, she glowered at Esther, as if demanding she defend her.

Esther just shrugged. Now that she was free from Uncle Ed's domination, she didn't have to appease her spoiled cousin. That time had passed. Tina had to learn she was responsible for what she said and how she acted.

When Tina didn't get her way, she resorted to the thing which always got what she wanted from her father. She cried. When no one paid any attention to her weeping, her crying grew louder.

"Oh, Miss Ernestina, you're helping so well. If Ray Miller is following us, he'll surely be convinced of my death by the depth of your mourning." Colin pulled a white folded handkerchief from his pocket and held it out to her. "Thank you for your assistance."

Esther bit back her smile. Tina batted the handkerchief away, then stopped crying, almost as quickly as she started. Silence filled the air. Well, there was a snicker or two from those on both benches, but other than that, silence.

Colin gripped his fist and concentrated on keeping the groans inside. His body ached. His chest pulled so tight he thought it'd bust apart if they hit another hole in the road. Four days of the constant jiggling around on the back of the wagon, and he wanted to jump out and grab the nearest horse. But he knew it'd do no good. The rest of the MacPhersons had deemed it necessary for him to stay where he was. He swallowed another groan and remembered how he'd started out the trip looking like an old man to fool Miller, if he was watching. But now Colin felt like an old man, pains, exhaustion, and all. He wasn't sure who would look older when they got to the ranch, him or his grandda.

Kerr pulled his horse alongside the wagon. "The main ranch house is a little ways over the next rise. I'm going ahead to let them know we're here." He waved and galloped off.

The only good thing was Esther sitting next to him. She handed him the canteen. "How are you doing?"

Colin took the water, but grunted from the weight of it. "I'll make it." He tried to grin. "But just barely."

Esther looked around the area. "Do you think we fooled those men?"

Her voice soaked into him, driving the pain away for a few moments. "Not sure. I figure they had to decide which group of people to follow. Adam's been checking around behind us and hasn't seen any evidence they picked us."

"Good. I just wish we knew what they wanted."

Colin couldn't agree more, but he still figured the connection had to be Linda's brother Jack. After all, Drew and Esther didn't seem to have any connections to the Millers.

CHAPTER TWENTY-ONE

Esther rubbed the small of her back as the wagon came over a rise. She could see a large house with smaller houses nearby, along with a barn and other outbuildings scattered even further back. At last, they had reached the MacPherson home.

She couldn't wait until Davey was with her again. She understood he was safer with the other children and all the guards surrounding them. And he probably had more fun playing with them in the wagon, but she longed to hold him in her arms now and not have to wait until the end of the day.

Colin let out a low whistle between his teeth while he stared at the house. "I'd no idea it was so large."

Gavenia nodded in agreement. "It took nearly a year to gather the materials needed, but Granny had her heart set on this house. She'd seen a picture and floorplans of it in a book years ago. Said when they got where they'd finally settle, she'd have her house and never leave it until they put her in the ground." She glanced toward the house as if looking for someone. "Granny already has her plot picked. And those who have passed away since we've moved here have been buried around it."

Esther remembered the way her grandmother had suffered after a stroke crippled her and left her unable to do anything for herself, but wait to die. And that day had been a bittersweet one, losing a loved one, but knowing she was in a better place. Esther's stomach clenched at the thought of her elderly grandmother, laid low and afflicted in such a way, slowly waiting to die. "I'm sorry your grandmother's feeling poorly. I'll do whatever I can to help."

Gavenia blinked a couple of times, then smiled. "I think Granny's going to like you."

A few minutes later, the wagons stopped in front of the large house. People poured out of it and the other buildings. Greetings were exchanged and children were lifted from the wagons.

Esther stood, but waited until those in front of her were helped down. Someone touched her arm. Gavenia pointed to the main door of the house. A white-haired man and woman came out.

"Grandda and Granny." Gavenia waved when the couple spotted her. The elderly man lifted his cane in salute.

Granny MacPherson stood on the steps while the children ran to her. Her laughter sounded like that of a young girl. The little ones waited for her to give them each a kiss.

Esther felt a knot ease in her middle. "She's not doing poorly?"

"Not at all. She rules the house with a loving, iron fist. She handles every birth on the ranch and oversees every new bride who marries here. She can tell you at any moment what's in the storehouse and how each family's doing. I just hope I can be like her when I reach her age."

"You coming?" Dougal held out his hand to help her. Colin stood beside him with his arm wrapped around his middle. The poor man's face was a bit pale.

As quickly as she could, Esther climbed down and was caught around the legs by Davey. "Mama gotta meet Granny. She's got cookies."

Dougal grinned. "She's always got cookies."

Davey pulled on her hand. "Know, but Benny says new boys get two." He grabbed hold of Colin's hand, too. "C'mon. You new boy, too."

This time Esther couldn't hold back a chuckle. She'd never thought of Colin as a boy. Man, yes, but not a boy.

He'd apparently thought so also, if the red on his face was any sign.

Moments later, they stood in front of the old couple. Esther watched as Colin grasped the old man's forearm the same way he'd done with his brother in Uncle Ed's kitchen.

The old man turned his green eyes on Esther. His lips rose into a large smile. "And this must be Miz Essie. Many words of yer kindness and good cooking ha' passed 'round our table by the mouth of Dougal. Welcome to our protection."

Esther swallowed a lump in her throat at the words, then followed Colin when he moved a few steps to his grandmother.

"Aye, me boy, ye look jest like me son, Alasdair."

Colin opened his arms and wrapped his grandmother in them. Esther couldn't keep a tear from her own eye. Oh, how much she missed her parents and grandparents.

Colin pulled back. Mrs. MacPherson turned to Esther with welcoming arms. They clasped hands. The old woman kissed Esther's cheek. "Welcome to MacPherson land. Ye're welcome to stay as long as ye want."

"Thank you. You all are so gracious."

"Bah, just being good Christians." She grinned. "And good MacPhersons." She glanced at Davey. "Have ye heard about the cookies?" She laughed a light, tinkling sound when Davey's head bobbed. A grin spread across his face. She pulled two cookies from the large pocket of her snow white apron and handed them to Davey. "Now be off with ye, lad. Benny awaiting for ye."

"Tank you" Davey held a cookie in each hand and looked at Esther. "Go wi' Benny, Mama?"

"Yes, you may since Mrs. MacPherson said you could."

"Oh, lassie, I'm Granny to all who come here. And he's Grandda." She nudged the old man beside her.

"Thank you, Granny, Grandda for having us here." Esther felt like she'd traveled to another world, where everyone was nice and smiled all the time.

Gavenia hooked arms with Esther. "Come with me. I'll show you where you and Davey are sleeping."

Esther wanted to say something to Colin. She just wasn't sure what it was.

Thorn joined them. "I'll be taking this cousin of mine to the bunkhouse. It's where all the single men sleep."

Colin struggled to smile while he kept his arm tight around his chest. "Sounds like a good idea." He looked at Esther. "Will you be all right?"

She nodded. "Try and get some rest. We'll see you for supper."

He grunted as Thorn led him away.

Gavenia tugged on Esther's arm. "Come on. You need to get a nap, too. You're in for a treat tonight after supper."

Colin stood on the front porch and watched for Esther to come out. The nap and the tea Granny had brought to him when she came to check his chest wound had restored a lot of his strength. At least until bedtime.

But he was feeling antsy to see how Esther was getting along with his family. He'd already seen Davey running around with the younger MacPherson children, but he hadn't seen a glimpse of Esther yet. And he needed to see her.

Dougal stopped beside Colin on the steps. "Adam's come in. He still hasn't found anything that makes him think we were followed."

Colin felt his muscles tighten again. "Good, but they still can come." He wanted to feel they were safe here, but he wouldn't put anything past Miller, not after the attack. "If they followed the Denver MacPhersons, and find out the boy they want isn't there, they'll come here. Ray Miller's not giving up on what he wants. Look how he followed his prey to Central City."

"If they step on MacPherson land, we'll know."

"They're good at hiding. How do you think the old man stayed ahead of the law for all these years?" Colin let his eyes wander over the part of the ranch closest to the house and knew the MacPherson land extended far beyond this. With all this land about, even the MacPhersons couldn't cover every single inch. Someone could still slip through.

Colin knew the part of helplessness he was feeling was the result of getting shot. He scanned the yard again. Only this time, he watched the families gather. The men set out the tables and benches while the women brought the food.

He glanced at his brother. "Seems like all the MacPhersons are here tonight."

Dougal chuckled. "Don't fear, big brother. There're always guards out watching, twenty-four hours a day. Linda and Esther, along with their kin, will stay here at the main house. No one'll harm them. They're under MacPherson protection. And what I've learned since I been here, MacPherson protection is a mighty powerful thing."

Tingling rippled on the back of Colin's neck. The girls might be under MacPherson protection, and the guards might always be out, but Ray Miller was going to find them. If he hadn't already.

Linda came around the side of the house, carrying a bowl of something and set it on the table. She looked around and waved when she spied Dougal.

He waved back. "Oh yeah, something else. The single men take the night watches. As soon as we're able, you and I'll take our turn. But only until I marry some willing gal." He gave a small salute and joined Linda.

Colin watched Esther walk to where Linda and Dougal stood. They laughed at something Dougal said. He wanted to join them, but something held him back, as surely as if a giant hand had wrapped itself around him. He didn't have to ask himself what the hand was. He knew—the vow he'd made to Matty. He only realized now how heavy the vow was, but he'd made it and had to keep it. No matter the cost.

His hunger disappeared.

He turned away.

Esther drummed her fingers on the table while she glanced over her shoulder. Where was Colin? She thought he'd be eating with her. During the hard trip, she'd gotten used to having him right beside her. And she missed being with him, missed taking care of him, if only to give him water or a shoulder to lean against when he drifted off to sleep. But now with all these people around, she felt the closeness seeping away. The meal was ending, and he wasn't anywhere about, at least as far as she could see.

A few minutes later, everyone began cleaning up. Esther helped the women as they took care of the leftover food and dirty dishes, while the men moved the tables out of the way and set the benches in a semi-circle around the front porch.

Once everything was taken care of, she gathered with the MacPhersons when they sat back on the benches. The children gathered between the first bench and the porch steps.

Three men moved to the porch, one with fiddle and one with a musical horn, while the other one carried something Esther had never seen before.

Gavenia leaned over and whispered, "I love this part of the family get-togethers. Grandda will tell the story of the clan, including Jamie MacPherson, then they'll play the bagpipes and everyone will join in and sing 'Jamie's Lament' as well as some other songs. But first he'll give Colin his clan shield."

The men sat and made some strange noises with their instruments. But before they played any tunes, Grandda MacPherson climbed the steps and stood on the porch.

"Tonight we gather to welcome one of our own into our midst." He held out his hand and signaled for Colin to join him. "I speak of Colin Niall MacPherson, son of Alasdair MacPherson, grandson of Angus MacPherson." At the last name, he raised his closed fist and laid it over his heart. He turned to Colin. "Son of me son, yer da named ye well, for yer name means 'victory of the people, champion' and ye served and protected the weak and needy."

He moved his fist and laid his now-opened palm on Colin's shoulder. "Colin has come to stay with the clan for a while. May it be a long, long while."

Grandda tucked his hand into his pocket and pulled something out. He raised it for all to see. "As is our tradition to all of the MacPherson blood, I give to ye the clan shield." He held up a small metal disk so everyone could see it. "It is yers and proclaims to all our family motto, 'Touch not the cat bot a glove'."

As the words were spoken, a cheer rose from those sitting on the benches.

Esther wasn't sure what they were cheering. It was different from anything she'd known, and she liked it. She looked at Colin and was shocked to see tears in his eyes.

Colin blinked several times. The only time he'd seen his pa's clan shield was at the weddings of his five sisters. No, there was another time—the day his pa was buried. His ma had pinned it to his shirt above the heart which no longer beat. Then. with her hand resting on the clan shield, she spoke her last words to him. "A MacPherson you were born. A MacPherson you'll be buried." The lid to the pine box was nailed closed and his pa was lowered into the ground.

Although he stood still while Grandda pinned the piece of metal to his shirt, a thought slipped into his mind. He had traded one type of badge for another. A job for a family. But something jabbed him deep inside near his heart. He may have left his job, but he couldn't take on his family, not yet.

He glanced at Esther. The jab hit harder. She could be his family. Her and Davey. And however many little MacPhersons they'd be blessed with. But not now. Not yet.

He swallowed hard. Maybe never.

After everything from supper was cleaned up, and the MacPhersons went to their different homes or to the bunkhouse, Esther took Davey to their room. It took a while to settle him down, as he told her all about the other children and said he wanted a puppy like Benny. Finally, he got drowsy. And once his head touched the pillow, he went right to sleep.

Still, she wasn't tired, even though she wished she were. If she went to bed now, all she'd do was think about Colin. She looked around her room. It was nice, but right now it seemed to press in on her. She needed to see the stars, to know God was out there, and to know she wasn't alone.

Since she hadn't changed for bed, all she needed was her shawl which hung on one of the pegs on the wall. Once she had it around her shoulders, she slipped out of her room and walked downstairs. Moonlight shone through the windows and guided her way to the front door. She hoped it wasn't locked.

When she turned the doorknob, she felt someone near. Without thinking, she reached for her knife, but she hadn't put it in her pocket. She'd felt too safe here.

"Calm yourself, lassie. 'Tis only Thorn."

She spread her hand against her chest and waited for her breathing to slow. "I couldn't sleep, so I thought I'd sit outside and watch the stars. Is it all right?"

He chuckled. "It's fine. You're free to go wherever you want. You'll be safe. We always post guards. Even if you don't see them, they're out there."

"I'm only going as far as the porch."

"Enjoy the peace." He turned and went back into the shadows.

As quietly as she could, she opened the door, slipped out, then closed it again. The chairs were where she remembered them. She sat and tucked her feet under her skirt.

Life was so confused right now. She had no home, no position, no family except Davey. She did have good friends in Linda and Dougal, money and jewelry, and the whole MacPherson clan to take in her and Davey.

Earlier, she'd taken the pins out and her hair hung around her shoulder and down her back. She ran her fingers through it. Little by little she pressed her fingertips along her scalp, squeezing and releasing. Slowly, tension which had been building ever since supper started eased. At last she dropped her hands onto her lap.

The tension was gone, but not what caused it—Colin. His distance tonight bothered her. No, it was further back than that. He'd changed after he thought those outlaws had died. She'd never really understood what it was all about. He seemed to care for her, had given up his star, although he still wore his gun. Then they were all shot. And now where did they stand?

Somewhere off to the left a door creaked, not much, just the tiniest bit. But she didn't fear the noise she heard in the nighttime. No, she feared the sound of the two faceless men who came in her sleep. And that's when fear grew into terror.

They never hurt her. They just kept repeating they were coming back for her. She'd been able to keep quiet in her terror, at least enough so she didn't wake her son next to her. But when she'd wake in the morning, her scarred arm would be sore where she'd scratched all night long. Fortunately, the dream only came once or twice a year.

Something caught her eye. A movement by the bunkhouse. A man walked from there toward the barn. He stopped. A moment later, he headed for the porch where she was sitting.

CHAPTER TWENTY-TWO

Colin gave up on sleeping. He crawled out of his bunk and pulled on his boots. Maybe a walk would help. He slipped out of the bunkhouse, then tried to decide which way to walk.

Someone moved out of the shadow cast by the nearby barn. A hand raised, then waved him over. As he got nearer, he recognized Grant, a cousin and younger brother to Thorn. He swallowed a chuckle as he realized he was sounding like Grandda.

"Notice something?" Grant held a rifle. Definitely one of the night guards. Maybe Dougal was right, and there was enough protection for Esther and Linda here on the ranch.

"Just couldn't sleep."

Grant nodded and turned back to the shadows. He stopped and looked over his shoulder with a grin. "Get tired of walking and want to sit and ponder a while, Granny's chairs on the front porch make mighty fine sitting."

Colin watched the young man disappear into the shadows. Looking to the left, then the right, he decided he might as well go and sit on the porch since it was in the shadows. If he paced anywhere in the yard, at least one man's eye would be on him, probably more than one.

When he reached the top of the porch, he realized someone was sitting in one of the chairs. Now he

understood the grin on Grant's face. He let out a small
sigh. It was the one person he didn't want to see right
now. Well, that wasn't really true. He wanted to see her,
to be with her, but he couldn't. It was why he'd stayed
away from her all night. He knew she was probably hurt,
but he needed to get his thoughts straight. And he
couldn't do that when he was with her.

"Evening, Esther. Can't sleep?"

"So much has happened and—and—things are so
uncertain." She touched the chair beside her. "Have a
seat."

He should leave her alone, but he couldn't.

Her fingers floated over his fist. He turned his hand
and linked fingers with her. "Oh, Es. For a while, I
thought everything was going to work out for us."

"What happened? Did I do something wrong?"

Her low, husky voice sent waves of longing through
him.

"Or did you realize I...I'm not right for your family?"
The last part came out in a rush. "Is it because of what
happened to me before, about...how I got Davey?"

He tightened his fingers on her. "No, never. You're the
one I want in my life. You and Davey." He sucked in a
deep breath. He needed to explain but how could he do it
without exposing her to the worst side of Ray Miller and
men like him?

"Es, I have feelings for you, strong feelings, but I can't
do anything about them."

Her fingers trembled against his, then her hand fell
away from his. "Is it your wife? Do you still love her?"

The question hit him in the gut. He hadn't expected it.
"No, it's nothing like that." He reached for her hand
again. But his past was ripping him apart inside. He had
to tell her, try to explain. "Years ago, I made a vow at my
son's grave. I thought the man who killed him was dead,
but now I know he's alive. And is willing to kill again."

His gut twisted again. "The vow has to come before anything else."

Silence closed around them like flooding waters. It was pulling her away from him. He felt the distance she was putting between them. And he didn't know how to stop it.

Esther tightened her hold on him. "Years ago for one of their wedding anniversaries, my father gave my mother a book of poetry by a man named Richard Lovelace. She loved the book, but let me read it whenever I wanted. It was one of the things I truly wished Uncle Ed had not sold."

She gave herself a little shake as if to clear away the bad thoughts of her uncle. "Anyway, there's a poem. The last lines go like this 'I could not love thee so much, Lov'd I not Honor more.' I understand. I don't like it, but I understand."

With a loosening of her fingers, she stood.

He stood beside her and lifted his fingers to her face. "One kiss. I've dreamed of one kiss from your lips."

"So have I." She rested her palms on his chest.

He dropped his hands and wrapped his arms around her. And inch by inch pulled her closer, then lowered his head. Their lips touched. He wanted more, so much more. At last, he stepped back and dropped his arms.

"You best go in. It's getting late." His voice came out low and thick.

She hesitated for a moment, then disappeared into the house without another word.

He wanted to go after her and tell her the past didn't matter. But he couldn't lie to her like that. She deserved more. Matty deserved more.

He headed back to the bunkhouse, a cold bed, and a sleepless night.

A few days later, Colin leaned against a post on the back porch. An empty cup dangled from his hand. Granny had just gone in the house after she declared Colin fit to get out and do some work. He probably could've gone back to work a day or two before, but it hadn't taken long to figure out no one, but no one, went against Granny when she laid down the law.

On one side of the yard, Davey and some of the younger boys played tag while on the other side, Esther and Linda filled tubs to do laundry. Tina stood near the women but wasn't helping much. He could see her lips moving, but couldn't hear the words. Not quite true. He couldn't hear the words she spoke, but in his mind he could make out everything she was saying. And they were all complaints.

His eyes were drawn to Esther. She fit in so well with his family here. And the thought filled a dry, empty place in his gut—both the woman and his family. After Jessie, he hadn't thought he could trust another woman, not with his heart and his name. But Esther had woven herself into him, into his heart and mind, along with Davey. He loved them both. They'd become a part of him. Still, he wasn't sure he could take them into his life. Would Esther tire of him like Jessie? Would she leave him then?

His fingers tightened around the cup's handle. Slowly, he relaxed his hand. There was no way he'd break one of Granny's china cups.

The door to the kitchen opened and closed. He looked over his shoulder. Thorn crossed the wooden floor and leaned against one of the posts.

"We're gonna start building a place for Dougal and Linda back of here. They'll be close enough to be safe, but have their own home. We could do the same for you. And Esther, if you want."

Colin's gut rolled. He upended his cup and let the last few drops dribble out onto the flowers surrounding the porch. What he wanted and what he had to do battled each other. "And do what? I've always been a lawman. I don't know how to ranch." He watched Esther for moment. "Besides, I still have something I have to finish."

Thorn gripped Colin's shoulder. "I've been there myself, so I understand. Just know there is a place for you here, whenever you want to claim it."

Colin had heard the story from several of the single men of how Thorn had searched for more than a year trying to find his brother-in-law so he could discover how his first wife had died. He nodded.

Thorn released his grip on Colin's shoulder, then slapped him on the back before he took the cup from Colin's hand. "May God be with you and bless you on your quest."

When Thorn returned to the kitchen and closed the door, a huff of air popped out between Colin's lips. Would God be with him as he held a gun on Ray Miller and squeezed the trigger? Would God bless him when he put a bullet into the heart of the man who killed Jessie and Matty?

He stepped off the porch. He had to get away and think, clear his head. He'd only gone a few steps when a little voice broke into his thoughts.

"Unca Collie, catch me."

Almost without thought, Colin bent and caught the little boy cannonball heading toward him. He grunted when the still healing muscles in his chest rebelled when he swung Davey above his head. The little boy giggled as only little ones can while he dangled above Colin's head. The muscles in his chest eased a bit when he settled the boy on his hip.

Davey wrapped his arms around Colin's neck, his brown eyes shining with interest. "Whatcha gonna do? Where ya going?"

Colin's gut tightened. He wanted this child and his mother in his life, but it might never happen. And that left a hole bigger in his chest than the one made by Miller's bullet.

From the corner of his eye, he spotted Esther heading toward him. She stopped before him and reached for her son, but he pulled away, clinging more tightly to Colin. "Come on, little man. Thorn said Colin was going to help them with the cattle, and the boys are waiting for you to go and collect the eggs."

Davey pouted. "I'm not little." He stretched upwards in Colin's arms and lifted his hand and touched his head then Colin's. "See. I'm big like Unca Collie."

Colin swallowed a chuckle, figuring Esther wouldn't appreciate the humor especially after their conversation several nights before. He set Davey on the ground. "Need to mind your ma." He tapped the little boy's nose. "Always."

At supper, Esther listened to the talk around her when it turned to planning a picnic to celebrate the engagement of Dougal and Linda. Everyone seemed to agree Saturday afternoon would be the best time.

Esther couldn't hold back a smile as she thought of the picnic they'd planned back in Central City. How that would be a time to get to know Colin better. How Linda had joined in with the plan. Then the smile no longer pulled at Esther's lips when she remembered why they hadn't gone. How the men had tried to kill them all.

She glanced past the barns, out to the foothills. Were the outlaws out there watching them? Granny said her grandson in Denver had sent several letters. So far, no one had seen any signs of those outlaws in Denver.

Linda scooted a bit nearer. "I'm thankful Jack's here with me, but I wish my sister was with us. She'd love all the goings-on with me and Dougal, but I know she's thrilled to be helping Drew and Linda with the babies."

She grinned. "But Dougal promised someone would bring her here before the wedding."

Esther nodded. "I heard Granny has a lace wedding veil she brought from Scotland and you'll get to wear it."

"That's right. She told me all her daughters and sons' brides wore it, as well as any granddaughter or grandson's bride who got married where she was." Linda let out a happy sigh. "Can you believe I'm going to be Mrs. Dougal MacPherson, and we'll be living here?"

Linda suddenly looked serious. "But there is something I have to ask you. Will you stand up with me? The MacPhersons are all wonderful people, and I love them all, but I need someone to stand with me who understands what this means to me. How hard accepting Dougal was. Of...of the fear I've overcome."

Esther grabbed Linda's hand. "Of course I'll stand with you. Thank you for asking me."

"Oh, Dougal's waving for me to join him." She stood, then whispered to Esther. "And I'll stand up for you when you marry Colin, if you want."

Esther watched her friend bounce off and join the man who loved her and whom she loved. All at once, she had to get by herself. Who said she'd ever marry, much less Colin? He had a vow to fulfill, and it must come before anything else, even a wedding vow.

For five years, she thought she'd never marry. But that was before she knew what it was to love a man, to love Colin.

How long would she have to wait for him?

The afternoon sun beat hot on Ray Miller and his boy, while they hid in some trees a ways from the ranch's main house. He stared through some kind of fancy eye thing called binoculars he'd taken from a dead man he'd left by the side of the road on the way from Missouri some time back. They were pretty good for watching from far away and seeing up close what was going on around the MacPherson's place.

Near as he could make out, the ranchers kept most of the guards around the main house and outbuildings. So it hadn't been too hard to slip in last night and hide in the trees. That way, they could get an idea of what they'd have to face when they came to get the boy. But they were going to have to wait until well after dark to slip away.

Ray growled, then stuffed a wad of cloth in his mouth to keep from coughing and giving away their location.

"What's the matter, Pa?" His worthless son sat there guzzling water from his canteen. Kid didn't have a lick of sense or the stomach for killing. Besides that, the boy was a lousy shot.

When he stopped coughing at last, he struggled to suck in enough air to breathe. As soon as he got the boy he'd come for, he'd find an old sawbones and get something for whatever was going on in his chest.

He looked back at the group of people gathering for some kind of picnic, then pulled the binoculars from his eyes and blinked a couple of times. He raised them back to his eyes and let out a string of curses. "It's those two MacPhersons, the marshal and his brother. They ain't dead. Now we're gonna have to kill them all over again 'cause they'll give us more trouble than all the rest of the group together.

"Really, Pa? They're still alive?" His youngest shifted and tried to grab the eye thing, but Ray shoved him aside. Worthless brat, he'd been moping around ever since they shot those MacPhersons. Seemed to think he'd done something unforgivable. Well, once Ray got who he'd come for, he wouldn't need this worthless one. The boy down there was all he needed. That boy and him would make a great team.

"Pa, why don't we just leave them be? The kid's got a good life."

Ray had to hold back and keep from giving his brat the back of his hand for fear his son would scream like a foolish woman and give away their location. But soon he wouldn't matter.

Gritting what was left of his teeth, Ray turned back and stared at the youngster again through the binoculars, dreaming of the time it'd be just the two of them.

"The kid'll be better off with me. If I leave him with those people, he'll just turn into a whinny no-good like you."

"Why don't you just let me go? I won't tell anyone where you are."

Ray wished he could just send Blake away, be shed of his complaining, but he needed him until he got the boy he'd come for. Then he'd put a bullet in Blake's back to make sure of his silence.

"One day. One day soon." Ray held back a chuckle. Yep, one day real soon.

CHAPTER TWENTY-THREE

Esther watched everyone having a good time preparing for the picnic—everyone except Tina. She wanted to help her cousin fit in somehow, if for no other reason than to keep peace with the MacPhersons. But Tina had grown more and more irritable and irritating with each passing day. The girl hated working in the kitchen, working in the gardens, helping with the children, anything and everything. And she'd made her feelings known to anyone who was around her.

Esther let out a deep sigh. Tina hated doing anything where she wasn't the center of attention. Aunt Bonny had often talked to Esther about the situation. But the older Tina got the more her father spoiled her.

Even now, Esther helped some women and older girls set out the food while others took care of the younger children. And all the time, Tina sat on the end of one of the benches next to a table, fanning herself. Not helping, not working, not smiling. As if she were the queen and all others were her servants.

Esther headed toward Tina. Her cousin needed to do something, anything to help those who were protecting her. Before Esther had gone five feet, Granny stepped to the table where Tina sat. The sweet woman kept her voice low, and no one took notice of her while she talked. But Tina's face grew redder and redder as words shot out of her mouth.

With responsibility sitting heavy on her, Esther hurried to them, hoping to keep Tina from saying any more hateful words, especially to the woman the whole MacPherson clan held in highest esteem.

Esther's heart sank as she joined the two of them. The words between them had stopped. She glanced at Tina's hard-set face with her glaring eyes and prayed Tina would control her temper. She sneaked a peek at Granny, afraid the old woman had been hurt by Tina's tirade. But instead of a pale, subdued look as she cowered before Tina's usual tirade, Granny MacPherson stood her ground and held herself as the one in control, the queen Tina had tried to be.

Tina let out a huff and stalked away. Granny gave a quick one-shouldered shrug and went the other direction.

Fearing the worst and knowing from past experiences how vengeful Tina could be if crossed, Esther started after her cousin. All at once she felt a tug on her elbow. She stopped and glanced to her side. Colin stood beside her.

"Let her go. She's grown and can take care of herself. Sooner or later she's going to have to face up to how she acts." He shrugged. "This might be the time and place. Her father can't ease her way here. She's going to have to learn to live with others, especially those who don't think the world revolves around her."

Esther knew he was right, but Uncle Ed had made it her responsibility for years to look after her cousin, to pick up after her, to take the blame for things she did. And some habits were hard to break. "You don't understand, Ti—"

Colin pressed his finger against her lips. "I understand perfectly. She's spoiled, and no one has ever held her to task for the way she acts."

She dropped her chin. Shame at her cousin's actions, ever since they'd arrived, rested heavy on her. "I know. I just don't want to cause problems for your family. You've all been so kind to us."

He raised her face with his finger while a smile spread across his face. "Why don't we take a walk and let her cool off a bit?"

A tingle of excitement ran around her middle. "I'd love to, but there's work to be done in order to have the meal ready. I'd hate for anything to go wrong and upset Dougal and Linda."

Colin chuckled and pointed to an area past the barn. The engaged couple stood there, arms around each other, the only two people in their world. "Don't think anything'll upset them." He tightened his fingers on her elbow just a tiny bit. "Take a walk? Just a short one?"

She answered with a nod and a smile of her own, then slid her hand into the crook of his elbow. While they walked in the opposite direction of the engaged couple, Esther took in the beauty around her. "I love it here. It's so peaceful."

Colin let out a deep chuckle. "Peaceful with all these MacPhersons about?"

"Umm. Loving. Caring for each other. That's peace, with shouting and bagpipes and singing."

She felt a tug on her arm. Colin stopped moving.

He lifted his hand and touched her cheek with his fingertips. "You're the peaceful one." He stepped closer and slipped his hand to the back of her neck.

Her hand had moved from his elbow and rested on his chest.

"I'm going to kiss you."

She couldn't say a word, so she nodded.

His face drew closer to her.

She moved upward on her toes.

Their lips were a hair's breadth apart when something shoved against her skirt. She jerked back a bit. They both looked down.

"Up, Mama, me want hugs too." Davey stood between them, his arms reaching upwards. A huge grin split his face.

Esther wanted to scream and laugh at the same time. Even more so when Colin muttered something she couldn't understand. But the man pulled Davey into his arms.

Her son wrapped one chubby arm around Colin's neck, then reached the other one out to her. "C'mere, Mama, c'mear."

Esther wrapped her arm around Davey. Colin spread his other arm around her back, pulling them all into a big hug. Her laughter echoed with deep, spreading warmth that went all the way to her center. This was what she wanted. And more.

But then the scar itched again.

The next day, Colin nodded when Dougal signaled him to follow him outside after breakfast. All the while they walked to the barn, Dougal's face grew more and more grim.

Once they were inside, Dougal moved to his horse. "Let's take a ride."

Not a question, no indication of his thoughts other than the look on his brother's face and the growl in his voice. Colin nodded and saddled his horse. He'd seen his brother in this mood growing up and knew he'd have to wait until Dougal was ready to talk.

In silence they rode away from the main house and on no particular trail Colin could make out. Half an hour later, Dougal stopped and dismounted. Colin followed his brother's action, but by now he was getting a mite irritated.

"What's bothering you, Dougal? You haven't acted like this since we left the home place."

Dougal swung around and glared at him. "What are your plans for Esther?"

His brother could have slugged him in the gut, and Colin wouldn't have been more surprised. It was the kind of question boys asked each other when they were fighting over a girl in the schoolyard. Unless Dougal really had his eye on Esther. "What's it to you? You've got Linda."

Dougal's hands formed into fists at his sides. "Like Grandda said, this is MacPherson land, and here we protect women. I've looked after Esther ever since her uncle moved them to Central City. I've bashed many a young idiot for not treating her right. And I watched you both last night. She and Davey have fallen for you. You could hurt her bad, maybe worse than those men years ago because you could destroy her inside."

Colin felt his hands ball into fists. He wanted to slug his brother. What was between him and Esther was none of his brother's concern.

Dougal shoved his fists on his hips. "I just don't want her hurt. Have you gotten over your need for vengeance against the Millers? Are you ready to make a life with her?"

"It wasn't vengeance. I'm a lawman. I'm just carrying out justice."

"No, you *were* a lawman. You gave up your badge. And you never wanted justice. You wanted vengeance for what happened to Jessie and Matty. So you just picked what you figured was the likeliest target—the Millers. Whether they did it or not." Dougal slashed his hand through the air. "But that's a whole different matter. You wouldn't listen to me years ago, and I doubt you'll listen to me now."

Dougal took a step or two closer, then raised his hand and jabbed Colin in the chest. "But you still didn't answer my question. What are your plans for Esther?"

The anger went out of Colin as he heard the same question that had haunted him ever since Ray Miller and his son gunned them down. What was he going to do about Esther? Sure, he'd given up his badge, but that was before he knew the Millers were still alive. But it didn't change how he felt about them.

He loved Esther and Davey. He'd admit that now, at least to himself. But he wasn't sure his love was greater than the hatred he felt for the Millers. Or if he did set it aside, would it return in years to come and poison the feelings he had for them?

He felt his shoulders drop. He didn't have the right to ask anything of Esther.

"That's what I thought." Dougal placed his hand on Colin's shoulder. "Brother, you have to get your thoughts straightened out. For your sake and for Esther's."

"I know." Colin grabbed the reins to his horse. "Let's get back and see what work Thorn says needs to be done."

He mounted his horse but kept his eyes turned away from his brother. Tonight he needed to talk to Thorn and Grandda. Make a plan. He was healed enough to travel. Esther and Davey were safe with his family. He could go after the Millers, hunt them down.

Questions shot through his mind which left him cold. *What if I never find them? What then?*

Esther stopped just before she entered the kitchen. She'd told Granny she'd help with the noonday meal, but the words being spoken in the kitchen kept her rooted to the spot in the hall.

"Of course you have to be careful around Esther. She's the most selfish person I have ever met. If it helps her, she'll twist your words around, as well as outright lying. No matter the situation, she makes sure everyone feels sorry for her and takes care of her and that son of hers."

She lowered her voice, but Esther could still hear the whispered conversation. "And speaking of her son, did you know she's never been married? She dyes her hair and talks like she does to draw the men's attention to herself."

Esther gritted her teeth to keep from shouting at her cousin. Her fingers itched to slap Tina's lying mouth. The girl had gone back to the way she was in Central City. Or maybe, she'd never changed in the first place. But one thing had changed. Esther no longer had to put up with the lies Tina told about her. She took a deep breath, then two. This was not the time to talk to Tina. She'd wait until after everyone ate and the dishes were cleaned.

She moved into the kitchen and watched two of the younger MacPherson girls stare at her as redness rose from their collars to their hair. They were embarrassed, either at getting caught talking about her, or at what Tina told them about her and Davey, or both. She wouldn't explain anything to these girls. If she did right now, it would make it seem everything Tina said about her was true. No, she'd have a talk with Granny first. Maybe she could help her know how to handle the things Tina said.

Esther's head started pounding soon after they sat to eat, so she was glad there were only Grandda, Granny, Linda, Gavenia, Tina, and the two younger girls who'd been in the kitchen earlier. But every time she looked across the table at the girls, they dropped their heads and seemed to be completely absorbed in their food. It didn't help that every time it happened, a smirk crossed Tina's face.

Her throat tightened more and more. There was no way she could swallow anything, so she just pushed her food around on her plate. She breathed a sigh of relief when Linda brought a pie to the table.

While it was being cut and served, Tina looked at Grandda. "When can I leave here and go back home?"

He smiled at her. "Patience, lass. Hopefully, ye'll hear from yer da soon."

Tina's face took on the look Esther had grown to hate. A look that usually preceded a temper tantrum—the kind only Uncle Ed could stop by promising his little darling some bauble or other.

"I am not a lass, and I want to go to my papa, not my da." She sneered the last word. "He's always taken care of me, and I want to be with him." All at once, her face lit up as if she had just solved all the problems in the world by herself. "I know. You have enough horses and men here. You can spare some to take me to Denver."

Grandda MacPherson shook his head. "Nay, that won't be possible. Yer da sent you to us for your protection. MacPhersons always fulfill the trust put in them."

"But I don't want to stay here." The whine started in her voice. Soon would come the tears and tantrum.

He stood and seemed to grow in size. "Lass, ye'll stay and do as ye're told. So be it." His voice hadn't risen in volume, but the law was laid out. With that said, he left the room.

Tina stared at his back with narrowed eyes. In her red face, her mouth pinched so tightly together that her lips were lost from the pressure. But she didn't say a word. Instead, she threw her napkin on the table and stomped out of the house, slamming the door as she went.

In the silence that followed, Granny stood. "Come lassies, I think it's time for another knitting lesson."

Esther stood and cleared the table. Linda poured hot water from the pot that had been heating on the stove into the small tub they used for washing the dishes. When the dishes were done, Linda left to visit Thorn's wife Sarah, who stayed close to home since she was expecting.

Esther paced the kitchen. She wanted to talk to Granny but knew she needed to wait until they finished the knitting lesson. The things she needed to talk over with Granny weren't things she wanted to discuss with those two girls present.

When she passed by the window, something caught her attention. Tina had changed her clothes. She had on the pants and shirt Esther had worn when they left Central City. There was only one reason she'd have done that. Of all the silly things to do. Tina was going to try to sneak away, or in this case, ride defiantly away. Didn't she know how dangerous that could be? Not only to her, but also to anyone who went after her to bring her back?

Esther hurried out the back door and walked to the barn. She slipped inside. Just as she suspected, Tina was getting a horse ready to ride. Foolish, selfish girl!

Stepping through the dust motes and past the first two stalls, Esther stopped by the one where her cousin was trying to put the bit between the horse's lips. "You know you can't go out riding by yourself. And you definitely can't go to Central City or Denver alone."

"You have no right to tell me what I can and can't do. You aren't my mother. Just get out of my way and leave me alone."

"So, because you didn't get your way, you're going out there into danger, maybe get captured by those outlaws. Do you really want to have done to you what that man in Central City threatened to do?"

Tina stood still for a moment, then looked stunned, as though something she hadn't thought about before had entered her mind. "You said something like that before we left Central City." She looked at Esther, questioning. "Is it what happened to you?"

Esther's stomach clenched. Tina knew exactly what had happened. After all, she'd taunted her with it for years. A thought burst into her mind, a possibility which hadn't occurred to her before. Was it possible that Tina really didn't know? Had Uncle Ed and Aunt Bonny never told her?

Memories flashed through Esther's mind—all the taunts of the last five years, all of the snide comments, the horrible words Tina spewed out the night Aunt Bonny died, none of those times had Tina said what really happened. Did she truly not know?

Tina took a step forward. "Is that why you had all those nightmares?"

"You didn't know?"

Tina's head shook. Her fingers fidgeted. "I was only twelve when you came to live with us. All I knew was that Mama Bonny spent all her time with you. And I hated you. She was my Mama Bonny. She didn't have time for me. She was always with you."

Esther slowly nodded her head. So many misunderstandings. So many words and thoughts aimed hatefully at the other. So much hurt which could have been avoided. But it was in the past. That was one thing Aunt Bonny had taught her. You could not undo the past. You could only go on from now. Correct what you could, ask forgiveness for what you couldn't correct, and try to live in peace with yourself, others, and God.

"I thought you knew. The men killed my parents, then took me. I don't remember much, other than screaming and fighting and pain. Aunt Bonny said it was my mind's way of protecting my sanity. I don't know who they were. I can't remember their faces." She wiped moisture from her cheek. "Uncle Ed took us all away shortly after that."

Tina scuffed her boot along the hay in the stall. "I hated you for making us move. I left all my friends. Papa said it was because of you we had to move." She shrugged. "So I blamed you." Raising her hand, she pointed to Esther's arm. "Did they do that?"

Esther placed her right hand over her left sleeve. "Yes, they said they were branding me and would come back and get me one day." She took in a quivering breath. "They said it's why they didn't kill me then."

She couldn't take any more talking about that horrible day. Stumbling to the barn door, she shoved it open with shaking hands. The sun felt good, healing. God was everywhere around her. His warmth surrounded her.

She knew she couldn't go back to the house yet. Peace, she needed to find peace. Off to the right, she spied the small apple orchard Granny and her daughters-in-law had started. She lifted her skirt and hurried to it. It wouldn't be long until the apples were ripe. The fragrance lifted her.

She touched the bark. God made the tree. He made the flowers of the field and the birds in the air. He made and loved her. She sank onto the dirt under a tree, pulled her knees to her chest, and wrapped her arms around them. In a low voice, she sang the one hymn which had always brought her peace. "Nearer, my God, to Thee, nearer to Thee! E'en though it be a cross that raiseth me; Still all my song shall be nearer, my God, to Thee, Nearer, my God, to Thee, nearer to Thee!"

Her voice stopped. Her head bowed in prayer, silent prayer without words, prayer where she trusted the Spirit to take her needs and pain to God.

CHAPTER TWENTY-FOUR

Colin rode up to the barn. He stopped for a moment and looked around. Warmth rolled around his insides as he watched Davey running and playing with the other boys on the ranch. It was the way boys should live, and if he stayed here, it'd be good to know Davey would have lots of friends around. Lots of MacPherson friends. Of course, he'd be a MacPherson too. He didn't think Esther would object to him adopting the boy, if they ever married.

He dismounted and led the horse into the barn. He stopped just inside the door. There was a sound—a sound that didn't belong in a barn, a sound that twisted his gut. A woman was crying. He dug his fingers into the palms of his hands. Not Esther. *Dear God, don't let Esther be hurt.*

His boots thudded on the ground as he raced to the stall at the far end of the barn, scattering dust motes out of his way. He dropped to one knee in the dim light, then drew back in surprise. "Tina!" He sucked in a deep breath, but coughed when the dusty air filled his nose. "What is the matter, Tina? Are you hurt?"

The young woman gazed at him, her tears making dirty streaks down her cheeks. "I didn't know. I always thought she was such a hypocrite, having done things with boys, then going to church like nothing happened. I didn't know."

Colin knew Tina was talking about Esther. The words she said the night Bonny Small died came back to him. Although they were spoken in anger and grief, Tina never mentioned an attack—just that Esther was unmarried with a child. Maybe this time, Tina was telling the truth.

Tina swiped her palms against her cheeks. "She's always been so pretty. Everyone loved her. They loved her smile, the way she sang in church, her beautiful red hair. I wanted to be like her, but when she came to live with us, everything changed. Those men changed everything. They hurt her so bad." She let out a wail. "The scar, that horrible scar on her arm."

Colin's head spun. He thought she'd been talking about Esther, but she had brown hair, not red. And he'd never seen a scar. Suddenly the word scar brought back other memories, ones of when he and Tuck had taken that first trip together. Miller had killed those miners and branded them on the forehead.

His gut twisted so tight he thought he'd be sick there in the barn. Swallowing back the bile rising in his throat, he grabbed Tina's arm. "Who are you talking about? Who has a scar?"

The girl's eyes grew wide and she trembled. She scooted around him as she tried to get out of the stall, but he still held her arm.

He hadn't meant to frighten the girl. He dropped her arm and stepped back. "Who are you talking about? Who has red hair?"

She edged along the side of the stall. "Esther. Papa made her dye her hair."

"Where is she?"

"Don't hurt her. She's been hurt enough already." She took a few steps backward toward the barn door. "I've been horrible to her, but I didn't know."

"I just need to talk with her."

The girl nodded, spun around, and ran out of the barn.

Colin leaned his head against the side of the stall. His whole world had just crashed around him. Had the Miller boys taken Esther? Was Davey the grandson of Ray Miller? Had the men who'd killed his son fathered the boy he'd planned to adopt and raise as his own?

The door jerked open. Thorn stomped inside. His eyes glittered in the dimness. "What did ye do to the girl? She ran into the house like fanged-toothed serpents were after her."

Colin rested his hands on his hips and let his head drop to his chest for a moment. A moment or two later, he looked at his cousin. "I didn't do anything to her. She was crying when I came into the barn. From what she said, Esther was attacked by men, who left her with Davey. I need to go find her."

He headed for the door. Answers, he needed answers, and only Esther could give him those. When he passed by Thorn, the other man stopped him by resting his hand against Colin's shoulder. "Does it matter? The past?"

Colin didn't fight his cousin. He needed a few minutes to think about what Tina revealed. "I'm not sure. If what Tina said is true, it's Davey they're after. He's Ray Miller's grandson."

Thorn tightened his grip on Colin's shoulder, then dropped his hand. "Go find Esther. Find out the truth. I saw her heading toward the orchard a bit ago."

Colin nodded and rushed out of the barn. He was torn, wanting to comfort her after her words with Tina, but needing to know why she hadn't told him about the Millers sooner. Why had she kept it a secret? Why hadn't she told him it was the Millers who attacked her? It would've saved them all so much time and pain. No one would have been shot.

With each step he took, pieces fell into place. The night they'd been chasing the Millers after they'd killed the miners, the outlaws had snuck back into town, and someone had broken into the boardinghouse. The Millers had tried to take Davey then, only Esther had moved out. Then, they had broken into the Hollingsworths' house, trying to get Davey again. Had she known the Millers were after Davey? Would she leave him after he got the Millers? Had she fooled him like Jessie had, making him think she loved him, then leaving with their son?

He stopped. Was he wrong about Esther? He loved her and thought she had deep feelings for him. And now he wasn't sure of anything.

He came to the edge of the orchard and saw her huddled under one of the trees. Her low, husky voice carried in the air. She sang to God, words of closeness, words of need.

His heart twisted. How long had it been since he felt the longing, the closeness, the need? He shook his head as if he could shove those thoughts away with that simple act.

Why hadn't Esther told him about her connection to the Millers? Hiding that information nearly cost him and Dougal their lives.

As the last words of the song drifted away, Esther felt someone sit on the ground to her left. She turned her head and smiled when she saw Colin beside her. It was almost as if God had sent the man to comfort her. But when she looked at his eyes, his mouth, his whole body, she drew into herself.

The dappled sunshine filtering through the apple leaves couldn't hide his clenched jaw or the way his nostrils flared with each breath he took.

She wanted to touch his hand which rested on his leg, but the anger radiating off of him in waves held her back. "What's the matter? What happened?"

He took her arm and pulled back her sleeve, revealing the ugly scar. The seconds ticked by while he stared at it. Slowly, he raised his eyes to hers. "Why didn't you tell me it was the Millers who attacked you? Why did you wait? Why keep it a secret?"

Her chest tightened. She couldn't breathe. Fingers ran over her arm, over the scar. She closed her eyes as faceless voices sounded around her, voices taunting her, voices claiming her, then the pain in her arm. No, no, no!

She tried to leave, but arms held her where she sat. Colin wouldn't hurt her, but she needed to get away. The memories gouged into her—hurting her, scaring her. The faceless men in her dreams telling her they were coming back for her. Her head couldn't take any more. Her stomach agreed. She lost what little lunch she'd been able to eat earlier.

Colin held her as waves of sickness rolled out of her body. The waves continued well after her stomach was empty. When her stomach stopped heaving, he lifted her and carried her several feet away. She felt limp as the rag doll her mama had made for her when she was just a little girl. She hadn't thought of the doll in years.

He sat her on his lap. She raised her head and stared into his eyes. Eyes not piercing now, not angry, but sorrowful.

Esther twisted her fingers together, round and round. "I didn't know who—who it was who killed my parents and—and hurt me. I don't their remember faces. I never knew their names. Aunt Bonny called them 'evil men' and Uncle Ed moved us away."

Colin didn't say anything. He just kept rubbing his thumb across her scar.

A thought slowly wormed its way through her mind, a thought so horrible she tried to fight it, but it kept coming. A thought which had a face with brown eyes and graying brown hair. The face of the man in the store who said he was playing hide-and-seek with Davey.

Colin said something, but Esther had been so lost in thought, she hadn't made out the words. "What?"

"Ray Miller wants his grandson. It's what this has all been about. Miller wants Davey."

Esther stood. "He can't have him. Davey's mine. He's going to grow up to be a good Christian man, not an outlaw, not a killer, not a ra—no! Davey and I'll leave and go someplace where this Miller can't find us."

Colin stood. His whole chest squeezed tight when she talked of leaving. He wasn't sure he could put what'd happened to her out of his thoughts, forget who'd hurt her. But he knew he didn't want her completely gone from his life. At least not until he could straighten out his thoughts. Besides, he felt she was safest here on the ranch with all the MacPhersons around her, now that they knew what the Millers wanted.

He touched her chin, tilting her face until he could look into her eyes. "Let's talk with Thorn and the other MacPherson men, give them all the information about what the Millers want and see what they have to say. All right?"

Tears filled her eyes. She nodded as her shoulders slumped. "Nothing bad can happen to Davey. Nothing."

His thumb shifted a little higher, and he rubbed it against her cheek.

"You have my word as a MacPherson, nothing'll happen to the boy." He'd lay his life down for Davey. And for Esther. "I love him like"—he swallowed hard—"like my own son."

During a quiet supper, Esther sat in the dining room of the main house. More of the MacPhersons had gathered for supper than usual, bringing pots and pans of food just like a potluck meal at church. Word about her connections to the Millers and the meeting that was to be held tonight had passed around the MacPhersons like a yellow fever epidemic. Memories—this whole night brought back so many memories of the days and months after the attack. Women talked, words whispered, gossip passed from person to person, and all eyes on her—looks which shamed her to her very soul. She hated those memories.

Even the children were more subdued than usual.

She kept her eyes on her plate while she moved the food around on it. She couldn't bear to see if the MacPherson women were staring at her.

The minutes dragged on.

At last the meal ended. She helped the women clear the tables. Some of the other women took the children outside. She headed to the tub filled with steaming water and dirty dishes, but Granny MacPherson pulled her aside.

"Lass, come with me." Granny MacPherson tugged on her hand. "Ye be needing to know what's happening."

When they slipped back onto chairs around one of the tables, Grandda grinned. Thorn looked resigned, but kept on talking to the men around him. Colin frowned at them and made little shooing motions with his hand.

Granny stretched out her small hand and laid her gnarled fingers on Esther's sleeve. "Let's hear what plan the men devise."

When Thorn stood, the others quieted. "Men." He turned and nodded toward the table where Esther and Granny sat. "And ladies. As most of you know by now, we've a serpent nearby, one who wants to snatch a child off MacPherson land. Everyone needs to keep a special lookout for strangers or anything out of the ordinary. These men are killers who seem to enjoy killing and hurting women. Keep your guns at the ready. Don't travel alone. If you're going to be away from your place, bring your families to the main house first."

With each word Thorn spoke, Esther's stomach rolled tighter into knots. She couldn't put these people in danger, especially now she knew it was Davey the

Millers were after. With the money left to her by her great-uncles, she had enough to take Davey and go east. They could start a new life there.

She wrapped her hands across her waist at the thought of leaving Colin. But if that was what must happen to protect her son, she'd do it. She couldn't bring harm to these people. And that meant only one solution.

Her chair scraped the wooden floor, and she stood. All eyes turned to her. Her throat dried. She licked her lips and forced the words out. "I appreciate your willingness to help us, but I can't let you do this. I, uh, I watched them kill my parents. I've heard what they did to those miners back in Central City. I won't let it happen here. If you can get me and Davey to Denver, we'll take a stagecoach back to where we can catch a train, then go and lose ourselves in some town where the Millers can never find us."

Grandda MacPherson stood. Fire filled his eyes. He gripped his cane to steady himself. "It matters not. Ye're on MacPherson land, welcomed by all, protected by all. When we first settled this land, we made a pact. All who bear the MacPherson name, all who carry MacPherson blood, and all unprotected women and children are welcomed here. As long as ye desire, ye're one of us. And we protect our own."

A roar of agreement sounded round the room.

Thorn smiled at her. "Ah, lass, it's not that simple for you. Ray Miller is determined to get his grandson. He trailed you hundreds of miles. How? I've no idea, but he did it. Add to that, there's no guarantee you'd make it safely to Denver, even with our help. Look at what it took just to get you to the ranch. And once you are on a stage, the Millers are known for their stagecoach holdups."

He shook his head. "'Tis best for you and your bairn to stay right here until we take care of the Millers."

Defeat wrapped itself around Esther's heart. She couldn't protect Davey if she left, but their very being here put the rest of the MacPhersons in danger. She glanced at Colin. The moment she met his eye, he turned away. Defeat gripped her chest. His vow to his son had kept them apart before, but now knowing that a Miller was Davey's father, that vow had changed—grown bigger, sprouted claws and fangs. It had become a monster and was feeding on their love. That pain was one she wasn't sure she could bear.

Colin looked away when Esther stared at him. The battle raged too deep in his heart, hatred against the Millers and love for Esther with two boys dancing between—one living and one dead. Even if they caught the Millers and they hung for their crimes, would he be able to deal with Davey every day and not see his son's murderer in the face of Ray Miller's grandson?

A few minutes later after several of the MacPherson men stopped and talked to her, Esther moved to the door leading to the stairs. Before she left the room, she gave him one last pleading glance, but Colin couldn't make himself go to her. His anger held him anchored to the wooden floor.

Her shoulders slumped. She turned and took her first step away from his anger. Granny wrapped her arm around Esther's waist and drew her close. Together they left the room.

Dougal nudged him with his elbow. "Go to her. She needs you."

"Not now, maybe not ever."

"Then you're a stubborn, stupid fool. If Esther can put what happened behind her, you can, too."

"Don't you understand? It's not what happened to her. It's who did it."

Dougal jerked the hat from his head and slammed it against his thigh. "Oh, I understand, big brother. I remember what it was like between you and Jessie, and because you couldn't fix your marriage, you figure you have to avenge their deaths. But Colin, you don't even know for sure it was the Millers. You've latched onto the idea they did it just because they were in the area. But no one saw them anywhere nearby that day."

Colin's hands balled into fists. He wanted to cram those words down his brother's throat. He and Dougal had been chasing Jessie for two days when they'd come across the overturned stagecoach. The local sheriff and a couple of his deputies were heading to the gully where it lay. Colin had climbed down after them.

Jessie and Matty were lifeless but still warm. If only he'd gotten there a little bit sooner, he would've been able to save them.

"I talked to the sheriff before I left Missouri. He said the doc told him that the driver's heart had gotten bad and it probably just gave out, and that's why the stage went over the edge."

Colin slung out his hand as he shook his head. "No. The stage was robbed. The Millers did it."

"You're even more stubborn than I thought. You've latched onto someone to blame and you're not going to let go. Colin, it's just plain stupid to do this. You might know one of the Millers is Davey's father, but you can't prove one of them killed Matty."

Dougal sucked in another breath and started again. "You have a chance to begin a new life here with a woman who loves you and a boy who wants you for a pa. Don't be a bigger fool than I already think you are."

He smashed his hat on his head. "It's all I have to say." He took a step away then stopped and peeked over his shoulder. "For now."

CHAPTER TWENTY-FIVE

With Davey in bed for the night, Esther had to get out of the house, out where she could see the stars and feel God watching over her, letting His peace seep through her thoughts and heart. She gripped the kitchen doorknob, opened the door, and went out into the darkness.

She could just make out the battered bench near the clothesline.

While she sat staring at the stars, the nighttime air flowed over her almost as if God were wrapping her in His arms. The Bible verses Aunt Bonny had taught her after she'd come to live in Uncle Ed's house came to her mind. The first one she'd memorized had helped her in the early days. *Rest in the LORD, and wait patiently for him: fret not thyself because of him who prospereth in his way, because of the man who bringeth wicked devices to pass.* Those words and Aunt Bonny's love helped her accept what those men—she knew their names now—what the Millers did to her and her parents.

She let another verse rest in her thoughts, one she'd discovered after she learned she was with child from the attack. *Be still, and know that I am God: I will be exalted among the heathen, I will be exalted in the earth.* But her favorite was the one she memorized after Davey was born, the one she'd clung to for the last four years. *For I know the thoughts that I think toward you, saith the*

LORD, *thoughts of peace, and not of evil, to give you an expected end.*

She whispered the verses again and again, drawing strength from them. God would take care of her. He had in the past, and He would in the future.

Peace slid into her heart. Her mind rested. God was with her. She trusted Him. All would be right, maybe not the way she wished it, but in His way. She'd trust, and she'd pray.

Boots sounded on the ground. Colin stopped not ten feet from her. And peace fought to hide. Esther took a deep breath.

Colin took a few steps closer and stared at her in the moonlight. "I wasn't sure it was you. Are you all right?"

She stood. "Fine. You don't need to worry about me. I'm going inside."

He caught her arm when she moved past him. "Don't go." He dropped his hand. "Please."

She stood still and waited for him to say what he would.

Silence filled the air for several moments, then he let out a deep sigh. "I'm sorry for the way I've been since we talked earlier. There's just been a lot to think about."

Esther raised her hand and touched his sleeve. "Colin, you don't have to explain. I've lived with this for five years—the gossip, the stares, the ugly words—especially before we came to Central City. I know many people think I'm used, unclean, no better than those women who work in the saloon. But I know better. I'm clean, and if no man, if no man…"

She swallowed the tears running down the back of her throat as she thought of a long, empty life without Colin. "And if no man wants to have a life with me, I can accept that. I might not like it, but with God's help, I've learned to be at peace with it."

"You don't understand."

"You're wrong. I've had years to understand. The only thing I ask is that you treat Davey kindly while we're here."

Without another word, she hurried into the house and closed the door. Once there, she raced past Grandda and up the stairs to her room. Hopefully, Davey would stay asleep and she could cry out her pain at Colin's rejection.

Colin leaned against the back porch post much the same way he had the night he'd first kissed Esther. He swallowed back the groan that came with the memory. His feelings that night had been strong, and they were so much stronger now. But the question remained. Would he ever be able to look at Esther and not remember the men who killed his wife? Would he ever be able to take care of Davey and not remember Davey's father killed Matty?

The door opened, and for a second, he thought Esther had come back. Instead, Grandda hobbled out, carrying two cups. "Will ye sit and have a cup with me?"

Colin nodded. Even though he preferred coffee, he'd drink the stuff and spend the time with Grandda. His own da had been gone a few years now, and he missed the talks they'd had, the wisdom he'd gained. Colin took one of the cups and sat in a nearby rocking chair while his grandfather sat in another one.

Not a word was spoken for a few minutes. They just rocked and sipped. The crickets chirped when a cat padded on the porch and jumped on the old man's lap. Peace, the first he'd felt since finding Tina in the barn, rolled over Colin. It was the way with Grandda. He brought peace wherever he went.

At last, Grandda set his cup on a nearby table. "Son, I know ye're troubled. Yer heart's a'war with wi' yer head." He stroked the cat again. "Thorn's wife, Sarah, had that same problem afore she came here. As did

Dougal's lass." Grandda spit on the ground. "Bah, 'tis a cursed thing, men hurting women like that."

"But how can one win the battle, find peace?"

"Thorn's Rose said it best, a lesson learned from her sister-in-law. 'Forgiveness 'tis a commitment ye make in yer mind, ye bind in yer heart, and ye live out in yer life.' Without forgiveness, ye'll never have peace, boy."

Grandda swallowed the last of his tea. "Well, it's enough preaching for this night. By the way, did yer da teach ye that MacPherson means 'son of the parson?' Something ta think 'bout."

The old man stood. "Ah, one more thing. Did yer da ever tell ye what Jamie said just afore they swung him from the gallows tree?"

"Not that I recall."

"Well, it went something like this, 'I spent me life in rioting, Debauch'd me health and strength. I squander'd fast as pillage came, and fell to shame at length. Me da was a gentleman, o' fame and honour high. Oh mother, would ye ne'er had borne the son so doom'd to die. The Laird of Grand, The Royal Majesty, pass'd his great word for Peter Brown. And let Macpherson die. But Braco Duff, with rage enough, first laid a snare for me, And if that death did not prevent, aveng'd I well could be. But vengeance I did ne'er wreak, when power was in me hand, And ye, dear friends, no vengeance seek, It is me last command. Forgive the man whose rage betray'd Macpherson's worthless life; when I am gone, be it not said, My legacy was strife.' Might be wanting to think about yer legacy, son."

The old man hobbled into the house.

Colin couldn't move. Was Grandda echoing Dougal? Were they both right? Had his life truly come to this one word—vengeance? Vengeance which would live past the killing of the Millers? Vengeance which would keep him from the ones he loved?

The next morning, Colin tied bags of grain and food to his saddle. He needed to get out of here, get by himself at least for a couple of days. After the talk with Dougal and Grandda the night before, he needed to get his thoughts cleared.

"I don't like the idea of you going out alone." Thorn rested his elbow on the top rail of the corral. "But with three of the hands out sick with retching and fever, we're a bit shorthanded, and I don't have anyone to spare to go with you."

"I'll watch out for the Millers. And those cows need to be brought back." Colin shook his head. "And I need to be by myself. "

Thorn chuckled. "I understand. I can remember when it was just a few of us MacPhersons, but now we seem to draw them like flies to a summer picnic with lemonade, cake, and cookies." He gazed over the land. "I'd like to take your place and enjoy the peace, but Rose is too close to her time, and she's lost too many bairns already."

"I remember when my son was born. Fear's not just for women."

Thorn nodded, then clasped forearms with Colin. "See you in a couple of days. May God ride with you."

Colin returned the grip and nodded. "May He be with you and your Rose as well."

Thorn walked back to the main house. As Colin gathered the reins, he heard a voice he loved yet needed to get away from.

"Unca Collie! Unca Collie!" Davey got off the pony he was allowed to ride in a nearby corral. The little boy dropped the reins, then crawled between the lower two rails and ran to Colin. Davey stopped and looked at the bulging saddlebag. He was puffing a bit and a bead of sweat rolled down his cheek. "You going 'way?"

Colin squatted to Davey's level. "No, I'm not leaving. I'm just going out to look for some cows for Thorn."

"I go, too?" The boy raised his hand above their heads. "See, I big like you."

"Maybe another time. Right now you need to stay around here and help your mother." Colin stood. "Best you get on back to the house now."

Davey's mouth dropped into a frown and his shoulders slumped. He kicked a small rock, then stared at Colin with such pleading in his eyes. "Please?"

"Not this time. Now go and see if your mother needs you to do anything. With all the folks sick, she could probably use your help." The boy moved back, and Colin mounted his horse. As he rode away, he forced himself not to look over his shoulder at Davey.

Esther stirred a pot of soup while Tina peeled potatoes. Like everyone in the world did when people were sick, they were fixing chicken soup for all those with sick stomachs and fever. Fortunately, those living a little further away were still healthy. Granny thought it might have been something tainted in the food last night with the way so many were getting sick so fast.

Tina set her knife on the table. "When do you think Papa'll come back?"

"I'm not sure, but it hasn't been that long."

"I know. It's just so different here."

Esther nodded. She understood why Tina felt the way she did. But Tina was different today, not complaining as much, helping more.

Before Esther could do anything else to help her cousin, Davey burst into the kitchen.

"Mama, Mama, need help?"

Esther smiled at her son, always so willing to come to her aid. "Not right now, honey. Why don't you go outside and play on the porch for a few minutes while I finish talking to Tina?"

Davey stared at her for a moment. "Help Unca Collie?"

Esther gave the soup another stir, then wiped the sweat from her son's face with the corner of her apron. Oh, how this little boy looked up to Colin. "And what's Unca Collie doing that you want to help with?"

"He watch cows."

She grinned at her son. "All right, just stay close to him. I wouldn't want you hurt."

"Yippee! Need apples and cookies." He grinned back. "Please?"

Esther kissed her son on the forehead. "All right."

Davey's grin grew bigger. "Tank you."

She handed him the bag and watched him shoot out of the kitchen. Before the door closed, Linda stepped through, carrying Thorn's two youngest girls, while the oldest one helped the other sister.

"We've got more sick. Where do you want me to put them?"

"Granny's made pallets in the parlor for the little ones. Take them in there. I'll be in with some more damp cloths and cool water to bathe them with."

Linda nodded and left the room.

Esther wiped her forehead with the sleeve of her dress, then looked out the window. With all these getting sick, she was thankful Davey was with Colin. But she'd need to check with Benny's mother later, and see if Davey could stay with them when Colin finished looking after the cows. Well, that could be a plan, as long as no one in Benny's house got sick.

Colin pulled his hat from his head and wiped his bandana over his face, getting rid of the sweat and dirt at least for a little bit. He'd been able to find a half dozen head of cattle and moved them toward the line shack Thorn had told him about.

But the work left him with too much time to think, too much time to remember, too much time to ponder what-ifs. He'd been less than twenty when he and Jessie married. Looking back, Jessie was ready to marry. He'd just been the man she'd chosen to complete her dream. That thought sickened him a bit. She hadn't really loved him. He wasn't sure he really loved her. He'd just started being a deputy, and it felt good to have someone to come home to. But she hadn't been ready for all the responsibilities that came with marriage. Then Matty was born before their first anniversary. What a mess they'd made of their marriage.

He pulled his canteen from the saddle horn, then took a mouthful of lukewarm water, swished it around in his mouth. Leaning over just a bit, he spit out the dust he'd been swallowing. He watched the dry ground snatch the moisture and hoped it'd rain soon. Thorn and the other MacPhersons would need it for the cattle and the gardens each house seemed to have.

After another drink, he put the canteen back and kept the cattle moving.

He tried to think of something else, anything else, but Jessie kept coming into his mind. For years, he'd blamed her for leaving him, for taking Matty away, maybe even for causing him to step away from his faith. Maybe—just maybe—Dougal could be a little right in what he'd said about guilt.

He looked ahead and spied the line shack. Maybe he could get settled in before it got too dark. Maybe he could leave the thoughts which haunted him out in the darkness, and they'd scatter in the night. Maybe he was an idiot to even think it'd help.

The sun beat on Ray Miller for the second day while he sat under an outcropping of rocks. He'd already cursed the hot sun, the dry wind, the horse that'd thrown him, the thigh bone he'd broken when he hit the ground, and his ungrateful son who'd left him here to die. The boy hadn't even stayed to help him set his leg. Said he was going to find a better life. Bah, what kind of better life could that namby-pamby kid find? His mother'd ruined him. He never should have left him with her. At least she was in the ground now, and the boy wouldn't go back to her.

He grabbed his canteen, and let the last few drops drip onto his dry tongue. Fortunately the stream wasn't far away. If he could only get to it, but the leg hurt something fierce every time he tried to drag himself anywhere. He smashed his fist on the ground near his broken leg.

He was so close to his grandson now. He had to find a way to get him, then he could raise the boy to be a real man, not a do-gooder like his mama or that marshal. After all, didn't he deserve something? He'd lost all his sons.

A horse nickered nearby. Ray swallowed the moans of pain and pulled closer to the outcropping. Moving his fingers, he wrapped his hand around his gun. He waited just a bit and snuck a peek to see who was coming.

He couldn't believe his own eyes. Brushing his dirty hand across his eyes, he took a breath, then took another look. Davey, his only grandson, the boy he'd been trying to snatch, sat on a pony, and the pony was headed toward him.

Ray bit back a chuckle. The boy had come to him, come right to him. As the pony came closer, Ray bit back the cry of pain and scooted out a bit. "Davey, Davey, can you come here? I need help."

The boy looked around. He bit his lips. His shoulders slumped. He tapped his heels to the pony's side and trotted to the outcropping.

"What's the matter, Davey?"

"I-I-I lost." His head jerked around as if trying to catch his mama playing hide-and-seek with him. Tears leaked out of his eyes. "Wanna go h-home."

"Well, come here. We'll talk about getting you home."

Davey gave him a long stare, then his face brightened. His hand reached out, and he pointed at Ray. "We played in the store."

"That's right, son, we did." Ray spied the bulging bag tied to the boy's saddle. "Whatcha got in there? Something to eat? Sure am hungry."

Davey perked up even more. He untied the bag. It fell to the ground as the boy slung his leg over the pony and dropped. The movement scared the pony, and it took off.

The kid screamed for the pony to come back and ran toward the disappearing animal.

"Davey, Davey, come back here. Your pony's gone. I'll help you get back home." A lie, Ray knew, even as the words left his lips. He was never taking the boy back. The kid was his now—finders keepers. Let his mama and the marshal weep.

"Really, truly, we go home?" The boy brought the sack and sat in the shade of the outcropping.

"Of course, we will."

"What your name?"

Ray now had what he'd been after ever since he'd learned the boy existed. "You can call me 'Grandpa.'"

"Don't gotta grandpa. Benny does." His face glowed. "Got grandpa now, like Benny."

Something moved in Ray's chest, not the pain which had grown deeper and more painful ever since he'd been hit by that knife. No, this was different. Something he hadn't felt since he was a little boy himself. An old man who had loved him and held him and told him exciting stories, who told him what a wonderful man he'd grow up to be. He called him "his little ray of sunshine."

But then Pa came and took him away, laughing at Grandpa when he begged him to leave the boy. After that, there was only pain from fists or kicks from boots. And when he asked to go back to Grandpa, Pa beat him until he couldn't stand.

Ray rubbed his chest. He hadn't thought about his own grandpa for more years than he could count. Rubbing his chest again, he almost wished he could see the old man again.

But what would his grandpa think about him now, "his little ray of sunshine?"

Sickening shame—the first he'd felt since he'd left his own pa with a knife stuck in his back—swept over Ray. He shook his head, trying to get rid of the thoughts about the past, about the only person who ever loved him.

His boys had done good, maybe for the first and only time in their lives, when they took the girl and created this boy.

He watched Davey pull apples and cookies from the bag. The boy rubbed one of the apples on his shirt until it shone and held it out.

"Here, Grandpa, yours."

Something twisted in his heart, something he hadn't felt for years, or maybe he'd never really felt it. The men and women he'd been around for years were never like this little one.

Something tickled around his heart when Davey smashed his hands together.

"Pray. Dear God in Heben, tank You for food. And tank You for Grandpa. Jesus name. Amen."

Tightness gripped Ray's chest now. Soon as he and the boy got away from here and found a place to settle, maybe he'd try to be more like his own grandpa. But first he'd have to rest up so he could steal a horse that could get them away from here.

CHAPTER TWENTY-SIX

Misty rain floated from the ever-darkening sky when the men came in for the day with all signs pointing to even greater storms coming before the sun rose in the morning. Esther pulled a large pan filled with roast, along with potatoes and carrots, from the oven. A couple of men waited to take the food out to the bunkhouse for the cowboys. After the men left, Esther dropped into a chair near the table. Linda brought a tray with a pot of tea and two cups. "Where's Granny?"

"Oh, hadn't you heard? Thorn came by a while back, all in a frenzy, begging Granny to come to his house. Seems his Rose is having her baby a little earlier than they thought." Linda's lips spread into a sweet smile. "I can't wait for me and Dougal to marry. I wish our house was built right now."

She touched her middle. "After what that man did to me, I was so scared I'd be in the family way. For a long time, I didn't even want to think about having a baby. But now with Dougal, I can't wait to have children who look like him. They can grow up here with all the other MacPhersons."

The back door opened. Granny stepped inside and pulled her dripping cape from her shoulders. She hung it on one of the pegs on the wall, then turned around, face all aglow. "The lass did good. We be having a new MacPherson bairn in the family now. A fine lad he be."

Esther stood and got a cup for Granny, then filled it with steaming tea. The old woman dropped onto a chair and sighed deeply as she lifted the cup to her lips.

After a few sips, Granny set the cup on the table. "Best be on my way. I told Thorn I'd let the lasses know about their brother."

When they finished the tea, Linda looked around the kitchen as though she was searching for something. She glanced at Esther. "I just realized I haven't seen Davey all day. I figured he'd be wanting his supper about now."

"He's been with Colin today. He even took out some apples and cookies for them to share. So when Daniel came in and got supper for the men, I asked him to see if Colin would keep Davey out in the barn with the men and older boys tonight. I don't want him to get sick along with the other children."

Linda's hands shook so hard the cups and saucers she held rattled. "But Dougal said—"

The back door burst open. Daniel stepped in, his face pale and his lips pinched below his dripping hat. "Colin went out this morning to search for some missing cattle. He planned to stay out overnight. Dougal saw him leave. Davey wasn't with him." He jerked his hat from his head. "But the pony Davey's been learning to ride is missing."

Esther's legs lost all strength. She dropped onto the wooden chair by the table and covered her mouth to keep from screaming. No, this couldn't be right. Davey was somewhere around here. He had to be. If he went out after Colin by himself, anything could happen to him— wolves, snakes, Ray Miller. No, not Miller.

Her legs gained strength again, and she stood. Not Miller. She wouldn't let the man have her precious son. "We have to go out and find him."

When she grabbed her shawl by the door, Daniel laid his hand on her shoulder. "Wait, Esther. We need to check out this house first, then the other houses. He might be there. The pony might have wandered off."

Esther wiggled her shoulder until Daniel's hand fell from it, then she headed for the back door. "No, Ray Miller has him. We have to find him before the man leaves or I'll never see my son again."

Daniel stood at the door as if to bar her way out. "Miss Essie, I can't let you go out there. It'll be raining near enough to float a boat out there before the night's over. Besides, it's already too dark to track him. We'll have to wait 'til the morning and send out search parties then. "

She tried to push him aside, but he didn't budge. "I can't wait until then. My son's out there. I've got to find him."

Thunder rocked the house and jagged flashes of lightning burst across the windows.

Esther tried to swallow the painful moans that started deep in her chest as she thought of Davey out in the storm. A comforting hand rested on her arm.

Granny stood beside her. "Come, lass. Sit for a moment." She turned to Daniel. "Get yer grandda."

Esther tried to lift the old woman's hand from her arm, but Granny wouldn't let go. "I have to get to Davey."

"Hush. Wait for Angus. We'll be needing a plan to find the bairn."

Esther longed to race out and find Davey, but she saw the sense in what Granny said. Which way would she have gone anyway? She didn't know where Davey had gone.

The door to the kitchen opened. The head of the clan walked in, using his cane to help his stumbling gait. "Daniel's headed out to get Thorn and Dougal. By the time the men can start in the morn, we'll have a plan ready."

"Morning." Esther forced herself to stand strong. "We need to go out now. He's just a little boy."

"Aye, that he is. But ye got to remember, lassie, we've nary an idea where he headed or where to search."

Another huge clap of thunder seemed to echo his words.

The back door opened. Three dripping men scrambled in. More flashes of lightning lit the sky, followed closely by loud claps of thunder. After giving a quick nod to her, the men quickly joined the old man around the table. Coffee boiled. Cups were filled. Cups were emptied. More coffee appeared.

Esther watched the men. No one asked her to join in, so she sat at the end of the table, her arms wrapped around her middle. Tears threatened, but didn't fall. Instead, they ran inside and bathed her breaking heart. *Oh, God, please protect Davey. I don't know where he is, but You do. Hold him, protect him, comfort him this night. Help us find him in the morning, safe and alive. Oh, please, God, help us find him alive."*

Gnarled fingers covered hers. Esther glanced to her side. Granny sat in the chair next to her. The old woman's head was bowed, her eyes closed. She prayed sweet, simple words, talking to her Friend, giving thanks for the blessing of Davey, for the joy he brought into their lives, for the love the boy already had for God through his mother's teachings. And then she prayed for his protection. On and on she prayed, not big fanciful words, just heartfelt ones.

The scraping of chairs brought both of their heads up.

"Get some rest. We'll leave at first light." Grandda MacPherson nodded to Thorn and Daniel, who then turned and left.

Esther stood. "I'll be going with them."

The old man smiled. "I know, child. I know. Get yer rest so ye can."

Granny stood and kissed Esther on the forehead. "God be wi' ye and yer bairn."

The old man took his wife's hand. "Come, Mary. Let's go to the Father." Together they hobbled out of the kitchen.

Esther hurried to her room. More prayer was needed tonight. Much, much more.

Colin shoved his shoulder against the door to the line shack. The sky had opened up while he was getting the cattle into the corral. If the water pouring down was any indication, an ark just might be passing by soon. He shook his head. It was a foolish thought, but then he'd been having foolish thoughts for quite a while.

He dumped his saddle on the floor by the bed which rested against the wall, while water ran off his hat and splashed on his boots. Grabbing the saddlebags from his shoulder, he set his supplies on the rickety table, then pulled off his slicker and hung it from a nail on the wall. Next, he built a fire in the small potbellied stove.

A few minutes later, he held out his hands to warm them from the heat of the stove. Without thought, he dropped one hand to pet Old Benson. He chuckled and drew back his hand. Old Benson had been dead for a good twelve years. But being caught in a rainstorm, then taking refuge in a line shack had brought back memories of his early years on his pa's place and the number of times he'd ridden out looking for strays.

Colin let out a deep sigh and paced around the small cabin. He couldn't get Dougal's words out of his mind. Well, he could get those words out of his mind, but then Grandda's took their place. And the questions kept jumping around—questions he'd never really asked himself. What proof did he really have that the Millers were the ones who'd tried to holdup the stage when Jessie and Matty died? Could it have been some other outlaws? Or like Dougal said, could it have just been an accident caused by the driver's heart giving out?

His stomach rolled. Had the last five years of his life really been driven by guilt? Had he been using his badge as a way to cover his guilt? He could still see the look on

Jessie's face when they'd had their last argument. She'd wanted him to quit being a lawman, to find a safer job. She'd choked back tears when she told him she didn't want to raise their son—and any other children they might have—alone.

He smashed one fist into the palm of his other hand. The memory of Jessie's sister shouting at him at the funeral still burned in his mind. He hadn't known Jessie had been with child when she'd left him. But her sister told him and everyone in earshot that his wife had left him because she couldn't take care of two children never knowing if she'd be a wife or a widow when he rode out. She said Jessie and Matty would still be alive if he'd just stayed home with her. And it ate at him because he knew it was true. He was the one guilty of killing his wife and son.

Colin paced again. But then Jessie always knew he wanted to be a lawman. It was just in the early years of their marriage that he'd been town sheriff. But when Matty was two, the chance came for him to be a deputy US marshal and that meant more traveling. At first, Jessie seemed to like it—the way she bragged to everyone about how important he was and how he was helping to make the state a better place.

He shoved another couple hunks of wood in the stove. Her family had come for a visit. He'd been gone for two or three weeks that time, missed the entire visit. Jessie changed then, talked about wanting them to move back closer to her parents.

Grabbing the coffee out of his saddlebags, he started a pot. As the smell filled the air, he sat at the table. After that, all he and Jessie seemed to do was argue. He hated the fussing, and he hated seeing Matty's face when they did it.

He bent over and covered his face with his hands. Thinking about it and put that way, he could see some of her way of thinking. But it still wasn't right when she took Matty and left him. They could have worked it out, couldn't they?

This time, when he thought about how it could've been different if she stayed, he wondered how he would've changed, what he would've changed.

Too antsy to stay seated, he stood and moved the few steps to the stove. He rested his shoulder against the wall and watched the steam roll out of the coffeepot's spout. All the what-ifs were like that steam, floating away and not turning into anything.

He needed to face some cold hard facts and see where he could go from there.

Dark clouds gathered in the sky. Another shiver shook Ray Miller as he lay on the ground. Curses shouted out in his mind. But for Davey's sake, he kept his lips pressed together. He'd make it out of here and get Davey somewhere they could live together, somewhere where no one knew of them, somewhere where no one would think to look for them.

They'd spent a good time together. The boy'd been a great help, taking the canteen to the small creek which ran nearby and filling it. Later, he found a couple of stout dead branches to bind his leg. It felt better once he got it bound.

"Grandpa, go home now?" Davey grinned, his wide brown eyes so trusting.

Ray rubbed the stubble on his chin. "Well now. It's getting a mite too dark to walk around. We'll need to wait until morning to head out." He figured by that time he'd have time to work out a plan.

"Stay in dark?" His small voice shook.

"Sure, boy, cowboys do it all the time. You want to be a cowboy, don't you?"

Davey's eyes sparkled. "Like Unca Thorn and Unca Dewy?"

Ray bit back another curse. Soon the boy would think of him with that look on his face. "Yep, like them, but right now we need to get tucked in under these rocks."

"Why?"

Ray never liked it when his boys asked that question and usually gave them a cuff to the shoulder. But he wanted it to be different with Davey, more like it was when he was a boy with his grandpa. "'Cause it's fixing to rain and we need to get under whatever cover we can."

Davey scooted back as far as he could. Ray pulled the near-empty food bag over their heads. He shielded the boy with his own body when the rain started pelting his back. As the storm grew wilder, Davey whimpered.

Ray rubbed Davey's back to warm the boy, as well as to comfort him. Strangely, he couldn't ever remember doing this with his sons. He'd always left it to the women. Now he wished he'd done it at least once with them. "Tell me about your ma."

"Love Mama. She makes...good...cookies."

Even in the dimness caused by the storm, Ray could see the boy's eyes lowering as he snuggled closer. In a few moments the boy was sound asleep. What trust Davey had. A feeling he'd never had with his own sons, spread through Ray's chest. He sucked in a deep breath when moisture filled his eyes as thoughts of his grandpa filled his thoughts again.

He lay there a long time, long after the storm passed, long after clouds passed and the moonlight shone on them. The temperature dropped and dampness settled in his bones. Pain raged in his leg and chest. It ripped through his throat every time he coughed. It was no longer just where the knife had stuck him. Now it spread from side to side. It got harder to breathe. Shiver after shiver passed through his body, covered by rain-soaked clothes.

He tried to sleep, but dreams of what he'd done in the past kept waking him.

While the moon moved across the sky, he realized it was better to struggle with the pain than try to sleep because the pain in his body was better than the pain of his dreams.

In the dimness before the sun started to rise, Davey stirred. His eyes opened. Confusion filled them, then excitement. "You here." He clapped his hands together. "Grandpa here."

Something shifted inside Ray. When had his sons ever shown such joy and excitement to see him? Never, and now they never would.

Davey coughed and rubbed his sleeve across his dripping nose, then wiggled. "Gotta go."

Ray chuckled. All little boys were the same. "Let me move, then you can get out and go behind the rocks."

Davey nodded and scampered out. Ray bit his lips to keep from grunting while he shifted. The grass rustled as the boy made his way to do his business. A few minutes later Davey called out. "Grandpa, bunny. Catch bunny."

Ray knew what lay a little ways from the outcropping of rocks. It was one reason he decided to hide out here. There was a drop-off close by, too near for a horse and rider to come up behind him. But a little boy like Davey wouldn't realize the danger. He tried to stand, but his busted leg wouldn't let him stand. "No, Davey, come back."

"Grandpa!" Davey's voice filled with fear.

Ray heard the thud when his grandson's body hit the ground. He crawled, tugging on the small tufts of grass and weeds that clung to the dirt. Hand over hand, he pulled himself across the ground. He bit his lips to keep from crying out from the pain in his leg. Elbows dug in the ground, he moved inch by inch. Silence surrounded him. No call for help. No crying or whimpering.

"Davey, I'm coming." The words puffed out from between tightly stretched lips. He saw Davey's footprints ahead in the damp dirt and pulled harder. Pain grew in his chest, a different kind of pain than before. It didn't matter. He had to get to his grandson.

His fingers dug into the mud. He strained. At last he reached the drop-off. He sucked in a deep breath and looked over the edge. At first he didn't see anything, but then something caught his attention. Below a small bush which grew on the side of the cliff was a tiny ledge just big enough for a little boy.

Ray tried to take a breath, but the pain in his chest ripped it away. For a moment everything got blurry. He blinked a time or two, then looked down again. There—a little bit of white was almost hidden by the overhanging bush.

Pain roared again. Ray struggled to breathe, to push the pain back, so he could think. When they came for the boy, they wouldn't see him. Not unless they knew where to look. Breathing hard and fighting the pain as dark spots danced in his eyes, he pulled his hand to the mud in front of him and scrawled out a message he hoped someone would see.

He finished the last mark. Pain came back and brought all its brothers with it, all ten or twenty of them. The pain ripped his chest apart. He fell into silent darkness.

CHAPTER TWENTY-SEVEN

The darkness outside hadn't lifted when Esther pulled on the split skirt Rose had loaned her shortly after she'd come to the ranch. She tucked her blouse into the waistband. Next, she pulled on the boots Granny had Daniel bring from the storehouse. She grabbed a jacket and headed for the door. Before she twisted the handle, she dropped her head, and as she'd done the whole night long, prayed. "Dear God in Heaven, You know where Davey is. Please wrap him in Your arms of protection until we find him. He is such a little boy. Please, please help him." She drew in a shuddery breath. "Amen."

As quietly as she could, she made it down the stairs. She'd waited long enough. Davey needed her. She must go now.

She jumped when a voice called out.

"Coffee's ready for ye, though I prefer tea meself."

Esther jerked around at the sound of Granny's voice. The old woman sat at the table.

Granny lit the lamp that rested in front of her. "Sit. Have a bite. Ye'll be needing it for where ye're going."

Esther gripped the top of the chair in front of her. "What, what do you mean? Has news come in during the night about Davey?"

"No, child, I just meant it's going to be a hard day for ye, searching for yer Davey boy. Sit, drink yer coffee, eat a bite. If ye hurry, ye'll be finished before the men get here."

"I'm going with them. They can't stop me."

Granny laid her gnarled old hand on Esther. "I know, dear. They won't be leaving without ye." She let out a tired laugh. "They wouldn't dare."

Before Esther finished her scone and cup of coffee, the sound of men's boots thudded on the wooden back porch. The door opened and Dougal, along with five other men, entered. They all grabbed cups, and Granny filled them.

Esther swallowed the last of her coffee and stashed the rest of the scone in her pocket, then stood.

Dougal gave her a hard look. "You going with us?"

"You can't keep me away. If you don't let me go with you, I'll just follow you."

One side of Dougal's mouth tilted upwards. "Figured as much." He turned toward his grandmother who held out a large stuffed bag and a smaller one.

"Food for yer bellies and doctoring things, if needed."

Dougal took the bags, then kissed his granny's wrinkled cheek. "Hopefully we'll be back by noon."

The rest of the men followed suit and kissed the old woman.

She waved them off. "Just be careful and let the good Lord guide ye."

Esther couldn't resist the urge and kissed Granny like the others.

"Be off with ye, lass, and bring the bonny boy home. We'll keep the fires burning and the coffee hot."

Esther followed the men out. Thorn, weary-eyed and stern-faced, stood by the saddled horses, giving men instructions on where to search. He looked at her riding clothes and gave a nod. One hurdle passed. Now to find Davey. She swallowed past a large lump in her throat. Hopefully alive and unhurt. *Oh, God, please let us find him unhurt.*

Colin sat on the bunk and tossed the thin blanket aside. Might as well get up. Sleep had been sparse during the night. Any chance of getting more had slipped out of the cabin an hour before.

He stoked the fire in the stove and put on another pot of coffee before he dressed. The questions that had haunted him all night still pounded in his head. Had he blamed the Millers because of his own guilt? What was he going to leave behind when he was gone, because of his vengeance?

He closed his eyes. Still, he could see Esther's sweet smile and Davey's bright eyes. They loved him, and he loved them. But would finding Ray Miller and sending him to prison, or worse, bring peace to the rage which lived in his chest? His whole body tightened as his need for revenge battled with his guilt. Ray Miller didn't deserve to live after all the killing he'd done. The man was guilty, and someone needed to see he was punished.

Colin bit his lower lip. But wasn't he guilty too? If he'd been a better husband, if he'd realized just how fearful Jessie had been every time he'd left to go after some outlaw, if only he'd gone after her sooner, she and Matty wouldn't have been on that stage.

Dougal was right. There was no proof the Millers tried to rob the stage Jessie was in. Colin gripped his hands into fists. His brother was right about something else: he was a stubborn, stupid fool. But that would end now.

Like the forgiveness Grandda had talked about, this letting go would have to start in his head until he could live it out in his heart. He knew he'd lived with the guilt and vengeance for too long to let it go all at once. It'd keep creeping back into his thoughts, and he'd have to keep shoving it out. But one day, and with God's help, he'd cut the last tie that his stubborn heart held onto. The anger and the vengeance would be a thing of the past.

He dropped into the chair and rested his head on his folded hands. "Dear God, I come to You. You see inside me. You know my heart and the struggle I'm having. Help me to let go of the anger, the vengeance I've had for so long against the Millers, especially Ray. It was me who caused Jessie to leave me. It has been my guilt that I've been running from. Oh, God, forgive me. Guide me. And like the prodigal son that I am, welcome me back into your fold. In the name of the One who died for my guilt. Amen."

At last, Colin stood. He poured out the over-boiled coffee sludge and cleaned the pot. It was time to get home, to get to the woman and boy he loved and wanted to live with for the rest of his life.

Within minutes, he had his horse saddled and the cattle moving. To the east, the sun was just peeking out, drying the rain-moistened ground. There was just a smearing of pinkish clouds against the blue sky. If the weather held, he should be back at the ranch house by midafternoon. Then he could talk with Esther.

An hour or so later, he'd just started the cattle over a small hill when he saw two riders racing toward a saddled pony.

Fear—black and cold and hungry—coiled around Colin's gut. *No. No. No.* The words kept pounding in his skull. The pony was the one Davey used. One of the riders was Esther.

Gripping the reins tighter and shoving the heels of his boots against his horse's side, he left the cattle and rushed toward Esther and the pony. Moments later, he pulled on the reins and jumped off his horse. Esther, her face pale with dark smudges under her eyes, watched while Thorn checked out the pony. She covered her mouth with her trembling fingers as tears ran down her cheeks.

Pain, wrestling with fear, rolled around in Colin's head, his chest, his gut. *Oh, God, please don't let anything happen to Davey. Please hold him, help him, keep him safe.* He wrapped his arm around Esther's stiff shoulders and pulled her to his chest. "Where's Davey? What's happened?"

She raised her head and stared into his eyes. "He asked me if he could go with you and watch the cows. I didn't know you'd left." She gripped his shirt in her gloved hands. "So many sick at the ranch. No one knew until last night." She let out a shrill laugh. Pulling one hand from his shirt, she pounded her own chest. "I gave him apples and cookies, then sent my baby out alone."

Colin pulled her closer. "We'll find Davey. We'll find him."

Thorn walked over, his eyes bleak, his jaw clenched. "Pony's in good shape. Nothing to make me think Davey's hurt."

"But he's out here somewhere all alone." Esther shuddered. "Where is he? Where's my Davey?"

Colin lifted her chin with his finger. "We'll find him. We know he's somewhere close by. We just need to search for him. Can you do that?"

She gave one last shudder, then moved away from him. After taking a deep breath, she drew her shoulders back and stood tall. "Yes."

Thorn nodded and pointed to the left. "Good. Let's spread out and check the area over there. It's a little rougher, but there's a small stream which flows a ways back there."

Without another word, Colin mounted his horse. The other two did the same. While Esther called out for Davey, Colin used his words to ask God to deliver Davey safely into his mother's arms.

An hour later, Esther continued calling out her son's name, even though her voice had grown hoarse. She'd already sent prayer after prayer to God, begging, pleading, crying for her son's safety. And though she waited for an answer, she kept praying.

Thorn, then Colin, called out Davey's name.

She came across the creek Thorn had mentioned and felt the need to follow it.

In the distance, she spotted an outcropping of rocks, not big, not far from the creek. She tapped her heels against her horse and headed for it. As she drew near, she tugged on the reins, and her horse stopped. Someone had been here.

She nudged her horse into a slow walk and scanned the ground. Then she saw it by a mound of rocks with a narrow overhanging ledge above it—the bag she'd given Davey for the apples and cookies the day before. At least it looked like the one she gave him.

Her hands shook as she dismounted. She stumbled to the rocky mound. The dirt under the ledge was dry. She grabbed the bag. It contained an apple and three cookies.

Davey had been here.

She studied the damp ground in front of the rocky mound. There in the dirt, a child's footprint. She looked and found several more leading to the back of the outcropping. There was something else—a man's handprints pressed into the dirt. Something or someone had been dragged around to the back of the rocks.

Her arm itched as she looked for Ray Miller, waiting for him to jump out at any minute and grab her. She stepped back and pulled the rifle from the scabbard tied to her horse's saddle, then followed the trail. When she came around the rocks, she saw a man lying on the ground. Moving slowly, she came around and saw his face.

With barely a thought, she raised the rifle and fired.

The sound of the rifle shot nearly jerked Colin out of his saddle. He slapped the ends of the reins against the side of his horse and headed toward the sound. His prayers for Esther and Davey joined the horse's pounding hooves. In the distance, he spotted Thorn galloping to the same spot.

Colin got to the outcropping first and pulled his horse to a halt next to Esther's. He dropped the reins and jumped from his saddle. He raced around the rocks, yelling for Esther.

With Thorn on his tail, Colin spied Esther kneeling next to a man's body on the ground at the edge of a drop-off. She raised her head, pain etched in her face. He got to her as quickly as he could. His heart beat even harder when he saw Miller on the ground.

Colin knelt down to check on Ray. From the stiffness already setting in, the man had been dead for a couple of hours or more. Colin stood and reached out to help Esther stand. She batted his hand away and crawled to the edge of the drop-off. He grabbed her, but she slapped his hands even harder.

"Davey's here somewhere. I saw his bag. Let me go. I've got to find my son." Her voice rose with each word.

Thorn joined them, his jaw clenched as he bent to examine Miller. "Look over the edge. See if you can see anything."

Colin gripped Esther's arm to keep her from falling. Together, they moved several feet from the body and examined the area below.

Esther let out a sob when they saw nothing out of the ordinary, no clothing, no little body. She turned to Colin with pain scarring her face.

He rubbed his hands across her back, hoping to give whatever comfort he could. After a moment, they stepped away from the edge.

"Look again." Thorn barked out.

"Why? There's nothing there." Colin couldn't keep the harshness out of his voice. Esther hurt, and he couldn't take her pain away.

Thorn waved them back to Miller's body. He pointed to Miller's dirty hand. "Look."

Esther pushed away from Colin and knelt beside Miller's body. "He wrote something in the damp ground."

"It's an arrow pointing to the edge. Is that a D?" Colin twisted his neck one way, then the other, trying to make out what the old man had written. "We looked there, but there was nothing."

Esther stared at the man. "What happened to him?"

Colin squatted beside the body. He checked him for any wounds. There weren't any, but the old man gripped the front of his shirt even in death. "Looks like his heart just gave out."

Esther continued to stare at the man, then shifted her gaze a few inches to where the drop-off began. She rushed over to the dead man. "Help me move him." She tugged on his legs. "From where he was lying, he must have seen something. Help me move him, so we can see what he saw."

They moved the body. She started to kneel, but Colin grabbed her around the middle. "I'll do it."

Esther clawed and shoved him, but he pushed her into Thorn's arms.

On his hands and knees, Colin crawled to the edge, then lay on his stomach and looked down. What had Miller seen? What was so important he crawled through the mud with his broken leg, then gave his last moments of life to leave a message? He tried to block out Esther's cries to find something as he looked bit by bit across the cliff wall. Nothing was out of the ordinary, just rock walls and plants growing out of the cracks here and there.

He searched everything twice, but couldn't find anything. He hated to pull back and let Esther know Davey wasn't there. It'd destroy her to never find her son, to never know what happened to him. He kept eyes downwards, so he couldn't see the hope in Esther's face, and rested his palms on the soft soil next to the marking the old man had made. He started to rise.

Halfway up, he stopped and stared to the side just a tad. There—beneath some bushes growing out of the rocky wall—was that a bit of white? He strained to get a better view. Almost hidden by the bush was a tiny ledge. Something white was on it. Could it be Davey? Was that what Miller was pointing to?

New strength filled his body. Colin pushed away from the ground and faced Esther. "I think I saw him. We'll need a horse and some rope."

A few minutes later, Colin eased down the rock wall, tied by a rope to the saddle horn on Thorn's saddle. Inch by inch he made his way, praying all the way. He caught his boots in the bush but pushed it aside. At last, the toe of his boot rested on the tiny ledge.

He heart nearly burst when he leaned over Davey's body. The boy was unconscious, but still breathing. "Davey's here. I'll need another rope to tie him to me."

The sounds above him flowed over the edge—Esther thanking God, Thorn running to get a rope from one of the other horse, Esther asking how Davey was.

Before he could answer any of the questions Esther kept asking about her son, the end of a rope slithered past the bush. Colin grabbed the end and gave a tug. Thorn let go of his end.

With great care, Colin tied Davey's feverish body to his. "Pull us up."

Inch by inch, the two of them rose along the rock wall. Colin protected Davey as best he could. When they got to the top, Esther's whimpers grew stronger. She reached for them.

A vision of her falling as she tried to get to her son flashed into Colin's mind. "Thorn, keep her back before she goes over."

She cried out when Thorn pulled her back.

Colin pulled himself and Davey farther onto solid ground. At last, he relaxed and sucked in a couple of deep breaths. Thorn must have let Esther go, because she was all over him, untying her son, crying for Davey to open his eyes, telling him how she loved the boy.

Once she got her son free of the ropes, she pulled him into her arms and rocked him back and forth, whispering to him all the time.

Thorn helped Colin to get the rest of the ropes off him. "We need to get him home pronto. He's burning up with fever."

Thorn went to get the other horses. Colin pulled the bedroll from the back of Thorn's horse and laid it on the ground beside Davey. "Let's wrap him. He needs to be kept warm until we get him home."

By the time they got him covered, Thorn was back with the other horses. He pulled out his rifle and shot into the air twice, waited several seconds, then fired two more shots.

Thorn nodded to Colin. "To let the others know we found Davey."

Colin moved closer to Thorn. "I've checked him as best I could. He doesn't seem to have any broken bones, but he's still unconscious and running a high fever. We need to get him back to the ranch house."

Thorn nodded and lowered his voice. "Granny'll have the right potions and herbs to help him." He rested his hand on Colin's shoulder. "But I'm gonna need your help to get the boy from her. I know the quickest way to get home and can make it faster by myself. Besides, we can't leave Miller's body out here for the buzzards and the wolves, not after the way he struggled to let us know where Davey was."

Colin swallowed hard. Here it was. The first challenge to his letting go of his vengeance against the Millers. He knew he was being tested, not only by God, but by his cousin. He knew it'd happen, he just didn't think it'd be

so soon. Two day ago—even yesterday—he would've
left the old man to rot in the dirt, but things had changed.
He'd changed, at least he was trying. Head to heart, head
to heart. He nodded. "I understand. Let's go."

"No. No. No. You can't take Davey and leave me. He
needs me." Pain ripped across Esther's chest with each
word she spoke. She pulled at Colin when he lifted her
baby to Thorn, sitting on his horse.

Colin turned and wrapped his arms around her. She
fought him. She screamed when Thorn tucked Davey
close to his chest and took off. Colin's arms held her
tighter.

"Sh, sh. Let's get done what we have to, so we can get
back."

"Why do you care what happens to Ray Miller? You
hate him." Esther shoved her fists against Colin's chest.

He dropped his arms. "No, not anymore."

Once loose, she moved to her horse and struggled to
untie the knots holding her bedroll on the back of the
saddle. The quicker they got this done, the quicker she
could get back to Davey. "Since when?"

He stepped over, brushed her fingers aside and undid
the knots. "Since last night."

She jerked the blanket from his hands and walked to
the body of the man who'd caused so much hurt to so
many people. She let out a sigh. But in death, he saved
Davey. She stood nearby while Colin wrapped the old
man in the blanket and tied him onto the back of her
horse.

When that was done, he mounted his own horse and
removed his gloves. He held out his hand to her. "You're
going to have to ride behind me."

She bit her lower lip and took his hand. Holding the
reins of the horse carrying Ray Miller's body, they
headed back to the ranch house and Davey.

Silence filled the air for some time, not an easy silence. No, more of a silence filled with words which hadn't been said yet, questions which hadn't been asked or answered. The longer she rode behind Colin with her arms wrapped around his middle, the louder the silence got.

Esther ended the silence. "What happened last night? What changed?"

"I was alone." He rubbed her hand. "I thought about things Dougal and Grandda said. I realized if I didn't come to peace with the Millers, I was going to drive you and Davey away." His hand gripped her hand for a moment, then he loosened his hold slightly. "I don't want that to happen."

"You don't want me to leave the MacPherson's ranch?"

"I don't want to drive you away from me."

Something that had been tucked away for so long opened inside Esther, like a rosebud opening to the morning sun, like a gift unwrapped on Christmas Day, like love blessed by God. *Thank you, Father, thank You, thank You, thank You.* She tightened her arms around him. She dropped her head and laid it against his back.

Colin slowed his horse when three cowboys rode toward them.

Daniel nodded to them. "Met up with Thorn on his way to the ranch. He said for us to come and get the, uh, body. Pete's going to go find Davey's pony."

Esther couldn't hold back the question. "How's Davey?"

Daniel gave her a slight smile. "By this time, he's at the house with Granny taking care of him."

"Has he woken up yet?"

"Sorry to say, he hadn't when I saw him. But don't worry, Granny's good as any doc out of the best medical school. She'll get him well. Her, with God's help."

Daniel tapped his finger to the edge of his hat. "Best be going. See you back at the house."

Colin handed the lead rope of the horse carrying Miller's body to one of the cowboys, then dropped his voice. "Hold on. We'll get home faster now."

Esther clung to him as Colin urged his horse into a full gallop. *Oh, God, I don't have the words. Look into my heart. Take care of my son. Please don't let him die."*

CHAPTER TWENTY-EIGHT

When they rode in, Esther watched Thorn frown. He stood next to his grandfather on the porch at the back of the house. Colin reined in his horse at the barn. She released her hold on his jacket, ready to jump to the ground. He reached back. "Grab my arm."

She did, and he helped swing her off the horse. Without a word, she headed for the house. Colin hurried close behind her. The two men on the porch stood still as statues. When she was close enough to talk without screeching like a banshee, she wet her lips and asked the one question which kept her heart pounding. "How's Davey?"

Thorn didn't meet her eyes. His grandfather shook his head just a bit.

Esther's heart almost stopped. No! She couldn't lose Davey. She grabbed Thorn's sleeve. Colin wrapped his arm around her shoulder and gently pried her fingers from the fabric.

He held her hand in his and pulled her to his side. "What'd Granny say?"

Thorn still didn't meet her eye. "She said he's in a bad way." He waved to the door. "Said for you to go right on up when you got here."

As Esther and Colin hurried past the two men, Grandda MacPherson touched her arm. "We'll be praying for ye and yer bairn."

Esther nodded, afraid that if she opened her mouth she'd either scream or howl out her pain and fear. Inside, they hurried through the kitchen to the back stairs. Linda met them on the stairs.

"Granny wants some willow bark tea. We're all praying."

Again Esther nodded. She needed to get to Davey. No matter how wonderful Granny was with herbs and medicines, Davey needed his mother. And Esther needed to be with her son. Colin seemed to understand and wrapped his arm around her, catching her when she slipped on the stairs.

After what seemed a hundred steps and miles of hallway, they reached the room Esther shared with Davey. Her small son barely made a bump on one side of the big bed, his face flushed against the white pillow. His eyes sealed shut.

Esther jerked away from Colin and ran to her son's side. She dropped to her knees by the side of the bed and rested her hand across his chest. Her fingers moved slightly, but enough to let her know her son lived. "Mama's here, Davey. Mama's here."

Tears dripped from her cheeks, but she didn't care. All that mattered was Davey and getting him well again. She stroked his cheek. "When you're better, you can play with all the boys around here and ride your pony. You'd like that, wouldn't you? And you can have a puppy just like you wanted. Just get well. Mama loves you so much."

Still holding his hand, she bowed her head. She continued to ask God to heal her son. It didn't matter that she had prayed while they were riding. Now that she was with Davey and could see how sick he was, she prayed again and again and again. She'd pray until God answered her prayers.

She just hoped He would answer her prayers with healing for Davey.

Colin wrapped his now empty arm around Granny and nudged her into the hall. "Is Davey going to make it?"

She patted his arm as it rested on her shoulder. "If God wills. Until then, I'll do what I can, knowing He's the Great Healer." She stepped back. "Why don't ye get in there and spend a bit with yer lady and the bairn. I'll be in when Linda brings the tea."

Colin kissed Granny on the top of her white head. How he wished he'd known her all of his life. Maybe then he wouldn't have had the problems he'd had with Jessie. "Thank you for all you're doing for Davey."

"Get along with ye. I'd do it for any of the bairns here. But he's a special one, he is. Take good care of them both."

"I plan to." Colin turned and slipped back into the bedroom. Esther was still on her knees. He moved to the bed and lowered himself to his knees, then slipped his hand on top of hers. He bowed his head and prayed.

Time passed as he went before God on behalf of Davey and Esther. He wasn't sure how long, but he turned when a light hand rested on his shoulder.

Granny smiled at him. She held a mug and spoon on a tray. "Take yer lady there." She nodded over her shoulder to a couple of wooden chairs against the wall. "She needs to rest while I tend to the boy."

Colin tugged on Esther's hand. She nodded and stood. He wrapped his arm around her shoulders and led her to the chairs. He wished it was a sofa, so he could sit closer to Esther, but once she sat, he scooted his chair as close as he could. She laid her head on his shoulder.

Together they watched Granny settle beside Davey and slip her arm behind his shoulders, then lift him slightly, so she could spoon some of the willow bark tea between his lips, blotting what didn't stay in his mouth.

Colin laid his hand on Esther's as she pleated the fabric of her split skirt between her fingers. She rolled her hand around and clung to his. He wanted to pull her onto his lap and hold her close, let her draw strength from him, soothe her in any way he could, but right now he didn't have the right.

He'd turned from her when she needed him the most. If only he'd stayed and talked to her after the MacPherson meeting. But his stubborn hurt and guilt had gotten in the way. God may have forgiven him for the way he acted, but he needed Esther to forgive him also.

But this wasn't the time to beg for her forgiveness. Now was the time for Davey and his healing. So he did the two things he could for her—he rubbed her wrist with his thumb to let her know he was here for her, and he prayed for her, for Davey, for Granny's healing hands, and for himself.

Still tense and hurting like a cow caught in a mess of tangled briars, Esther strained forward every time Granny lifted the spoon to the boy's face, as if she were giving the medicine herself.

After several minutes, Granny moved her arm from behind Davey and eased him onto the pillow again. When Granny left the room, Esther moved and lay on the bed next to Davey. She whispered, but only a few words of her prayer reached Colin—words filled with a mother's love asking—no, begging—for a blessing, for healing. When she finished, she lifted Davey's hand to her lips and pressed a small kiss there. With dark smudges beneath her eyes and a slight smile on her face, she closed her eyes. The tension eased from her body, and she slept.

Colin couldn't look away from the image before him. He didn't know if he'd ever felt the trust and peace Esther showed. He just knew he wanted it in his life and was thankful God was such a forgiving Father and had given him a second chance to win Esther's love and hopefully have a life with her and Davey.

And with that in mind, he bowed before his God once again.

Esther opened her eyes and shifted to get a better look at Davey. His body shook as he coughed. His breath rattled in his chest. She touched his cheek with her fingers, then jerked back as waves of fear rolled through her. His fever was high, so much higher than it'd been when she laid next to him. "Oh, Davey."

The legs of a chair thumped on the floor. Colin was beside the bed in seconds. "What's the matter?"

"Davey's worse. He's burning up."

"I'll get Granny." He raced out of the room. His boots echoed in the hallway and down the stairs.

Sometime later, it seemed years to Esther, while she held Davey's fingers in her hand, Granny entered the room. The old woman bent over Davey's small body, touched his forehead, checked his eyes, and listened to his chest. "Need ta get the fever down."

As she straightened, Colin thumped back into the room carrying a bucket of ice chunks, a slicker, and some kind of awl. He knelt by the bucket and beat the ice chunks into smaller pieces. "More's on the way. Daniel's still at the icehouse, but I wanted to get some to you as fast as I could."

Esther jumped off the bed and grabbed the towel hanging on the washstand and took it to Colin. He heaped the tiny bits of ice in the towel. While they worked with the ice, Granny pulled a thick quilt under Davey, then covered him with the slicker. When the towel was loaded with the ice, Colin gathered the four ends of the towel and carried it to the bed. Esther helped pack the crushed ice on top of the slicker and around her son.

Colin returned to chipping at the ice chunks.

By the time Esther and Granny had used all the ice in the towel, another batch was ready. Esther touched Colin's hand as he poured the crushed ice onto the towel as it lay on the bed. She tried to smile. "Thank you."

Granny turned to them both. "Sit. Now is the time to watch and wait." She sat on the chair by the bed. "And pray."

Again, the seconds stretched into weeks as Esther watched over her son. She prayed. Colin held her hand and prayed. Someone brought another bucket of ice and set it inside the bedroom door, while someone else brought more dry towels as well as another bucket to hold the melted ice.

As the early morning sun battled with the light from the oil lamp on the table, Granny deemed the fever low enough to remove the ice. Once it was done, she left them to watch over Davey, while she went to check on the ones who still hadn't recovered from the stomach upsets.

Esther couldn't stay back. She crawled back on the bed and lay beside Davey. Her little boy murmured something and snuggled closer to her.

Colin took Granny's chair by Davey's head. "Sleep, darling. God and I'll watch after you and Davey."

"Thank…" She wasn't sure if she'd even finish before her eyelids closed.

Colin's eyes felt gritty. He rubbed his palm against the two-day-old bristles on his chin. As soon as Esther woke and he could assure her Davey was sleeping peacefully, he'd go and clean up. But there was no way he could leave until she woke and could see he was still with them.

The one thing he'd learned, beyond all doubt during the last twenty-four hours was that he loved this woman and wanted her for his wife. He knew he'd have to be careful with her, after the way she'd been treated by the Miller brothers. But she'd survived and gone on to build a good and happy life for herself and Davey. He just hoped she had room in her life for him.

Davey shifted but continued to sleep.

Colin's heart tightened a bit. The love he felt for Esther was matched only by the love he felt for her son. Davey wouldn't be a replacement for Matty, but would be a second son, each having a place in his heart.

His fingers itched to touch Esther's face, to wake her and see her brown eyes, to see her lips lift into a smile. He wanted to start the morning with a kiss but knew it was too soon. There were things that needed to be said, needed to be explained. But soon, very soon, he hoped he'd be able to begin the day with her in just that way.

As if his thoughts called her from sleep, Esther opened her eyes, touched her fingers to Davey's face and smiled. "Fever's gone. He's sleeping."

Then she looked at him. "Good morning."

Colin couldn't keep back a grin. Yes, it certainly was a good morning.

Several days later, Esther sat in one of Granny's rocking chairs on the front porch with Davey on her lap. He'd been asking about his grandpa. She'd told him the old man had died, but she wasn't sure how much a four-year-old understood about death.

She kissed the top of his head while he lay against her chest. She knew he didn't truly understand, but he missed the man who'd been nice to him, the man he could claim as grandpa.

All at once, Davey sat straighter, then bounced up and down. She glanced around to see what he'd seen that caused him to move like that. Suddenly, he jerked out of her arms and scrambled off her lap.

Colin stepped on the porch, a yipping little puppy in his arms. "Look what I found. Think he needs a good friend?"

"I'm good friend." Never taking his eyes off the dog, Davey raised his arms as his feet did a little tap dance on the wooden porch.

Colin raised an eyebrow in question and looked at Esther. She held back a chuckle. What could she do when the puppy was already presented? Nothing, absolutely nothing. She nodded to Colin. "Yes, Davey, you would be a good friend to the puppy."

Colin squatted to Davey's level and put the puppy in her son's arms. Davey dropped to his bottom on the porch, giggling as the puppy licked his face. "You know a puppy's good friend needs to take care of him, make sure he has food and water, and take him outside so he can do his business."

"I be good friend."

"I know you will. Just take good care of him every day. And play with him lots, and he'll always be your friend."

Esther held her hand across her mouth to keep from laughing. The joy in Davey's face was something she'd always keep tucked in her heart.

Davey's eyes grew wide as if he had just realized something. "He mine?"

"If your mama says you can keep him." Colin turned to her, his eyes oh-so-innocent.

"Mama, Mama, ple-e-e-a-a-se. Keep puppy?" Davey and the dog both looked at her.

"Of course, you can, darling. Be sure and thank Uncle Collie for the nice dog." She made sure to stress the name and knew she touched the right spot when his lips spread out just a bit, and not into a smile. And she knew the next question she wanted to ask, for she'd read a book about dogs that Drew had had. "And ask Uncle Collie what kind of dog your puppy is."

Colin choked, then burst out laughing. He sat on the porch and pulled Davey onto his lap with the dog jumping on both of them.

"Tank you." Davey scrunched up his face as he tried to ask the right question. "What kind is puppy?"

"He's a border, ah, collie."

Davey's eyes lit even more. He touched Colin's chest. "Unca Collie." He then patted the dog's head. "Bord collie."

Colin leaned his head back against the post which supported the overhang on the porch and groaned.

When Esther couldn't hold back her laughter any longer, Colin glared at her, but his eyes twinkled. "Just you wait. You'll get yours."

"Sweet promises, sweet promises." Esther laughed a little more. But her middle tightened just waiting for those promises.

CHAPTER TWENTY-NINE

After supper, Colin waited for Esther. She had agreed to take a walk with him after she put Davey to bed. He needed to tell her things about his life and why he'd chased after the Millers like he had.

The door opened. He stood ready to greet Esther. But she didn't step outside. It was his brother.

"Nice night."

"It'll be better when Esther joins me." Colin held his tongue on the rest. He loved his brother, but he wished the man would mosey farther along or go back inside. Either way, just so he didn't tag along. Dougal needed to go get his lady and spend some time with her.

Dougal stretched his arms high above his head and let out a loud sigh. "Well, since you're occupied, think I'll see what Kerr's doing."

"Fine idea." Colin turned as the latch to the door sounded in the evening air. The sound joined Dougal's chuckle. "Give Star my best."

Colin started to say something, but his brother had already slipped away.

The door opened again. This time, Esther came out, with her shawl resting on her shoulders. "Sorry, it took me a little longer than I'd planned. Davey begged to have his puppy sleep with him, but there's no way I'm having a dog in my bed. I made a pallet on the floor for them. Tomorrow, we'll figure out how we'll go from there."

Colin slipped his hand around her elbow. They walked to the apple orchard. "I'm glad he's happy with the pup. Did he ever think of a name for him?"

"Oh, he thought of many for the puppy." Esther tried to swallow a chuckle, but the sound came out just the same. "He began with dog, then moved on to puppy, him, paws, and Collie. The last one I knew just wouldn't work. We'd never know if he was calling you or his puppy."

Colin groaned. "Maybe we can come up with a new name for me." And he had just the one he wanted.

"Well, it didn't matter. Your grandfather came out, and Davey discussed it with him. When he suggested the name 'Wyne' and told Davey it meant 'friend', Davey agreed to the name. So it's settled, we only have one Collie around here now."

He groaned again and found the bench Granny told him about, on the back side of the orchard overlooking a small pond. The talk of puppies and names had been fun, but now it was time to get to what he needed to say. "Let's sit a bit. There's something I need to tell you."

"Nothing's wrong is there?" A little tremor wove around her husky voice.

"No, I just need to explain some things about me."

"All right." She clasped his hand tighter. "Go ahead."

He started from the beginning about Jessie, how they met and courted, then married. It was harder when he got to the problems they'd had, but she needed to know all about them to understand the rest. Then he told how Jessie had left him.

Now for the hard part, the part he was ashamed of. Colin let go of her hand and paced. "The thing is, we had a son—Matthew—but we called him Matty. She took him with her the day she left me to go back to her folks. Only I didn't know for a few days that she'd left. I'd gone hunting some outlaw or another. I can't even remember the man's name. But when I got home, I found her letter telling me what she was doing and why."

He pulled off his hat and ran his fingers through his hair. "Dougal had come by to see me, and together we went after her and Matty. I didn't want to lose my family, my son. We found them. The stage had gone off the side of the road into a deep gully. Jess...Jessie and Matty were dead."

Esther sucked in a quick breath. "Go on."

He dropped back on the bench. "I blamed the Millers for robbing the stage. Vengeance, or what I called justice, against them filled my life. That's why I came to Central City. I heard they were coming here. Didn't know the reason then, just they were headed here."

He sat silent for a moment, then drew in a deep breath. "I'm telling you all this for three reasons. One, I want you to know my past—the good and the bad. Matty was the best and the way I treated Jessie, not taking her fears into account, was the worst. Second, I want you to know I've given the vengeance to God. It was always His to mete out. I just tried to take His place, and I've asked His forgiveness for trying to take that from Him. And third, I want you to know why I rejected you after I learned one of the Miller boys was Davey's father."

Esther sat silent for a moment, then stood and paced once, twice in front of him, before she stopped and bowed her head. Only the night birds and the crickets made any sound.

All the time, Colin's gut churned. He'd rejected her when he learned her past. Would she reject him now? He loved her and didn't want to let her go, but he'd have to if she couldn't accept and forgive.

At last, she sat beside him. "How old was Matty when he...when it happened?"

"Four."

She sucked in another gasp, then laid her hand on his arm. "How could you deal with Davey like you did? Didn't he remind you of your son?"

He shook his head. "Davey is Davey, not my son reborn. I never thought of him that way." He fidgeted with the side of his hat as it sat on his knee. "The thing was, I already loved you and Davey when I found out Davey's father was the man I thought had killed my son. I wasn't sure I could live with the thought every day, if we married."

A deep shudder ran through him. "That day my dream of the three of us being a family fell apart, and I got angry. Thankfully, Dougal and Grandda each talked to me, one making me see I held the Millers responsible when I had no proof, because I felt guilty for driving my wife away. Then Grandda talked to me about leaving a legacy of vengeance. I don't want to do that either."

He rested his palm against her cheek. "I want to live a life of love with you and leave a legacy of love to our children and grandchildren. I love you, and I want to spend the rest of our lives together. I want to adopt Davey and give him the MacPherson name. Will you marry me?"

She covered his palm with hers. "I—I need you to know that with God's help, and Aunt Bonny's, I've forgiven those men. But I'm not sure—I mean, I enjoy our kisses and the way I feel when you touch me. I just don't know how I'll handle...how my wifely—"

He touched her lips with his finger. "I know what you mean. Together we'll work that out. With you, me, and God's love surrounding us, we'll work it out."

"Then if you can put my past behind me as I can put yours behind you, yes, I'll marry you. Oh, Colin, I love you so much."

With more tenderness than he'd ever felt before, Colin wrapped his arms around the woman he loved and showed her love, not lust.

EPILOGUE

Esther stood at the upstairs window watching the people gather below. Linda and Dougal had a beautiful spring day for their wedding.

"Is that Granny's veil?" Linda's voice filtered through several layers of fabric as Sarah helped her into her wedding gown. Linda had feared this day would never come after Dougal got hurt when he was thrown from a horse, but with a few months of Granny's nursing, he was ready to stand before his family and claim his bride.

"Yes, Granny asked me to bring it to you." Esther ran her fingers over the old lacy veil. It was the same one she'd worn six months before when she married Colin. They hadn't wanted to wait for the MacPhersons to build them a house, so they had Uncle Kirk, an ordained minister who had retired to the ranch, marry them. When the Homestead Act came into effect at the first of the year, Colin and Dougal had filed for land near each other. Cousins and uncles had all joined in and helped build two houses. Thankfully, soon after their wedding, Uncle Ed had come and taken Tina back to Central City where she was learning to run the boardinghouse.

Esther set the veil on the bed and touched the small bulge just below her middle. One day, her daughter—or if this was a boy then his wife—would wear Granny MacPherson's veil at her wedding—a tradition spanning at least six generations.

Someone knocked on the bedroom door.

"It better not be Dougal. He knows he can't see me until the wedding." Linda's voice was clearer now that the dress hung from her shoulders and not her head.

Esther moved and opened the door just a bit, then swung it all the way open.

A loud squeal sounded behind her. "Nancy! I'm so glad you finally got here."

Linda's younger sister, who'd remained with Drew and his family so she could help with the twins, ran into the room and hugged the bride. They stood there, arms around each other, babbling like schoolgirls.

Esther started to close the bedroom door when she heard her name whispered in the hall, and her heart raced a little. She'd know that voice in the middle of the night, in the darkest thunderstorm, from the depths of the deepest sleep. She stepped out of the room and into Colin's arms.

He pulled her close, as close as the mound at her waist would let him. "Duncan has arrived."

"I know. He brought Nancy like he said he would. I just hope the wedding happens on time. The way those two are talking, it might be hours before they finish."

Colin chuckled. "I think Dougal would have something to say about that. But with the girls busy gabbing, do you have a couple of minutes?" He held out a small metal piece.

Excitement shot through her. "Duncan brought the papers?"

Colin grinned. "Yep. Grandda has Davey waiting on the porch."

She grabbed his hand. "Let's go."

When they stepped out on the front porch, Grandda stood with his arm on Davey's shoulder.

Grandda nodded and turned to her son. "Davey, there's a tradition here in the MacPherson clan. Every MacPherson who lives on our ranch is given a clan shield, whether he's born or married in. That also holds true for one adopted by a MacPherson. Today, ye are a MacPherson. Davey MacPherson. I'll always be yer Grandda, and ye'll be me great-grandson."

Esther tried to blink away the tears when the old man bent low and pinned a clan shield on Davey's shirt.

Davey raised a finger and touched the metal disk. "I'm a MacPherson, just like Da." He ran to Colin and was lifted into his arms. Davey then reached for Esther. "C'mere. We all MacPhersons."

When the three of them wrapped their arms around each other, the family let out a cheer to welcome the newest MacPherson. Esther laughed to herself. The newest MacPherson—at least, until Linda said her vows and took that honor.

Esther smiled at her husband, the man who had given her a home, his name, and all the love her heart could hold.

THE END

OTHER BOOKS

The Rose and The Thorn
The Hawk and The Eagle

AUTHORS BIO

Mischelle Creager writes inspirational historical romances set in the mid-1800s. She's not sure which she loves more—researching or writing. When she's not doing one of those two things, she can probably be found reading or baking.

She is a wife whose wonderful husband told her, when he retired several years ago, that he wanted to support her in her writing and took over all the household chores, including sweeping, dusting, and laundry. He even cleans up for her after she bakes! Her son and daughter are always available to help with social media questions.

Mischelle loves to share her historical research and has a website, Under the Attic Eaves, filled with tidbits she's found in books written in the 19th Century. She also "reprints" a historical magazine, Worbly's Family Monthly Magazine, filled with items from books and magazines published in the middle of the 1800s. You can visit these two sites at http://undertheatticeaves.com/ and http://worblysmagazine.com/

If you would like to know more about Mischelle and her family, please visit her blog, Families Across the Generations at

http://familiesacrossthegenerations.blogspot.com/

You can contact her at http://mischellecreager.com/

CPSIA information can be obtained
at www.ICGtesting.com
Printed in the USA
FSHW022037250819
61410FS